Tough Girl in the Jam

LARRY LOEBELL

MILFORD HOUSE

Milford House Press

Mechanicsburg, Pennsylvania

MILFORD
HOUSE

an imprint of Sunbury Press, Inc.
Mechanicsburg, PA USA

For information about special discounts for bulk purchases, please contact Sunbury Press Orders Dept. at (855) 338-8359 or orders@sunburypress.com.

To request one of our authors for speaking engagements or book signings, please contact Sunbury Press Publicity Dept. at publicity@sunburypress.com.

ISBN: 978-1-62006-320-0 (Trade paperback)

Library of Congress Control Number:

FIRST MILFORD HOUSE PRESS EDITION: July 2019

Product of the United States of America
0 1 1 2 3 5 8 13 21 34 55

Set in Bookman Old Style
Designed by Chris Fenwick
Cover by Chris Fenwick
Edited by Chris Fenwick

Continue the Enlightenment!

"When you love, you wish to do things for. You wish to sacrifice for. You wish to serve."

— Ernest Hemingway, A Farewell to Arms

"The most sublime act is to set another before you."

— William Blake

PROLOGUE

NINA'S RECOVERY JOURNAL

The oval is my home. No. Not my home. My church. Not one of those airless sarcophagi you were dragged to as a kid, with the dead guy hanging over your head, or the eternal light menorah blinking dully like a distant star to remind you of miracles the likes of which no one you know has ever witnessed in their meager lives. No. Think instead of the rock clubs and crush bars where music changed your life forever, where you were lifted by the crowd out of the quotidian boredom of your dazed existence and into the weed-wet air of the divine. Think of the theaters where your heart broke, the hockey arenas where skaters slammed the boards streaking toward mathematically improbable victories, the gridirons where gladiators did furious grunt battle over inches, in no-guts-no-glory it-ain't-no-game games, where you wept and died watching helpless as contests played out in slow slogs or breakneck dashes like they were the essential metaphors of life. Think of all the places where you cheered your lungs out for something the value of which you could barely defend in your un-ecstatic moments, but which you knew, deep down, meant everything, that captivated your imagination for reasons as dark as your attraction to violence, and as sunny as your hope for love. Think of any place that propelled you out of yourself, into the abracadabra spirit of the mob, everyone hoping for the same magic, and sometimes seeing it – in the simple glory of your favorite band playing your favorite song as their last encore, or in an event as grand as your team's stunning come-from-behind retribution for seasons of shameful losses, crafting an improbable victory out of thin air, their win gutted out by the outclassed underdog survivors of last year's debacle who are your home team, who crush their nemesis opponents with a last-second Hail Mary miracle. When that happens, when you blow into that ecstatic collective exhalation of breath, the roof of the hall nearly shot off by the explosion of a thousand-thousand up-lifted hearts, the crashing tidal wave of cheers – you become changed – a charged particle, gleaming, and radioactive, in-fected forever with a fan's fierce devotion, a conversion as pure as any saint's. And better, if you are part of it, playing on that loser winning team, it's heroin. Nothing else in your life lives up. You want that high again and again, jonesing for the rush of it.

I was on one of those teams, one of last year's shamed un-derdogs, practicing with all my heart for redemption.

On that oval, circling and circling and circling, was the clos-est I ever came to touching god.

7 WEEKS BEFORE THE CHAMPIONSHIP BOUT

There is something you ought to know right here at the start. We are in the most intense practice period of our team's history. The "we" I'm talking about is the *Philadelphia Freedoms*, the city's premiere roller derby team. We used to be called *The Philadelphia Lizzies*, after eighteenth-century Philadelphia feminist Elizabeth Powel, the woman who was reputed to have asked Ben Franklin on the day the Constitutional Convention ended, "Dr. Franklin, what have you given us?" To which the famous statesman was supposed to have answered, "A Republic, Madam, if you can keep it." Historians debunk this encounter, though locals love it, but the team managers thought *the Lizzies* might be mistaken by the unenlightened as a euphemism for lesbians, so they up-scaled the name, even though a lot of us who are lesbians on the team thought the managers were running scared from something they shouldn't have run from. The important thing to know right now is that we *Freedoms* are tied for first place in the East Coast Divisional League with the Manhattan team, *Hot Broadway*. There's a pun in their name, the same as there is in ours, that harkens back to the old days of derby, when sex and gender jokes were rife, the buried "broads" and "doms" seeming innocent enough in context. But there's a winking aspect to both names that I'm sure everyone gets that I don't need to spell out.

We are seven weeks from the national playoffs, busting our asses to click into our winning groove, and we stink. I don't mean our team play stinks. As a team, we're pretty fucking great. We've been in first place in our region all season. I mean we stink physically, olfactorily, personally, bodily. Each and every one of us. We practice four nights a week from seven to ten, and for the next six weeks, we're adding four hours on Saturdays, ten to two. Practice is not for wimps. Roller derby is not for wimps. The stink is part of it. Everyone on the squad has a gear bag with her skates and helmet, skate tools and extra trucks, toiletries, and deodorant, and we all shower when we go from our practice duds back to our street clothes. But those practice clothes, they get washed once a week. Maybe. And that's the fastidious girls. If you're lazy about domestic stuff or don't care, like me, it's less. It's part of the *fierce*; that's the thing you need to understand. We're jocks, as much as any football-playing guys are, as much as hockey players or basketball guys, and we have the skank to prove it. Maybe we have the skank so we don't have to prove it. You just get it. Like osmosis. It hits you before we do. It bucks you up.

My practice gear, in addition to my knee and elbow pads, includes a pair of Lycra *Athleta* sports bottoms, a *Brooks Embody* sports bra, some *New Balance Breathe Sport Hipsters*, and a tee shirt that says "Tough Titty" on it. That's another double-entendre, sort of a sad private joke. Everyone thinks its derby jive. It's really the name of a play about breast cancer by Oni Faida Lampley, but hardly anyone reads the fine print, so it seems like just more semi-snarky, half-offensive, sexually-explicit derby wear. The shirt was from the play's premiere production. The girl I was dating then was the lighting designer for the production. I loved the shirt so much she gave it to me. I loved the play, too. Oni died, but not without a fight. I met her. She was in remission when she wrote the play. She was smart and beautiful and, like the shirt says, tough. There's something about women who try to beat the odds. Who step up to defy the naysayers, even if they lose. They speak to me. They're my kind of women. Like the women on this team. We weren't even supposed to get to the championship round. We were ranked fourth in our division when the season began, in one of four divisions with twelve teams each. But we gutted it out, and here we are.

Some of the women on the *Freedoms* skate practice in the skivvies they slide in with, but I'm not comfortable skating in my street wear, so it's either sports undies or commando under the Lycra pants. I chafe, so unless I'm going to wear three for ten buck cotton grannies, this is my wrap. I swap the sports undies out when it occurs to me that they need it, which given my indifference to laundry is sometimes weeks. I tell Rachel, my girlfriend, that I do it once a week whether they need it or not. That's a lie. They always need it, pretty much after a single practice. Everything else in the bag gets the sniff test, the tops and the pads and the socks. If they don't offend me, though as you've probably guessed by now, I have a high offense threshold, they go back in the bag for next workout.

There's no audience for practice, except for an occasional girlfriend like Rachel, who comes semi-regularly to swoon, so no one balks at the shirt logos. For actual bouts, we have uniforms with our derby names stenciled onto our jerseys. It used to be that the dirty, double-entendre handles were *de riguer* everywhere in derby. Not anymore. There're still skate names, but they're a lot tamer. The sport has gone through a lot of stages and, right now, it's in its family-friendly, audience-development stage, and a lot of the tough dyke and queer nomenclature and sexual sloganeering has been toned down, to the consternation of some of us old-timers, which includes any woman who was skating professionally more than three years ago. There's a conflict. Do we want to be a bunch of outcast athletes skating for our own amusement and the pleasure of a few hundred hardcore fans who share our worldview and taste for outré clothing, in-your-face rhetoric, and what the straight world thinks is wham-bam physicality and kinky sex, or do we want to move toward the mainstream, try to make some real money, and become establishment? To make that move, the conventional wisdom says, we have to tone things down. It used to be that derby equaled unbridled permission to do or say whatever you wanted. I mean, it was queer girls slamming around with other girls, for Christ's sake. The rest of the world hardly cared. You could be anyone in your derby persona, the queen bitch you couldn't be to your boss at work or to your so-called 'loved ones,' or the sexually aggressive dyke whose in-your-face shit you knew would freak your parents totally the fuck out, or the smarty-pants purple prose punster, or the high-on-language geek girl, or the steam-punk badass, or anything else. You could be anything in derby, as long as you were a killer in the jam. Well, used to. Not anymore. Now there are bone-fide superstars, and the sexual derby names and the sly fucking and gender puns that have survived commercial censorship are a lot less wild. Or obvious. And, sadly, to my way of thinking, a lot more hetero. Don't get me wrong. I'm not knocking the straight world, and I'm not knocking the straight girls who play derby. A lot of them are hell on wheels, and I love them as teammates and friends. But when I see Suzy Skategirl's naked picture on the *ESPN Bodies* website, I'm thinking it's not only gay or bi or queer girls getting their ya-yas off looking at her. It's a lot of straight dudes, too. Straight dudes who think chicks with tats and muscles ripping it up on blades are hot. Especially if they're willing to get naked on horny-dude-oriented websites and in magazines. And that's all right with me, except in all the ways it isn't.

The first thing that happens in practice is warm-ups. That's individual skating to get the kinks out, to loosen up, snap the back, pop the knees. It goes on for maybe twenty minutes, the time it takes for all the girls to arrive and suit up in their gear. On practice days that follow matches, the club chiro doc shows up during warm-ups and works on the girls who come in with leftover pain from last week's or yesterday's bang-ups. He does table or bench work, and then has them try things out, ways to bend and shift and such, getting them in shape for the workout, or telling them to ride the bench for a day or two so they'll be healed by the next match. When everyone who's certified good-to-go has warmed up, and done a bunch of laps, and feels sufficiently loose, Coach whistles us in for the shape-up.

"All right, girls. Let's get this party started." There's a collective groan of protest, but it dies quickly. We let Coach get away with calling us girls, but as a club, we've tried to move away from gender-based monikers, even though this is a women's league. There were controversies over the inclusion of trans women on the squad when they first started showing up, and there were arguments in our team meetings a few years back, and in the league congress, about born-as vs. identify-as, but we have come to agree that insisting on the primacy of birth gender as determining anything is an idea whose time has come and gone. What you identify with is what you are, and for us on the *Freedoms*, at least, that's the end of the story. That Coach says "girls" matters less than how he treats us as a team, and if his play strategy works. We're in the playoffs, so we give him sass but also a lot of props. We know "girls" is shorthand for him, and no one gets bent out of shape when he says it, but no one is exactly willing to let it go by either. He used to call us "you guys," but we broke him of that habit by not responding to his instructions until he stopped saying it. Some old dogs, it turns out, you really can teach a few new tricks. When we all groan at "girls," we're reminding him we haven't stopped trying.

"First of all, who's missing?" Coach doesn't call roll in the traditional way, by looking at the roster and saying everyone's name. He looks for who's not there. We're supposed to let him know. Rogers, standing behind me, pipes up.

"Diaz," she says. Rogers has a kid but never misses practices. It pisses her off when other players use their kids as an excuse, like Diaz has been known to do.

"Diaz?" Coach repeats, looking around.

"Diaz," someone says, louder, as if Coach was hard of hearing. He looks around to see who said it, but then he remembers.

"Diaz. Broken finger. She's not ditching. Out for a minimum of two weeks, maybe longer. Remember when she crashed at practice last week?"

There are a lot of cringe faces, but someone, not sure who but someone, says, "Boo-hoo." There's some laughter.

Someone else says, "She never heard of adhesive tape? Just strap her fingers together, and pretend you're putting two in the pink." There's more laughter. We all know that reminding Coach about our anatomy sometimes embarrasses him and makes him blush.

Coach says, "Let's be nice."

"Sayola," someone else says before anyone takes another shot at Diaz.

Coach looks around for her. "What the hell," he says. "She call anyone?" There's silence. "Anyone know anything? Like what the hell is going on with her?" Silence again. "That's her second strike." Then suddenly, Sayola is rocketing toward us from the women's locker room. She skid-stops next to the pack.

"I'm here. I'm here. Fucking subway. No eastbound trains for a half hour."

"Fuck that shit. Practice starts at six. You're late. You come late once more you're benched."

"I'll bring a note from the conductor next time." Under her breath, she says, "Asshole." Then Coach makes a count. The rest of the people he expects to be here are, so he puts down his clipboard and starts to crank us up. "All right. You know what you're here for. You know the mantra. Drills build skills. Drills build skills. Everyone with me? Let's hear it. Drills build skills. Come on."

Everyone chants along, not particularly enthusiastically. "Drills build skills." Like blah, blah, blah. This is football huddle shit, carried over from some idea of his about how guys get worked up. It never truly works for us, though that doesn't keep Coach from sticking with it. He's a good guy, I guess, doing his job, trying to be righteous. He's got his method, and he's got real coaching chops. His game instincts got us this far this season. And it's not his style we're all antsy about. We're all just waiting to get into hard drills so we can shake some the tension out. Finally, he gives us the order. "All right. Interval sprints. Then snakes. Then lap the line. Then partner up for pushes and pulls. Then falls, single knee, then double, then four point. Then booty blocks and body checks. And if we have time, whips. First a two-minute race, with total squats at the whistles. Ready?"

Interval sprints are short timed races. The snake is two or more skaters holding each other's hips and moving as one. Lap the line has a snake made of a group of blockers. A jammer is chosen to try to get past the girls in the snake. When we partner up for pushes and pulls, we're in twos, with one chugging and the other steering. Falls are what they sound like. When you're on the track in a real bout, you go down. A lot. And you must know how to fall so you don't hurt yourself. We all have protective gear – knee pads and elbow pads and helmets and gloves and wrist straps and ankle guards – but learning to fall fearlessly and not tensing up when you bounce is a big part of staying healthy. So, we practice. Falls to one knee. Then falls to the other. Then to both. Then hands and knees. By the time we get to booty blocks and body checks we're pumped, ready to be banging into each other full force.

We practice these slams because this happens in the jam. Women going at full speed rocket into other women moving just as fast. Whips are the same as snakes, but with all of us hooked together with the purpose of flinging the skater playing jammer off the end to give her some extra go. Squats are torture at the end of the drills. Squat thrusts like we all used to do in gym class but coming out of speed drives. At the whistle, no matter where we are on the track, we all fall to our hands and knees, do a thrust and then get back up and race on. By the time we get to them, our muscles are stretched, and our skin is warm to the touch. After we're through with warmups, we divide into squads and play practice bouts. For the last several weeks Coach has broken us into fixed squads, with me as jammer on one and Marianne as the jammer for the other. We play regulation-length practice bouts, two thirty-minute periods. When it's all done, Coach gives us his critique and his final words of wisdom, things to think about for the next practice and to keep in mind for the championship.

For me, practice is heaven and hell. If I do a good workout, and then we play a couple of hard practice bouts, and I score like I mean it, I am wrecked for hours. Heading home afterward, every muscle burns. I ache head to toe. But I walk home smug and tight, it feels so good. I have never wanted anything as much as I want this championship. I've never worked harder for anything either. My name is Nina Gordon. I'm thirty-one years old. I can push as hard as any seventeen-year-old up-and-comer who thinks she's gonna be the next skating phenom. Harder. I've never been stronger in my life.

7 WEEKS BEFORE THE CHAMPIONSHIP BOUT

I walk through the door and the phone is ringing. "Nina?" I call into the apartment, but I know she's not likely to be here yet. I have my hands full, grocery bags from a stop at the Third Street bodega, that I drop on the counter. I slide my backpack off my shoulder. All that's in it is my empty thermos and my stainless-steel bento box, a gift from Nina, and some insurance forms in a folder with paperwork from today's sessions I need to get done tonight to get paid. It's a relief to shuck the thing off.

The phone keeps ringing. I let the machine pick up, which is what Nina would do. I hear the click, then the message starts. "Hello. This is Nina." And then my voice, "And Rachel. We're not here to take your call right now, but we probably want to talk to you." Then Nina again, "Probably. So here comes the beep." Then both of us together, "You know what to do." Then the beep sounds. It took us forever to get that down. Nina was so particular about it. She listened to each version we recorded like she was auditioning us for *America's Got Talent,* but she kept rejecting them. "Too serious," she said. Or "too unfriendly." We must have recited her silly little script a dozen times. Recorded, listened, critiqued, re-recorded. That's Nina. Perfectionist. Well, about some things. Most things.

From the kitchen where I start unbagging groceries onto the counter before putting them away – Nina has particular places in the cabinets and fridge where everything goes, and since I moved in with her, I try to respect her compulsive need for order – I hear Nina's mother through the answering machine speaker. "Nina? Rachel? Are you there? If you're screening, will you please, please, please pick up." There's a pause, then she says, "Nina, I need to consult with you about a serious medical issue. We need to talk. It's somewhat urgent. Please pick up if you're there." Then there's another pause while she waits to see if one of us might oblige her. After maybe ten more seconds, she says, "Okay. I guess you're not home." I can't tell if she's being sarcastic from the tone of her voice, but I assume she is. She's sarcastic about a lot of things, particularly us as a couple. She's especially snarky about me, "Nina's *shiksa*" she once said about me, loud enough for me to hear her, standing in the next room. She thought she was being cute, trading on the joke that every Jewish boy supposedly secretly wants to marry a blond, blue-eyed Nordic babe. Which, in my experience is not true or funny, but whatever. I am a blond and blue-eyed Nordic-looking woman but explaining to me that it was a joke didn't make it feel any less dismissive. As if who I am is readable in my hair color and facial bone structure. Or that being blond, I'm stupid or predictable. "Please call me as soon as you get this," I hear her say through the warble-y machine speaker. "It's important." She hangs up, the machine goes through its clicks, the outgoing tape rewinds and resets.

Ten minutes later, Nina pushes through the door. I hear her key in the lock and come out of our bedroom, where I have stripped out of my work clothes and put on sweats. Because I work in a medical facility, I wear scrubs to work. It's dumb. I'm not a medical professional, but it's the house rules. If it was up to me, I'd live, work, and sleep in sweats. Except maybe when I get dressed up to go out. Nina kisses me.

"Hi, sweetie," she says. I kiss her back, wrap my arms around her, pull her close. Then I recoil.

"You smell like food sweat and cheese farts," I tell her. "Cauliflower. And garlic, maybe? Did you eat Chinese for lunch?"

"Sweet of you to notice. That's my vegetarian eau-de-cologne, the personal scent I wear just for you. I splash it on whenever I know I'm on my way home, to cover up any other scents that might be stuck to me, you know from icky human contact at work or on the subway, and also to celebrate your dietary convictions. I also splash it on whenever I'm feeling, I don't know, kicky. Sixty-one-fifty a quarter ounce on Parfum-dot-com."

"I think I saw that same scent on guttersnipe-dot-biz for a dollar seventy-five a gallon." I let her go. She moves toward the bedroom. I follow her. "How was work? Your mother called."

Nina says, "My mother called you?"

"No. Well, maybe me. She did ask me to pick up if it was me screening."

"Did you?"

"Are you kidding? She left an endless message. She said it was urgent. Messages, I think. There's one from before I came in, I'd bet my eye teeth is also from her. I'm sure she thinks you're ignoring her."

"She should get a clue."

"You know that we're the last people on the planet who have an actual tape-to-tape answering *machine*?"

"You don't like it? I would think you would. It's recycled. It's seriously retro. Right up your political alleyway."

"I don't think I have a 'political alleyway.'" I pause, giving her time to rebut, but she just waits for me to go on. "It works fine, that machine. I'll admit that." I say, "except for that waver that makes everyone sound like they're talking while gargling."

"I doubt we're the last people to use a vintage machine. Those things were built like tanks. I bet lots of people still have them. They keep going and going. They're the Energizer Bunnies of call-screening devices. Built to last you until your parents get a clue. Or die. Built the way things were once made when America was the workbench of the world."

"Vintage is one way to look at it, I suppose. Or you might say 'obsolete' or 'stubbornly Luddite,' if we were on the reverse sides of this argument, which we normally would be. Maybe you should just hire an amanuensis to take your messages. That would give your mother someone to blab to and insulate you even further from ever having to talk to her. Oh, and by the way, about the quality of American craftsmanship, I'm pretty sure that Panasonic is a Japanese company."

"You love that word, don't you?"

"Amanuensis? I really do."

"I inherited that machine from my roommate in college, who got it from her brother, I think. Or maybe her uncle."

"You've told me this before," I say, knowing there is no stopping her.

"And anyway, we're not the last people on the planet to use these kinds of machines because we are not the last people on the planet who have parents. Lots of people still use these because of their excellent screening capabilities. You can't even find a machine like this in a thrift store anymore without paying a premium. Everyone with family-of-origin issues wants one. They get snapped up. You can't screen voice mail on your smartphone."

"You're ridiculous and full of shit. You know that, right?"

"What did she want? Did she say?"

"She wants to 'consult' with you. Something medical."

"My mother, the world's greatest unlicensed diagnostician, wants to consult with me?"

"That was the word she used. Listen to the message."

"She has an iPhone. Why can't she just text me?"

"That would require you to give her the number of your iPhone." I wait for Nina to respond. She doesn't. "How was your day?" When she still doesn't say anything, I say, "I love you. Despite your mother."

Then she says, "My workday was crap. A paperwork tsunami. They're making us justify every session in fifteen-minute intervals. You'd think documenting results would be enough without having to write about every baby step between – you don't want to hear this, do you?" Nina works for the county health department, in a rehab facility that deals with people with genetic or congenital problems. She's a physical therapist, which means when she's focused on kids, that she deals with a lot walking, coordination, or what was once called spastic problems. A lot of her kids have cerebral palsy, spina bifida, or digital deformities. Physical therapy is a misnomer since she spends more of her time doing evaluations and working on adaptive devices than doing actual therapy.

I've heard this complaint about treatment paperwork from her before. "It's taxpayers' money," I tell her. "They want to know how you're spending it."

"So, I should take time from actually doing my job and spend it writing reports on how I'm doing it? I'm sure that will help James deal with his scoliosis or help Juan get a fitted wheelchair seat so he can function with his spina bifida. Or get any of my kids the computers they need to be able to communicate with the world."

"I'm a taxpayer. I want to know what you're doing every second."

"Okay. For you."

"Call your mother, you want to have something to be pissed off about."

I really do love her always-slightly-agitated personality, her jangly edge. It thrills me that anyone would want to be so tuned-in all the time, so hyper-aware of every kind of stimulus that in an instant, if the situation requires it, she can get so cranked up as to be near apoplectic. It makes me feel safe to be around her. Which is funny to say, in some ways, since she's mercurial, even explosive in ways that can feel threatening, even dangerous. But never to me. With me, she's tender and protective. Okay, sometimes she's as sarcastic as her mother, but I get it when she is. I think of her explosiveness as her superpower. I watch her be a badass on the derby track, and I'm awed at how strong and fearless she is. I hear her talking on the phone to pencil pushers from state agencies and insurance companies and government bureaus that want to skimp on her clients' care, and then I see how often she comes home gloating about some win she's engineered for some kid who needs something, "deserves it" she would say, and I'm so proud of her. She's tough. She won't take no for an answer. She calls herself bull-headed. I think she just has the justice gene. Or maybe I should say it's the fighting-for-justice gene. She likes the fight. Maybe it's not really a superpower. Maybe it's just her. But whatever it is, it makes me crazy about her. And wary of her. I know she'd kick anyone's ass for me if it ever came to that. And I know that she is more self-involved than anyone I know. "How was practice?" I call to her as she heads down the hall to shower.

"I'm a little creaky. We're all pushing hard. We want that trophy."

"You're gonna get it. You're great."

"You're such a fan girl."

"What do you want for dinner?"

"Whatever," she says. But she knows I never do whatever. Tonight, I'll make something fast but impressive, something I know she'll like, a Mexican bean salad with *queso añejo* and chorizo chunks on the side. She eats flesh. I don't.

When she reappears, also in sweats and a tee, plates are out, wine is poured, dinner is ready. She smells great. No workout sweat base note, no practice-clothes stink, no stale vegetable overtone. Clean as rain. We sit at the counter side by side. She is to the left of me. She's a southpaw, and I'm a righty and this way we don't bang elbows. Sometimes when we eat together, we even hold hands. She reaches for the TV mounted on the wall and pulls the articulating arm out so we can both see it while we eat. She clicks through the cable channels past *FOX* and *MSNBC* to one of the twenty-four-hour news channels that plays the top stories on a half-hour loop. This is part of our dinnertime ritual – if you can call something a ritual that two people do when they've only been living together for eleven months – eating and watching the news. I sometimes wish we could just sit quietly through a meal and not listen to everything awful that's going on in the world or in politics, or maybe just talk about our days and our plans for tomorrow. Not that we don't do that. We sit together and talk a lot, often right after dinner, or when we're in bed, and sometimes even first thing in the morning before we get up and start the day.

Talking like that never happened in my family, but I used to visit a friend's house sometimes where there was a kind of verbal show and tell around the dinner table, with everyone reporting what they did that day, even the kids. I liked listening to the rest of them, but it terrified me when they expected me to join the conversation. Coming from a family where no one talked about anything significant, it felt like torture finding the right words to tell my friend's parents what I thought was important about my mundane daily activities. I had no experience at conversing that way, and what I said was usually brief and halting. I felt lucky if no one asked for more details. When the conversation moved on past me, and it was my friend's mother or brother talking, and everyone's attention was on one of them, I relaxed. But I vowed if I ever had a family, we would learn to talk to each other the way my friend's family did. We would describe our days and our activities, and we would share the details of our lives. How I would engineer this, I hadn't a clue, though I knew that was what I wanted. With Nina, the conversations don't usually happen at supper, but whenever they do, there isn't much we don't talk about. Eventually.

Most of the time at dinner, while we watch the news, Nina talks back to the TV. We might be the last people among our friends who think television news-watching is necessary, but we like being informed and TV news is a fast way to get the basics. The problem is, the news, when it's bad, has the same effect on Nina that the bad bureaucrats and insurance adjusters she deals with at work have on her. It cranks her up into high-indignity mode. She loves to rant about the stupidity of politicians who voted the wrong way in Congress on issues we care about, or rail at some immoral businessman who is being perp-walked on camera to humiliate him in public. Her anger thrills me. Most politicians and businessmen seem unfixably smarmy to me, but I can't muster the energy to care about them personally. Nina can. Enough, I tell myself, for both of us. And I have to say, I love being the audience for her rants.

"This asshole, who never set foot in a public school, is lecturing the Congress about cutting school funding? He wants his constituents dumb, so they keep voting for him," she sneered at Mitch McConnell. Or, "Here we go again with the white men who want to stick their noses in our pussies. The fuckers. I mean, they harass us, fuck us, impregnate us, not to mention how often they rape or abuse us, but they don't want to take any responsibility for what comes after? Or hold other guys responsible?" This was after some judge let a guy walk who raped and impregnated a semi-comatose woman behind a trash dumpster after a frat party. "They care about the unborn so much, but half of the born aren't of any concern to them?"

We don't argue about much of anything. I agree with her about almost everything she believes. I just don't come from a family where I learned to express my feelings about those things the way she does. Both of her parents are these super verbal, compulsively argumentative people. They have opinions about everything, from art and theater to politics, to religion to social issues, to what wines to drink with swordfish versus flounder, to which restaurants in New York serve the best *osso buco*. Or so she tells me. I've never met her dad. She calls him occasionally, but she never visits him, at least she hasn't since we've been together. He lives just over the bridge in New Jersey, a quick train ride away, but she avoids him like the plague. When she talks to him on the phone, it's mostly when I'm not around. The few conversations I've overheard seem cordial and sometimes teasing, which I gather is what most of their interactions are like, but they're also short. They're check-ins, not substantial conversations. She doesn't let them go on long enough for anything deep.

Her mom, on the other hand, calls all the time, and she comes over, usually unannounced, so I have talked to her. I've gotten to know her; I have an impression of her personality, believe me. And she does have a lot of opinions, like Nina says, which she is not shy about sharing. She's always giving Nina advice about things, from what stores have the best sales to what movies she has just seen and we "just must see," to books we should read, to diets we should try, to cosmetics we should rub on ourselves, to where we should go on our next vacation. As if our economics allow for trips to the places she thinks we ought to go. She offers these opinions without any recognition that they are opinions. She says them like she's reciting facts, not open for dispute, and that's that. She had some choice things to say about me when Nina and I first got together, but she's given up telling Nina what a "schlepper" I am because I don't care all that much about fashion or clothes, and how I "could use a better hairdresser" or how "mousy" I seem to her, or how being a vegetarian means I am not getting some essential nutrition. Sometimes she tells Nina she thinks I have too much influence on her, and sometimes she seems to be saying that if only I was a stronger personality, she would respect me as Nina's mate more.

I see where some of Nina's personality comes from. Sometimes she seems a lot like her mother, though I know if I ever said that aloud she would deny it and probably storm off and be pissed at me for hours. My father would have called Nina's mother "a pushy New York Jew," which is what he called any woman who was smarter than he was, expressed an opinion he disagreed with in his presence or on television, lived anywhere within a hundred miles of the Atlantic seaboard, or had ever set foot in any city between Boston and Washington, whether the woman was Jewish or not. To him, "Jewlandia" was dangerous, a geographical and political nexus full of "Hebrews, coloreds, and women's libbers," designed to keep people like him oppressed. He believed that Jews owned the banks, and controlled insurance companies, hospitals, and every other social institution that had ruined America by forcing liberal politics down everyone's throats, teaching radical ideas in schools and colleges, opening the government to foreigners and outsiders, and always raising taxes. He also believed that everyone else in America except white people were getting handouts of free stuff – from medical care to college educations – and that he was paying for it with his taxes. No amount of facts ever dissuaded him from these convictions.

After dinner tonight, Nina takes my hand and walks me to the living room. "How was your day?" she asks focusing on me at last, as I hoped she would. I work as a masseuse. Not the sex kind, the therapeutic kind. I'm a massage therapist in a chiropractor's office, in a group practice that offers physical therapy, chiropractic services, massage, and dietary counseling. I have an undergraduate degree in communications, but I couldn't figure out what I wanted to do to make a living when

I graduated, so I got a massage license. Once I had a dream of being a radio disc jockey, playing music and doing news on an alternative rock station. I had a late-night shift doing that for two years on my college station. After a while, the program manager asked me to come up with a new format, one that included commentary and call-ins. I became a kind of late-night dorm buddy, the kind you could tell anything to, and whose advice you trusted and sought. I had a following on campus and even a little in the community beyond. Sometimes I talked about current campus events, about how I felt about things going on in our very small collegiate world. It was the first time in my life anyone paid attention to what I said. I didn't trust myself to comment on the world outside of our campus, but I imagined myself one day having to do that. Sometimes I talked about sports because that's what many of my listeners called in to talk about. Most wanted to talk about games our teams had played. Sometimes someone wanted to talk about how much money was spent on men's versus women's athletics. I went to the all main sporting events, basketball and football, track and field, and rugby, which on our campus had passionate fans following both the men's and women's teams. I sometimes imagined having a job as a sports reporter. But by the time I graduated, radio had contracted to mostly computerized national programming, something my teachers, who had been out of the business for years, neglected to warn us communication majors was happening, and the few sports jobs out there weren't offered to me, probably because I was not a dude. Shock jocks and morning-ride bloviators, sports guys and political pundits ate up most of the diminishing amount of live airtime. On most urban stations, the jocks were all guys. Satellite radio was only hiring celebrities. Thoughtful, informed record spinners who loved music or favored non-confrontational news analysis and other obsolete ways of communicating had all but disappeared from local markets. There were one or two women in sports; the ones on television were mostly babes who played to men's fantasies about women sidekicks who would love sports as much as they did. There were a few sidekicks in radio, in the Robin

Quivers mold, who were supposed to laugh along with the male jock's sexism and inanity. That was not for me.

I was offered a job at one station, doing a late-night program playing love songs, giving shallow advice to the lovelorn and making sexy comments to call-in listeners. I had a hard time imagining myself telling lovesick divorcees and horny middle-aged straight men how to orchestrate their love lives. That was what Arbitron said the middle-of-the-night audience wanted. I considered taking it, but it would have required a move to Dayton, Ohio. I flew there to take a look, but the city seemed fusty. And the playlist was lame. How many times a night can you play The Carpenters' *We've Only Just Begun*, or Foreigner's *I Want to Know What Love Is*, or Peter Gabriel's *In Your Eyes* before you want to scream, gouge your eyes out, or shoot someone?

I don't mind doing massage. It's like any other job; it has its great moments and its crappy ones. I'm not crazy about certain of my clients, men mostly, who despite the quasi-medical surroundings of our office, think once they get into the room alone with me, they can show me their dicks and I'll just consent to blowing them or jerking them off. I mean, we hand them a consent form that spells out explicitly what we do and don't do. It says there is never any sexual contact between massage therapist and client. But that doesn't stop some people. The shock for me was the first time a woman grabbed my hand and put it on her crotch. Not that I have any illusions that some women aren't as needy and badly behaved as men. It's just that with men, it tends to be more blatant and more frequent, in my experience, and with women less so. Or maybe that's changing and I'm just now noticing. So that happens. And some clients, both men, and women, smell bad. But the thing people ask me about most is if I get turned off by fat or ugly bodies, sometimes while they are apologizing for the shape of their own body or telling me that their own shape is why they're embarrassed to get massaged. That question always surprises me. The thing I like best about my job is the way people's bodies are different in shape and feel. I love that there are surprising places in the folds of skin I can touch which wake people's senses up. Nina says I am a natural sensualist. She's right. I like the feel of skin. When I oil up my hands and start to work my fingers into the sinew structures and muscle masses of my clients, I feel like I am touching something divine. I know, I know. That sounds new-agey and spiritually fuzzy. But I believe there are mysteries that just don't yield to easy explanations.

When I saw my father die – I was in the room when it happened – I was shocked by the difference between his live body and his dead one. Whatever I thought of him, and it wasn't much, when he was alive, even as he was fading out at the end when he was sick, the spirit that animated his flesh was a familiar if strange comfort. He was my parent, however bad he had been at that, and my life was connected to his life through that animating spirit, and that meant something, for better or worse. But at the moment he died, when that animation was gone and his flesh instantly started to go cold and his lips turned from pink to grey, in that fraction of a second between life and not life, something awful and powerful had transpired. Some force had left his flesh, call it life force or soul or whatever you want. Whatever we say about the natural cycle of life and death, however clearly, we understand it physiologically, the force that animates us carries with it a mystery. When it's gone, the mystery is gone and we're just "ugly bags of mostly water," as a character on Star Trek once said. I feel that mystery when I touch my clients; what I am encountering in their flesh is the true mystery of life, of their lives.

"My day," I say, thinking back on it, putting my head in Nina's lap. "Pretty regular. I'm seeing this guy, I think I told you about him, who has a skin graft from a burn. The doctors think he might get feeling and sensation back into the skin over time. The burn is on his back, so he can't really treat it himself. It needs to be moisturized and cleaned. It's angry looking, red and pitted, but he's a real striver. He doesn't have a partner, so he comes to see me three times a week. He's paying with his own money; his insurance cut him off."

"The fuckers."

"I don't know. I guess. There's only so much to go around. Should he get unlimited sessions if someone else would end up getting none?"

"In the ideal world? There should be health care, and if that's part of it, then yes."

"I admire him for his commitment to being as healthy as he can be, having as much sensation as he can. I mean, on his back, where no one sees it, so who cares, right? The skin heals, what difference does it make if you can feel anything an inch below your shoulder blades? But he wants to be back where he was before it happened. He wants to feel whole."

And he likes getting touched. I can tell this is true. I don't say this to Nina, but I have a kind of special feeling for him. It's not about sex. He craves what we all crave, some bodily warmth, forgiveness for his flaws, intimate care. He never does anything untoward, never pushes the limits at all, but I'm drawn to take care of him, to respond to his need. It's my need, too. He wants what all humans want, and he's figured out how to get it. For him, there's a monetary cost. But I can't help wondering if there isn't a cost for everyone, compromises we make in relationships, ways we bend ourselves to fit to the people we want to respond to us, to touch us, to love us. I look across at Nina. She bends the least of anyone I know.

"I get it," she says. "It's good to have clients like that."

"The graft is healed up at this point, so I know it's as much psychological as physical for him."

"How'd it happen? The burn, I mean."

"Stupid accident. He was reaching for something in a cabinet in his kitchen, lost his balance and fell back against the stove where there was a pot of water boiling for pasta. He caught the handle and it flipped up."

"Ugh."

"There's a weird irony. The graft over the burn is ropey; it looks sort of like *fusilli*, which he told me was what he was going to cook, except it's cold to the touch."

"How does that make sense?"

I shrug. "Not getting as much blood near the surface. There's thick scarring. The mysteries of the body. I'm not a doctor."

"You should be. You should go to med school. You'd be great a great doctor. Focused and compassionate. We need more women docs."

"I wish someone had said that to me ten years ago. I would have taken harder math and science courses in high school."

"It's not too late."

"Yea. I think it is. Besides, I'm not all that hot to be a student again. And where would I get the money?"

"If you wanted to do it, you'd find the money. You'd promise the government you'd spend five years on an Indian Reservation or something. You'd figure it out."

"You want me to spend five years on an Indian reservation?"

"You know what I mean."

"I guess. I appreciate your confidence."

"You sell yourself short."

"I'm happy with the work I'm doing right now."

"You spend too much energy trying to make other people happy. To make me happy."

"That's what makes me happy."

Then I leaned up and kissed her. The conversation could have gone on, I know, but it was making me uncomfortable. Somehow, underneath every conversation where Nina is encouraging me, there is a little kernel of something else, some hint of dissatisfaction, as if, were it not for my love of her, I could be more than I am. This feeling is fraught with contradictions, I know. When she says stuff like that, is she drawing a line between us, or making a prediction that someday I am going to wake up and head out of Dodge? Or she is? Is she judging me for loving her, or simply acknowledging how much I do? Does she want me to be something more than I am? Something other? Or is she just exclaiming on the obvious, that I am happy to be with her and content to be who and what I am right now? I don't know. Even when the way she says things confuse me, I can't always tell whether the feeling generates from me or her. But it's easy enough to derail. Kissing leads to fooling around, which leads to focused sex. I take the evidence of our physical contact as the final word; she loves me enough to want to make love to me. Tonight, we stay on the couch until we have made our fingers sticky with each other's juices, and then move to the bedroom, where we can stretch out more comfortably and get our faces into each other. After we are both sweaty and satisfied, I get out of bed, turn off the lights we have left burning all over the apartment, wash my face and brush my teeth, and return to bed. Nina is fast asleep by the time I get there, and I lean over to kiss her, smelling myself on her lips and chin. Then I wiggle up next to her, my breasts to her back, with one arm threaded under her and one over. I listen to her breath until my breathing matches hers and I drift off toward sleep.

THREE

NINA'S RECOVERY JOURNAL

The modern sport of Roller Derby was invented by Damon Runyon, the guy who wrote the stories that became <u>Guys and Dolls</u>. This was in the nineteen thirties. He had a friend, a promoter, who was producing roller races and Runyon convinced him to make it a contact sport. I Googled it back when I first started skating in bouts. I may be on the sidelines right now, but I know my derby history. Runyon wrote the original rules, and it caught on. It's had its ups and downs for nearly 80 years, but these days, it's the only sport run by women, and though there are men's leagues, women's professional teams dominate. Once I discovered derby, I was hooked pretty quick. These girls kick ass and take names. Pretty soon I was rumbling with them every weekend and practicing solo every day. I was on skates from the minute I got home from work until it was too dark out to see. And then we got organized, got corporate. I was a shareholder, a fractional owner. Somewhere along the way, the girlfriend who got me started got off the train, and then she was off me, and then about a year ago, I met Rachel. In between, the women I was skating with organized a team, started having regulation matches, joined a league, organized a traveling team, and then there were funky uniforms and roller names and coaches and events and tickets to sell and concessions to peddle. It was a life. Well, my life. Exactly like the kind of thing you hear people say about being seriously religious. "It's a life." The place you devote your time, your thought, your energy. Where you invest your belief. My mother, who considers herself devoutly religious, told me that a devout life is hard work. She taught me the demands of faith require adherence to ritual, that the rewards are great though the attainment might be slow. She practiced her religion daily, and I practice mine. This was my mother's best lesson.

6 WEEKS AND 5 DAYS BEFORE THE CHAMPIONSHIP BOUT

After beginning to feel these last few weeks like we were locked into our focus, tonight in our intramural jams at practice we're all over the place, missing blocks, falling, failing to score. Mostly me. I fail to scorc. It's like we've all become a package of fresh meat. Fresh meat is what we call newbies, skaters who are just starting out in training for the sport. Tonight, everything is going spectacularly wrong, with me leading the pack. The half squad I'm on for practice bungled basic moves, and we let the other squad get way ahead in points, scoring on us almost at will. By all reckoning, we should be killing them. We have the best and most experienced players on our squad; we will probably start the championship game together and will play the crucial opening jams before Coach starts substituting. At least that's been his strategy in practice up until now. He likes having us get out ahead of the opposing team early, open a comfortable lead to have a cushion in case we slow down. He pumps us up in the pregame warmup so we're in kick-ass mode from the jump. If we get a good start, it gives us momentum, and momentum is what we're going to need if we're going to beat New York. Coach has honed the starting pack over the last several weeks of practice, moving people into and out of the jammer, pivot, and blocker positions to see who works best doing what.

Roller derby rules can seem confusing the first time you watch the game. The first time I went, with the girl I was sccing years ago who was playing in a pickup league, I couldn't follow the play all. It was fast and furious, and though there were things that attracted me right away, like the speed and the slamming-into-each-other contact of it, how the scoring worked, or what the strategies were for winning, I didn't understand just from watching. The two teams skate in the same direction, and it seems like a race at the beginning, since there is a lineup. But if you look closely, it's more like how football players line up at scrimmage. There's a group in front, blockers, and some folks behind them, jammers. When the ref blows the whistle to start the jam, everyone takes off in the same direction, counterclockwise. Then what looked like a race for the first few minutes turns into something else. No race you've ever seen has body blocks and the people elbowing in front of each other and using the speed of their teammates to whip around and increase their own speed. Its energy might suck you in, but if you don't know the meaning of the hats, it's all a jumble. The hats are the key, though if you don't know to see it, you might not even notice they're different.

Eventually, you can figure it out. The track is oval, with straightaways on either side and hard turns on the ends. The play is a series of short matches called jams. There are three types of players on each five-person team – jammers, pivots, and blockers. The jammer is like the ball in football; her movement determines the scoring. It is her job to pass all the members of the opposing team – "lap them" in derby-speak – with the help of her own teammates, and each time she does, she scores points for her side. The rest of the team members try to hinder the opposing jammer from lapping her teammates while helping their own jammer advance by blocking and obstructing the opposing team's jammer as she tries to pass them. The tricky thing about the game is that every player is on defense and offense at the same time. Scoring doesn't begin until the jammer has passed every member of the opposing team once.

The jam is two minutes long, and each bout is two thirty-minute periods. Lead jammers can end a jam in the middle of the two minutes by signaling a stop – there are hand signals that tell the refs to whistle down a jam – and jammers can change positions during the jam. That's where the hats come in. Each jammer wears a kind of cap over her helmet that has her team's colored star on it. This is uniform for all the teams in all leagues. If the jammer passes the star cap (which most of us call "passing the panty" since the star cap somewhat resembles panties without leg holes but with an elastic waist) to a designated pivot (who is also wearing a designated pivot panty over her helmet, with a bright colored stripe on it instead of a star) the play changes and the pivot becomes the jammer. This is a tactical move made during the jam that sometimes gets the original jammer out of trouble and allows for points to be scored by the new jammer. Pivots serve as blockers unless they are called upon to be jammers. Blockers have two functions. They inhibit the other team's jammers from lapping their own teammates, and they create openings for their own jammers to pass through.

Roller derby is fast, and there is always a lot of action on the oval. Once you learn to keep your eyes on the jammers and you get familiar with the rules, you can begin to focus on the finer parts of the strategy. Like when it's appropriate for a jammer to end a jam. Or why blockers skate backward to keep opposing team members from lapping them, or why blockers back up after penalties. Or when it's worth drawing a penalty.

I'm at my best in the first half of the game. Not that I can't rack up a good run of points in the second half, but I feel it more, and I think it's true statistically, that I'm a little less reliable when I get nearer the one-hour mark and the end of the bout. If we get behind early, our tendency as a team is to push extra hard, sometimes overcompensating and doing ourselves damage. It's easy to get sloppy. That's what the coach has worked on with us for weeks. To keep our heads in the game. To make the other team play *our* game. To be sure we are doing the fundamentals well. He's not a big one for go-for-broke antics. He likes sticking to the game plan. We have practiced all season how to begin fast and score early. But tonight, in practice, the second squad blockers are a curtain wall, and I just can't seem to break through them. I'm impressed with how totally they stopped me, and if I'm impressed, I know Coach is impressed.

When it becomes clear about fifteen minutes in that things are not going well for the starting five, Coach pulls me aside and asks what the hell is going on. "I'm stinking up the place tonight," I tell him, trying to be cute, taking the blame on myself, trying to deflect his anger by copping to the team's failure.

"Well, yeah, I can see that. But what I'm asking is, why?"

"I don't have an answer. I feel all right, but my moves are just not cutting it. Maybe Marianne has just gotten really good while I wasn't watching."

"Yeah, well, the way she's playing, I'm gonna let her squad start and your squad sit on the bench until the second half unless you step it up."

"I hear you," I say, but I don't know what to do. Rachel thinks when things are going against me it gets me charged up, and I just get pumped, but sometimes the opposite happens, and I deflate. I fill with anger at myself, and I can't find the way out, and that just makes things worse.

Coach sees that berating me is not getting anywhere. He asks me if I need to take a longer break.

"That might be a good idea," I tell him since I can't seem to figure out what to do to make things better. I pull off my helmet and walk around the perimeter of the track. I know everyone is looking at me, so I keep my eyes down. Coach has already given the jammer cap to Marianne, who skates under the name *So Long Marianne*. She's nearly six feet tall and making a pun on the name of an early Leonard Cohen song. She's new on the team, just over a year, and she's young, maybe twenty-two, but she's been my primary competition for lead jammer since she got here. She's originally from Finland and skated for a semi-pro team in Helsinki before moving to the US for college. She wants to write for TV and already has spent two seasons in the writers' room of a Finnish political satire show on one of their state-run television stations. We like each other, but we're wary. Our rivalry is healthy, but I'm not ready to accede my lead jammer status to her youth and vigor. She's breathing down my neck, but as long as I can feel her breath behind me, I'm still ahead. Or at least that's what I'm telling myself.

Walking the ring, I think about how I felt as a kid when I failed at something. My parents didn't think failure at anything was an option, but they also didn't like it when I chose to do things at which I might fail. They wanted me to win, but they wanted me to win at what *they* thought was worth winning. Because my parents stopped living together when I was a kid, about many things I could end-run one by asking the other. But about what was worthy of my time and what was not, they were a solid wall of intractable parenting, though often for opposite reasons.

My mother's tactic to discourage me from doing something I was contemplating was undermining. If she disapproved, she would tell me it was beyond me. "That's not in your skill set, honey," I heard from her more than once. She told me that when I wanted to try out for a musical in high school. "You don't have the right talents for the stage," she said, dismissing my desire to audition.

"But I like to sing," I told her.

"You have a pretty voice but singing along with your CDs is not the same as standing up in front of an audience full of your friends and teachers and pretending to be an orphan." I was planning to try out for a part in my high school's production of *Annie*. I thought *Annie* was a terrible play, and my father was downright scornful about its treacly narrative, but what my mother shot down when she derided my desire to try out was not my desire to sing but my desire to sing in front of that audience, to be seen as something other than the strange, awkward nerdy, good girl everyone thought I was in high school. And there was something else in it for my mother. She imagined me failing, forgetting my lines or blocking, or seizing up, and she didn't want my performance to reflect badly on her.

My father, on the other hand, venerated the arts. He had, in some subtle way, communicated that a career in the arts, as an actor or writer or creative person, was a meaningful aspiration. He was the one who took me to shows and museums, who gave me books that were way above my reading level, who expected me to understand that, unlike my mother's insistence that defining myself as a good person came from being a religious and obedient girl, there were moral lessons in books, in the language spoken on stage, and in the music of the symphony hall. If my mother hated the idea that I might embarrass myself dressed in rags while playing a poor orphan on stage, as if that reflected on her somehow, she hated more that my father approved of it. When I didn't even get selected for the chorus, I felt ashamed for my failure as well as disappointed. For my father's part, he was relieved that I was not lending my talents to "something so unworthy of you. People will recognize your talents someday," he told me, "but please do not waste them on inferior work like this." It was the double whammy. My mother's disparagement was somehow based on my inferiority, my father's on my superiority. In the end, it didn't matter what their reasons were. They were in agreement that I shouldn't do what they didn't approve of. My inability to land a role convinced me they were both right.

When one of the teams I joined in high school, in defiance of their scorn, field hockey, and track, won a game or a tournament, each of them was proud enough after the fact to take me out for a celebratory meal, but they never came to the games themselves. My mother claimed she didn't want to see me get hurt, something she was sure would happen. My father claimed to be bored by all sports and said he "could not fathom my interest." They were each willing to display my trophies, just not in their living rooms where the parents of my friends displayed the booty their kids won. But if I came home dejected after a loss, or actually got hurt during a game, like I did one time when I got clobbered in the teeth by an opposing player's stick in a field hockey game, they were severe in their judgments. My mother said that if I wasn't good enough to play the game without getting injured then maybe I shouldn't be doing it. My father simply asked whether or not I had gotten injured on the way to a team win. When I told him I had, he told me, "Well, at least there's that." Winning gold stars in arithmetic made my mother happy when I was in elementary school. Getting A's on my essays made my father delirious when I was in junior high school. Signing up to play field hockey in high school distressed them both.

So protected from failure was I by their discouragement and disapproval, that the first time I utterly bombed at something was in college, over a dozen years ago. I think about this every time something I think is in my control turns out to not to be. I was in the middle of my sophomore year, nearing the point when I would have to declare a major. I was contemplating the things I loved. Literature. Music. Sports. Movies. I'd taken all the required general education classes I needed and it was time to commit to something. I thought maybe I had the chops and the physique to be a dancer, though I never had any formal training. I wasn't interested in ballet, which the few dancers I knew from around campus seemed to feel was necessary as a basic skill even if what you wanted to do was modern dance, but I decided that dance was something I was naturally good at and wanted to pursue anyway. I pretty much killed it at clubs and parties, and people were always complimenting me on my moves. "Graceful," I heard often, and "funky" or "slinky." Even though I was a bit of a daredevil, I wasn't attracted to the kinds of sports where I might have used my physical skills – baseball, soccer, or basketball – and I was no gymnast, tennis player, or lacrosse player, or any of the traditional female sports. I didn't really want to major in physical education anyway. I had a lot of snobby ideas about who went into that field. But I was graceful, and I was strong, and I had moves. I attracted attention when I was dancing. So, defying my friends' warnings, and against the advice of the dancers I knew, I went to the audition to be a dance major.

I was practically laughed out of the place. It wasn't what I didn't know that was the problem, so much as what I couldn't do. I wasn't limber. Not dance-major limber. I wasn't prepared. I took too long to learn the steps in the routines they made us perform. I was good at finding a groove at a club, but when I had to duplicate the steps the dance captain was calling, I was a mess. I kept picturing myself at the audition in that Bob Fosse film, *All That Jazz,* where the dancers get eliminated first in groups and then painfully, one by one. I somehow snuck through the first round, but before most of the auditioners were cut, I was out. I was awful and I knew it.

When it was over, I sat in the hall of the dance studio to catch my breath and contemplate my future. I was nineteen years old, and in that moment, it felt like nothing I could ever do would redeem me from my own foolishness. After I sat for a while, gulping water to replenish what I sweated out attempting to follow the dance calls, and trying to figure out what I needed to do next, someone sat down next to me. It was one of the professors who had been rating us in the audition. She sat in silence for a while and then she said, "I saw you working really hard in there. You have a lot of grace." Now I hated hearing that word.

"Really? Thanks." I was surprised she was being complimentary when I knew I sucked. "Why didn't you pick me?"

"Because I could see you weren't ready, which said to me you didn't really want to be doing this. Almost every other girl in there has worked hard for this, and they came in with things to show me. Some of them were disappointed at my reaction to them, but none of them were pretending. You were."

I was shocked at how direct she was being. Adults, other than my mother, who usually came at things in her own twisted way pretty much straight on, were always dissembling, trying not to hurt anyone's feelings; teachers were like that especially. My mother didn't give a shit about anyone's feelings, but this was different. The woman was right. I had been pretending. I had no idea why I thought I wanted this.

"Maybe this is your calling, but if it isn't, you'll only disappoint yourself if you pretend it is. If you want something badly enough to work at it, then do it. Prepare. If you're not willing to do that, you're always going to look the way you looked in there, like you're not committed enough to it to put your all into it. You need to take some time and think about what you really want to do. If you decide you want this enough to try again, come and see me. We'll figure out what you need to do to get there." I never talked to her again.

Another big failure was when I came out to my parents. I had a feeling that they knew already what my sexual and relationship preference was, but we had never discussed it. They had each made comments about my "tomboy" look and my short hair, my lack of boyfriends and my apparent lack of interest in the normal social life of a teenage girl. I went to parties and hung out with friends, but my mother caught on to the fact that I didn't date and in my senior year of high school, after asking me over and over who I was likely to take to the prom, made a joke that if I waited too long the only date I would be able to get was with Jodi Pennell, who everyone assumed was gay. She was. Though Jodi had not asked me, I told my mother she had. We were in the kitchen of her apartment and she slapped me across the face and said, "Don't even joke about that." But I dug in. I knew that there was a better way to tell her, but the slap outraged me. "She's my girlfriend," I told my mother. "We're lovers. And I haven't told you because I knew you'd react like this." Then I ran out of there, slamming the door behind me as hard as I could.

The lie trapped me. I went to Jodi's house and told her what I had told my mother. Jodi was mortified. "I can't go to the prom with you. I'm not out to my parents."

"What are you going to do?" I asked her. "Are you even going? Are you staying home?"

"I'm going with Paul Boyer."

I was stunned. "Why?"

"Because he asked."

I decided that I had to tell my father the truth about what I had told my mother so I could hang out at his house and pretend I had gone. He was no more enthusiastic than my mother had been, but he kept his judgment to himself. Verbally, I mean. I knew what he thought. He let me pretend I had gone to the dance, took a picture of me in a fancy dress I bought second hand for the occasion, and told my mother he had seen me off. But I was despondent. I hadn't *prepared* to tell them this essential truth about myself and because I hadn't, I felt like a liar and a phony. It took me weeks to get past it. Or, at least, to calm down about it. Somehow, just because of the way I talked about it, or rather didn't talk about it, it became impossible to discuss it with either of them with any sense of reasonable proportion. My mother was angry that I deceived her about my sexuality as much as she was angry that I was gay. My father was angry I had put him in the position that he had to lie for me, *and* he was angry that I was gay. The only positive outcome was that I did end up having sex with Jodi Pennell. She took my virginity and made me sure I was who I said I was. We saw each other on the sly all summer, and then we both headed off to college. It was nice while it lasted, but after that, I never saw her again.

After I walk the perimeter of the track for a while, Coach calls me over. It is well into the second half. He asks me if I want to go back in. He's made a bunch of unusual substitutions and none of them seem to have perked up the play, so he tells me he's inclined to go back to the starting lineup. I tell him I'm ready to try again and I go in for the final 15 minutes with my usual squad. We don't fully recover our momentum, but we play well enough to not fall further behind, and we even gain some ground before regulation ends. When it is all over, Coach sends us home without any notes on our play, telling us all to get some rest and come back prepared to kick ass next time. The second squad gathers in the parking lot. They're headed out for drinks, despite the Coach's orders not to drink while we're training for the championship. Marianne asks me if I want to join them, but I tell her no, that she should go and enjoy herself. It's a kindness that makes me feel bad, though I don't blame her. I blame myself for not being good enough. I know I need to let it go, but that's what I carry home. I'm stewing when I get there, and I have the fleeting thought to just go to bed and not inflict myself on Rachel in this crappy state of mind, but she is waiting for me when I get inside, and I collapse into her arms. I can't explain any of this to her and so I don't try. I let her hold me, and after a while I let her lead me to bed.

FIVE

NINA'S RECOVERY JOURNAL

Twice last night, I had death dreams. They woke me up terrified both times. Not dreams of my death, which you might expect after the pain of major surgery and the drugged aftermath of having an organ extracted. No. In my dreams, the deaths were anonymous strangers. They were strewn across a blistered and wrecked landscape, their bodies scattered and broken like fatalities from a terror attack, or an earthquake, or a terrible aerial bombardment. I was wandering through this landscape, a place I did not know. It was impossible to walk without stepping on bodies. There were limbs and torsos all over the ground. They were charred and bruised and ruined from this horrible, fiery event, but they also looked odd, hard to make sense of, in some ways like the parts had not come from real bodies at all, but from semi-realistic mannequins, or from a Hollywood prop closet, pieces created to simulate the look of dismembered human limbs. They were unreal, but terrifying, monstrous, devastated by the explosive death that had been visited upon them. They were lying in contorted positions, bones broken in the most excruciating of ways. The bodies were scattered along with the evidence of their everyday lives, cooking utensils and school bags, casual clothing and bedroom furniture. These were not warriors who died in battle but citizens who were slaughtered perhaps as collateral damage, or in a genocide too horrible to fathom.

When I woke up, feeling the sharp pain from the incision or the stitches or the internal tearing or all of it, I was shaken. I am taking pain killers, Tylenol with codeine now, but high-octane morphine right after the operation, and then a step-down to Oxycodone for a few days. They all disorient me, tricking my senses. I have to remind myself where I am, and how I got here. "I am home in my own bed recovering after donating a kidney

to my father," I say aloud to myself, adjusting my internal physical experience to life on a single organ, adjusting my mental
state to this diminishment.

The death dreams started two days after the operation, by
which time I knew that I would survive, and that the operation
seemed successful for my father. At least as far as the implan-
tation part went. He has a long recovery ahead, but "indications
are good," or so say the doctors. I remember from one of the
psychology courses I took in college that death dreams indicate
the symbolic end of something as often as they are about any
kind of literal death. I'm not going to die from this, and hope-
fully, my father will now be able to live normally. I don't know
how my life will be changed by this operation, what I will have
to give up or what, in time, I will recover. What I wasn't prepared for was how totally I would be knocked on my ass.
"Insult to the system" are the words all the doctors and nurses
use to talk about the aftermath, which is a way of saying nothing specific about pain, tiredness, or just plain lack of
inclination to move. I think about calling out to Rachel and asking her to make me something to eat, soup or something else
easy to digest and light on the stomach, but then I remember
that she's at work. I turn my head to see the bedside clock. Two
thirty. It must be afternoon because there is light in the room,
and besides that, she is not next to me in bed. Has she been in
bed with me at all since I came home? I have a hard time remembering. Then I remember that she has not been sleeping
with me. Where is she sleeping? Couch? Cot in the living room?
Is this the first time since the operation I have asked myself
these questions? I don't remember. I'm typing this one finger at
a time on my iPad, lifting my head just enough to see the screen
propped against a pillow on my abdomen I think I have been
clutching against the pain. I realize I have drifted back to sleep
when I drop the device and it hits my chest, startling me awake.
I'm groggy, logy, but also afraid to let myself go back to sleep.
There's a residue of fear I feel has infected me deep in my
bones. I'm tired and I'm alone, and despite knowing I'm well
into my recovery, I'm scared if I go back to sleep, I'll die.

6 WEEKS AND 4 DAYS BEFORE THE CHAMPIONSHIP BOUT

Nina beats me home from work. This is unusual. The minute I come in the door I can tell something's bugging her. She's standing at the kitchen counter drinking a beer. This goes against team protocol. They've all vowed not to drink, so I know something's going on. I put my backpack down in the kitchen and hug her. "You all right?" I ask. "Why are you home so early?"

"My last appointment canceled. I just bugged out early. My mother called me at work. I've asked her a million times never to do that. She doesn't get it. There are boundaries. She's relentless."

"Call her back."

"She'll just bust my balls about something."

"News flash. You don't have balls."

"Shit. I don't?" She grabs her crotch to check. This is a kind of joking we both do these days, though I think she got it from me, where we take something stupid literally. After she pulls her hand out of her crotch she reaches over and pulls me in, kisses my neck. "Don't worry about it. Whatever this is, by the time practice is over I'll be too tired to worry about it."

"I thought practice didn't start 'til seven. There's more of the pasta salad I made us last night. If you're going to break training, I can open that Pinot you like.

"No. I am off alcohol. This beer is medication. I'll burn it off at practice. It won't slow me down. I'm going to head over and skate some laps. I'll eat after practice."

"You want company?"

"You're such a fan-girl."

"I just want to always be everywhere you are. No, wait. I just remembered. I have my appointment with Dr. Gray at 7:30. I'll meet you somewhere after for eats."

"She's your new shrink?" She says this with an air of disdain. No one has ever dragged Nina to a shrink, and she would never go without kicking and screaming the whole way.

"She's not a shrink. She's a Clinical Psychologist. And you make it sound like I've had ten before her. She's only my second therapist since junior high. They save the actual medical doctors for the serious nut-bags, and for prescribing. My primary's already dealing me Zoloft. I only get eight sessions. Insurance rules. I better be better by then."

"Or what happens?"

I make an explosion sound and make a motion like my head is blowing up.

She watches this demonstration and then says, "Only your second one? I'm surprised." She waits for me to laugh. When I don't, she says, "Sorry. Didn't mean to strike a chord. Just trying to lighten the mood."

"Yeah, well. I'm not so crazy that I have like a whole suitcase full of therapists."

"Suitcase of Therapists. What a great band name. 'Ladies and Gentlemen, let's bring on with one great roar, Suitcase of Therapists." She makes a sound that approximates a cheering crowd. Then I laugh. Nina says, "So Dave and Buster's? After? The upstairs bar?"

"I've been meaning to ask. Are those two queer?"

"Out of here."

I know I am treading into dangerous water, but as Nina is about to wheel out of the door I say, "Call your mother. But not between now and seven. She's out at her minyan."

"You know more about her life than I do."

"She talks to me more than she talks to you. She likes me better, too, even though I'm, you know, not in the tribe." I drop my voice to a fake whisper when I say that last part. But the minute it's out of my mouth, I think it was a mistake to say it, even teasing.

Nina turns serious. "No, she doesn't. Being nice to you is social behavior. She doesn't like you at all. If she liked you, she'd give you shit. She thinks you're the *shiksa* devil dyke who turned my head from the handsome Jewish doctor she believes it's my destiny to marry."

"Because our kids won't be Jewish if you marry me and I carry them. Oh, wait…" I know I'm keeping her from heading to the roller rink. But I know she'll take the bait of that comment and stay a while longer. She does.

"Yeah well, if you believe that bat shit crazy stuff. It's never going to happen anyway."

"Marrying or kids?" Nina doesn't answer me. "She's just freaked you're dating a Buddhist."

"There's a holy trinity in Buddhism?"

"I gave them up."

"Nnnaa." Nina makes a buzzer sound. "There's no giving them up. There's no wishing them away or washing them off. For my mother, it's like original sin or a port wine birthmark. Besides, you have the map of Ireland…Never mind. You just need to know that to my mother, once a believer, always–"

I interrupt her. "She just wants our kids to be *landsman.* Or *landsgals*, if there's such a thing."

"Where'd that word come from? You amaze me. How do you come up with this shit?"

I admit, I am a little flattered. "Phillip Roth. Or maybe Henry Roth. You recommended them, remember? I read them. Both very good."

"Your retention of these non-events never ceases…but it wasn't me. It was my mother that time we went out to dinner at, what kosher restaurant was that? Oh, yeah. Giuseppe's Bacon, Lobster, Cheese, and Treif Meat Pie Bistro."

"Funny. As I recall the *treif* latkes there were the best part of that meal. I hate to disappoint you, but it was you. We talked about those books that time at Zahav, an actual kosher restaurant. Your mother was testing me, but it was you who gave me the details about them when we got home. You just think I don't listen to you, but I take in every word –"

"The last thing I want is someone else telling me how to live."

"Are you talking about me or her, because I'm not telling you anything. And your mother's not having much of an impact, so what's your actual beef here?" I realize that we are now having a serious conversation about the religion of the kids Nina has never agreed to even talk about having with me.

"I was raised with all that stuff, my mother's feminist minyan I was dragged to every other weekend, the divorced kid's nightmare. Worship, but with the traditional pieties turned on their asses by her coven of orthodox Jewish witches, if you'll forgive the oxymoron."

"I'll forgive you anything."

"Trust me, imposed or implied, all that stuff is about should-have and ought-to, and don't."

"Yeah, but you blew that up a long time ago, the first time you put your fingers into that girl's pussy. What was her name? Jodi Pencil? You just have to keep reminding yourself."

"Pennell," she mumbles. "Jodi Pennell." Then she is out the door. I never know if she gets herself worked up sparring with me or being pissed at her mother, so she has something to grind against at practice, or if there's more going on behind it that matters. I know she won't bring it home. She'll be too tired for arguing. After practicing, and breaking training again by drinking another beer at D&B's, she'll be a rag doll. But the minute we get back here she'll want to fuck, which always amazes me, not that I'm complaining. She can drag in the door with about a half a cylinder firing and then somehow find the energy to fuck me into oblivion.

SEVEN

INTAKE, RACHEL WILLIAMS

CONCLUSORY NOTES: Initial evaluation
PATIENT NAME: WILLIAMS, RACHEL   SESSION # 1
DSM CODE: Record # 447/17
DESCRIPTION:
PRESENTING ISSUE(S): (From pre-treatment phone conversation) Trouble sleeping with bruxism; anxiety about the future; fear of loss of primary relationship; self-doubt
REFERRING ENTITY: Self
INSURANCE: Fonterra Healthcare HMO
SESSION: $175
  CO-PAY: $40

6 WEEKS AND 4 DAYS BEFORE THE CHAMPIONSHIP BOUT

When Dr. Gray shows me into her office, I hardly look around. I admit I'm nervous about being here, more than I expected to be. The last time I was in therapy – the first time – I was fifteen and just starting to come to terms with the fact that I was gay. I was unnerved by my attraction to girls, and I felt terrified and sinful and isolated and judged. I knew my parents and pretty much everyone I knew would think it was wrong, immoral. People think that by 2009 or 2010 it was easy to just come out, that there was "so much social information and political support" but no one has an easy time understanding their sexuality or gender at age fifteen, I don't care how relaxed their parents are and how cool their town or neighborhood is. In my case, because my father was such a conservative asshat, and my mother such a cowed dishrag, if you'll excuse the mixed metaphor, the idea of my father figuring out who I was, let alone imagining me trying to tell him, or trying to get my mother to be in any way sympathetic when I knew what her reactions would be, was terrifying. And no one in my town or school or community was likely to be much help.

I saw a counselor I got sent to through school. I think she was a psychologist, but her title was counselor. Someone figured out, my English teacher I think, that something had changed about me. I wasn't participating very much, and I was more than a little checked out, and so I got this referral. I was probably depressed; I was certainly stressed out, guilty and conflicted. And I was terrified that if I told anyone I was gay it would get back to my parents. I was not ready to have it out with them. When I first went to her, I worried the counselor would have to tell them. I didn't understand that she was bound by law to keep what I said in our sessions confidential. Or maybe I knew she was but didn't trust she would. Most adults I knew told small lies all the time so they could do whatever they wanted when it came to kids; I was habituated to not believe much of what adults said. My parents lied all the time, mostly by omission but sometimes to my face. Most often about their drinking habits or money or their own relationship, which they always said was "fine" even after a night of screaming at each other.

The counselor's office scared me because it felt like the interrogation rooms I had seen on police shows on television, white boxes with metal desks and chairs. Nothing to suggest that anything caring could happen there. I didn't understand that institutions like school didn't have the money to spend on decorating counselors' offices or buying comfortable chairs. Anyway, despite my fears, going to see that counselor helped. I was lucky. She was a good listener; she did not seem to want to judge me. After a few weeks of seeing her, I had told her pretty much everything, the way I felt about girls, the crush I had on Lori from the *Gilmore Girls*, not to mention Tasha Yar from *Star Trek: The Next Generation,* which I watched religiously in reruns on cable. I thought Tasha was beautiful and hot, and I masturbated thinking about her every night my entire junior year of high school. It occurs to me to wonder if I am going to need to tell this new shrink about stuff like this, or rehash the whole deal with my parents, or if we can just start with the now. I guess I'll see. In high school, just having someone to talk to, just being able to say things about myself out loud, was a gift. A picture of Mrs. Lewiston's austere office comes back into my mind. That was her name, my high school counselor: Alma Lewiston.

Dr. Gray's space is palatial compared to where Mrs. Lewiston had to work. I start to take in the colors on the wall, muted melon-orange, and the coordinated curtains and pillows on the couch, but before I take in all the details, Dr. Gray settles into the chair facing me. She has shaken my hand at the door, telling me her name, confirming I am her next appointment, but she introduces herself again, very formally using her title, but then asks what I'll be comfortable calling her. "You can call me Elaine," she tells me, earnestly, "if you would prefer in our sessions. Or Dr. Gray is fine if not. Either way, I want you to decide to call me something. Some of my patients never decide, and never find a way to address me."

"I'll stay with Dr. Gray for now," I tell her. "If that's okay."

"Sure," she says. "I'm going to ask you some questions to get started, to get a basic picture of your background and why you're here, and to give me some insight into your personal history. These questions are designed to elucidate aspects of your early relationships and will help me get to know you a little and to know what you're carrying with you into these sessions. Some of the questions are very general, and some might seem irrelevant, but they give me basic information without taking up too much of the time we have together. They're a good starting point."

I like that she is telling me this. I like to know how things work. It makes what she's doing feel transparent, a word I heard a lot in my communication courses at school. Transparency allows the listener to make judgments, though there are some theorists of communication who think the idea is a sham, feeling that there are always hidden agendas in communication no matter how transparent one tries to be. I try to see if there's guile in the things people say, and I trust my instincts about whether to believe they're telling the truth. I give people the benefit of the doubt, I suppose. The opposite of what Nina does. She's suspicious until she's satisfied she doesn't need to be.

Dr. Gray finishes explaining the questions. "They're designed to elicit broad but not necessarily deep answers. I promise we'll go deeper into all your specific concerns and everything you want to explore, and the things I think could yield something beneficial, starting with your next session. Make sense so far?"

"Sure."

"Okay. Let me begin by asking you about your childhood. Where were you born? Where did you grow up? What did your parents do for a living?"

"I was born in Schuylkill Haven, in central Pennsylvania. My grandfather was a third-generation coal miner. My dad worked for a tool-and-die maker up there because my grand-parents wanted him to have a vocation and did not want him in the mines, but we moved to Quakertown when I was a kid. Really a suburb of Quakertown, a suburb of a suburb. My father hated cities, or so he said, but I think he just hated people. He didn't want to be around anyone who wasn't the same as us, race, religion, all that."

"What age?" she asks me.

"My father's age?"

"What age were you when you moved there?"

"I was nine. The summer before fourth grade. I was lonely that year. I had left all my friends behind. I think my mom was lonely, too, but my dad kept telling us it was a good thing we had moved because the mines were all closing and soon there wouldn't have been any work and we would have starved. My mother was from up there, born and bred in the coal region she used to tell people, and she never liked Quak-ertown, but when they argued about moving back up near Scranton that's what he'd say, that we would have starved to death if we stayed up there because all the machine shops were only there because of mining, and without mining there was nothing to do and no business supporting anyone. In Quakertown, we lived in a small subdivision where all the houses looked the same, and my dad worked at a shop that made spare parts for trucks and some parts for trolleys, big vehicles, you know. Philly still had a trolley system, and they were the big client for some of the stuff he worked on. There's still trolleys to this day, which is amazing considering how old fashioned it seems."

I realize I am wandering on and off the point. I stop talking and look at Dr. Gray. She is taking notes while I talk, or at least she seems to be; I can't see what she's writing. She might be doodling for all I know. I wonder if all this preliminary stuff is boring for her, the recitation of the normal background of all her patients, before she catches up to the now.

When she finishes writing she looks up at me. "Which of your parents would you say was most responsible for taking care of you growing up?" she asks.

"My mother stayed home with me when I was in elementary school, and then got a job as a receptionist in an insurance office a few blocks from our house when I was in junior high. One of those storefront places that was originally a candy store or an in-home dentist's office or something. There were like six people who worked in one room. I never understood why they needed an actual receptionist since everyone was right there when you walked in, but whatever. She went to work after I left for school and got home around the same time I did. I'm sure she did other things than greeting people who came in. I know she answered phones and did some paper-work kind of stuff."

"So, your mom was the one who was most responsible for raising you," she said, reminding me I'd drifted off the question.

"I guess I would say my mom was around most on a daily basis. But if you're asking who made the rules, that was my father. He was strict; he had a lot of specific ideas about how the house should be run. One thing that was ironclad was we had dinner at the same time every night, five-thirty, and my bedtime was the same every night. No exceptions. I remember one time he made me stop working on a school project even though I wasn't finished, and it was due the next day. My mother argued with him, but he wasn't having any of it. Those were the rules. I should have planned my time better. I went to bed crying, and I think my mother called my teacher and explained what happened the next day.'

"How did that make you feel?"

"I thought my father was being unfair. But if you're asking me if I was angry at him, the answer is no. It was my fault. I didn't get the job done on time. I learned my lesson. To this day, I am never late for anything, and if some outside force makes me late, I get pretty wound up about it, even if it's not my fault. I did all my work on time in high school and college. I got the message."

"Okay. Not angry. Interesting." She wrote something down. "What else? Anything else he was regimented about?"

"We had the same foods on the same days of the week every

week. My mom tried to vary the ways she prepared things, but it was chicken on Monday, chicken leftovers on Wednesday, meat on Tuesday, meat leftovers on Thursday, fish on Friday, and spaghetti or some macaroni casserole on Saturday and sometimes again on Sunday if she made a big pot of it. Long after the Church stopped insisting everyone eat fish on Friday, we still did. That's how my father was raised, and he didn't think there was any good reason to change. We went to church for the same mass every Sunday. He liked things to run smoothly, and he was unhappy with us when they didn't."

"Here's another story about how regimented my family life was. When I was a junior in high school, my father had his first heart attack. It was the last day of May, the first warm day after a long winter. My mother and I sat down at the table waiting for him to come in the door at five-twenty-five, his usual arrival time, just long enough before dinner to take off his jacket and tie, wash his hands, and make it to the table at five-thirty. When he wasn't there by five-thirty, I think we knew something was wrong but hoped he was just delayed. At five-thirty-five my mother looked up and said, 'Your father has had a heart attack. Call Mercy General.' Sure enough, he'd just been brought in by ambulance. She didn't say, 'I wonder if something's wrong, or I wonder if he's stuck in traffic. She knew that the only thing that would have kept him from arriving on time to have dinner with us was a myocardial infarction."

"Who is 'us'? Do you have siblings?"

"No. It's just me. My mom told me she tried to get pregnant after she had me, but she never did. I don't know why."

"Was there anyone else living with you?"

"No. Both sets of grandparents lived all their lives near Schuylkill Haven, and they stayed there after we moved to Philly. They all died young. Both men died of lung disease. My grandmothers didn't stick around long after their husbands were gone. There was a period when I was in junior high when we were going to funerals every six months."

"Is there anything else you remember about your father's heart attack? Was it a bad time for you?"

"He was in the hospital for a while, maybe a week, and then he was home in bed for a while, I'm not sure how long, and then he went back to work. My mother hovered around him, and I wasn't supposed to do anything that bothered him or made noise and disturbed him, but things went back to normal after that. After the heart attack, he tried to stop smoking and was grumpy for a while. I suppose it was a big deal, scary for him. And maybe they protected me from the worst of it, but I don't remember anything being all that much different once he went back to work."

Dr. Gray turns her eyes to her notes and jots some things down, then says, "I want to get back on track here. I know this seems like I am jumping around, but there is a logic to all of this. If you had **to choose a few words or a phrase to describe your relationship with your mother, what would those words be? Start as far back as you can remember. Age five, perhaps.**"

"I don't know. Normal. We were like everyone else. That's what he wanted."

"Your father."

"I know you asked about my mother, but she wanted what he wanted."

"Do you remember any specific events that might give me a picture of what that meant?"

"Okay. Here's an example. My mother always fixed herself up before my father got home. Every day. When I was little, she used to sit me up on the bench next to the dressing table in her bedroom so I could watch her put on makeup in the mirror. I might have been a little older when she told me it was important never to let your husband see you 'without your face on.' I was born in 1994. You'd think that kind of corny stuff would have gone out the window by then. I mean what with feminism and all. But not for my mother. She spouted a lot of nonsense about men and husbands and sex she learned from her mother and never reconsidered. When I was older, in high school, and I knew I was attracted to girls, I didn't feel the need to get made up to pretend to be beautiful for boys. But if I went out of the house without makeup on, my mother gave me a hard time."

"I want to come back to some of that, but let's finish these questions first. Do you feel close to your mother?"

"As little kid, I sure did. I guess in some funny way I still do. She's irrelevant now. I don't think about her that much. I know that sounds awful, but it's the truth. But back then, she was the one who was always there."

"How about your father? Can you give me a word or phrase to describe him?"

"I think I said the one I'd use already. Strict."

"Did you feel you lived up to what he wanted?"

"No. I mean, sure, when I was a kid. He never made me feel bad when I was little. I was pretty, obedient, and girly, and that's what he wanted. It was later that I wasn't able to live up to what he wanted. As a kid, I wished he was different, more like my friends' dads or the dads I saw on TV. You know, friendly and open-minded, or goofy and good-humored. But he wasn't going to change. He was who he was. I don't blame him for anything."

"Did you feel growing up that your parents loved you?"

"I don't know if I ever thought about it. That word wasn't used much in my house. We were a family. They were my parents, and parents love their kids, right? So, I guess I thought they loved me. I felt secure. I knew my parents would stay together. My parents didn't believe in divorce, which is more than I can say for the parents of half the kids I grew up with. I think I believed that that was proof of something."

"Not a ringing endorsement for the concept of meaningful relationships. Or love."

"No, I suppose not."

"But you felt secure? Your house felt safe and your place in your parent's world seemed stable?"

"Yeah."

"When you think about your parents now, which one would you say you were closest to?"

"My mom. My dad and I didn't share much. And when I was older, I mean in high school, he didn't seem to like me very much. I know for sure he didn't like the fact that I was attracted to girls when that started. But he was one of those men who shows his disapproval by saying nothing. He was a big one for the silent treatment. He folded his arms across his chest and shook his head and held his tongue. At least with me. He yelled at my mom, but he didn't bark at me. For which I guess I should be thankful. He could have said the things he was thinking, which I'm sure would have been worse."

"Sometimes having it out can be a great catharsis and leads to things being more open, and sometimes things said in anger become the whole story. It's hard to know which would have been better."

"I'm pretty sure it wouldn't have had the effect of getting us talking in my house. That just wasn't his style. Even if he opened that particular can of worms, he wasn't likely to go fishing with them."

"You like metaphors. That's a good one."

"I think I have to blame Nina for that. She's my girlfriend. She's a metaphor junkie."

"Just a few more questions. When you got upset as a child what would you do?"

"As a young child? I don't remember getting upset that much. Later I did, but by then I'd just leave the house and walk around the neighborhood or go over to a friend's house."

"Did you talk to those friends about what was upsetting you?"

"No. I wanted to get away from whatever it was. I tried to put stuff behind me."

"Did you ever talk to your mother if your father upset you, or visa-versa?"

"No. No one would have been comfortable with that."

"If either of your parents realized you were upset, would they ever respond to that physically? Hug you, or hold you?"

"Not that I remember, no."

"You mentioned that you figured out in high school you liked girls. Is that when you told them?"

"Yeah. It was awkward and complicated, but I guess you could say I came out to them. I mean, the conversation was more abstract than confessional, and I had a lot of help from a counselor about what to say, but they got the gist."

"Before you came out to them, did you ever feel rejected in any other way by your parents?"

"My father once said, 'No kid of mine would ever behave that way.' Is that what you mean?"

"Yes. Why did he say that?"

"I was horsing around at a family gathering with some of my cousins. We stomped through a flower bed or through a vegetable patch. Something like that."

"How did you feel when he said that?"

"I guess it hurt because I remember that he said it. But I don't remember exactly what I was doing that made him scold me. Maybe I had already done something I shouldn't have, or maybe he was trying to keep me from doing something. That part I don't remember."

"Were your parents ever violent or threatening to you? Did they ever spank you?"

"I remember getting swatted by my mother a few times, but I have no idea what for. I don't remember my dad ever hitting me. He wasn't like that at all. I think the worst punishment I ever got was being sent to bed without any dinner. He'd tell me to go up to my room and think about what I did wrong, and then he'd come up like an hour later and stand in the doorway waiting for me to say I was sorry."

"Did you?"

"Of course."

Dr. Gray writes again.

"Were there any other adults you were close to when you were a kid?"

"My grandparents, until they died, but we only saw them a few times a year."

"Was it hard to lose your grandparents?"

"It was sad, but I don't remember it having much of an impact on anything in our day-to-day lives. I think when my mom's father died, we inherited some money. We got a new car."

"Did you lose any other important people during your childhood? Friends? Other relatives?"

"My father came from a large family; there were lots of uncles. But they weren't close. I remember we went to a family reunion picnic in Scranton one time when I was maybe ten. All these men came up to us and told him I was the spitting image of some aunt or cousin, Joanie something-or-other. My father didn't like it, because he had some beef with her or her family. I don't remember the details. On the way home, he told my mother I was way prettier than Joanie ever was."

"Are there any experiences from your childhood you would say were traumatic? Anything you remember as terrifying?"

"I came home one day, and the house was empty. I was little, maybe six or seven. I remember that it was the fall, and I walked home and there were lots of leaves on the ground. Maybe it was near Halloween, which always scared me. I don't like cats, and stories about ghosts and zombies always freaked me out. This was the height of the time that zombies were showing up in movies and on TV and all the kids were talking about them. When I got home and my house was empty, I didn't know what that meant. I called for my mother and went looking through the house for her, but she wasn't there. I don't know if it was my imagination or I saw something that scared me, but I remember I started to cry and by the time she came home I had convinced myself something horrible had happened to her. It was the same thing that made her so sure my dad had a heart attack when he was late that time. Their regularity. She was always there and if she wasn't it must mean something awful. I got myself worked up. I think I might have even thrown up. When my father got home and my mother told him about it, he laughed. By that time, I think I was over it, and I might have laughed as well. I had dreams about zombies for a long time after that."

"Did your relationship with your parents change as you got older?"

"Well, my dad was pretty disapproving of my interest in girls, which he figured out was not just theoretical by the time I was a senior and went to prom with one. I think it embarrassed him. He had expected me to have boyfriends and be dating boys and I wasn't. I think he didn't know what to do with that, so he just stopped talking to me about much of anything. But I knew he didn't like it. I don't think he liked much of anything about me by then."

"What do you mean?"

"He made comments about the way I dressed and said things like I didn't do a very good job looking like a boy. I never wanted to look like a boy, I'm pretty femme, but to him lesbian meant mannish. But mostly I think he didn't even know how to be angry about it. He was just disappointed. I was his only kid, and I turned out wrong. That's how I took it, anyway. I just wasn't what I was supposed to be."

"How much do you see your parents now?"

"Well, my dad's dead. He had another heart attack during my sophomore year in college. I almost never see my mother. She won't come down to the city so if I want to see her, I have to go up to Quakertown. She believes all the bullshit my father told her about how dangerous the city is. She thinks if she comes down here, she'll wind up dead. When I left for college, I knew I was leaving for good. We talk maybe twice a year. She's retired and very involved with the church now. We have nothing in common and nothing to talk about."

"Do you want to have children, Rachel?"

"I do, but my girlfriend doesn't. Or she says she doesn't. The first time it came up she was pretty adamant. She said, 'No way I'm letting an alien invade this body I worked so hard for.' She's pretty buff. We were at a bar, drinking and joking. I didn't take her all that seriously. I had just started staying at her place regularly. I didn't know where our relationship was going and I wasn't sure we were all that serious, so I didn't put all that much stock in what she was saying. But we're coming up on a year and when having kids comes up as maybe part of some future plan, she says things that confuse me. Sometimes she's just as adamant as she was the first time we talked about it, and sometimes she seems more open to the idea, and sometimes she just changes the subject."

"When you think about having children, what dreams do you have for them?"

"I want them to love me. That's all. I want them to feel all right about themselves no matter what, and I want them to be my friend. I want us to be friends for life."

After I say this, I notice Dr. Gray glance at her watch. My internal clock says we have been here nearly an hour and that the session will be over soon, but I feel comfortable enough with her to come back for more. I do not relish auditioning more doctors, and I'm not sure how I would pay for that anyway. I know that's what you're supposed to do, see a bunch of therapists until you find one you like, but my insurance makes that nearly impossible. Dr. Gray has put me at my ease and doesn't seem like she'll push me harder than I want to be pushed. When she closes the leatherette cover on her notebook, I reach for my checkbook. She stands and goes to her desk as I write out the copay fee. We agree she'll see me at this time every week, and she hands me an appointment reminder card. On the way out the door she says, "I look forward to talking more next week." Though I know this is just her way of saying goodbye, I am startled to realize that she has done very little talking herself. I did most of the talking, and I revealed more than I have to anyone in a long time, maybe even to Nina.

NINE

NINA'S RECOVERY JOURNAL

Coach blows his whistle. We move back into practicing. We are doing falls, first to one knee, then to the opposite, then to both. Suddenly, Coach signals me to the side. Butchy Trucks is there. He's this guy Rachel made up, or no, had a dream about in the days before the championship match. Butchy was her idea of a color commentator and interviewer for an ESPN-style sports show about derby. The name's a joke, a pun, but I loved it, and now I've started to visualize Butchy and claim him for my own. He begins to interview me about derby as if he was Boomer Esiason, or Bill Cowher on the panel that's a cross between a late-night talk show and a sports-themed game show.

"This is Butchy Trucks coming to you live and direct from the CBS Sports Studios, which I have hijacked tonight because these pinheads won't cover the fastest rising sport in the country: roller derby. With me tonight is Nina Gordon, who skates under the name Knickers the Knife, and is the star Jammer and national all-time points leader for the Philadelphia Roller Girls professional team the Philadelphia Freedom. Welcome Nina."

I do not skate under the name Knickers the Knife, but I let this go. "Thanks, Mr. Trucks," I say.

"Call me Butchy."

"Ok. Butchy."

"So, give us the inside scoop on Nina, rather on The Knife. How'd you get started in this slammin' sport?"

"I started skating in September 2002. Back then it was just a bunch of women who loved to jam. My girlfriend at the time got me into it. She spent the summer of 2002 in Austin and there was a derby club there, and someone took her to see them, and that was it. A full body contact sport for women? What's not to love?"

"Snagged, bagged and tagged, eh Nina?"

"When I brought my girlfriend home to Philly she found a gym in a former Catholic school that the priests were only too

happy to rent out on Saturdays to a bunch of dykes and queers who wanted to slam into each other, Catholic school attendance being what it is, money being tight, old ethnic neighborhoods in decay and all that. Never mind that on Sundays those same priests were all about the evils of women like us."

Butchy hits the kill button on his mic and says, "Nina, cool it with the queer talk. Don't you get it that the promoters want this to become a family sport? Can you give that answer again without the, you know, D-word?" He releases the button.

"On Saturday afternoons, with Jesus looking down from the rafters, they jammed. At first, I was like, roller derby? Really? Like Raquel Welch in Kansas City Bomber?"

"And that was the start of it? The first you'd heard of the sport?"

"Well, Butchy, I had one other encounter with it. It was a long time ago, when I was little. I remember staying home from school sick one day when I was ten and the woman my mother hired to clean our house had on this cheesy UHF station – my mother was way too cheap to get cable – and she was watching videotaped banked track matches from the 1960s. Her favorite player was Moose Kaboosky. I remember the name. 'Moose Kaboosky' the announcer would say, elongating every syllable. 'Moose Kaboosky.'"

"That's rich. Moooose Kaaa-boooo-skeee."

"Yea. Like that. She was scary wonderful. A brawler. I loved her at first sight. I named one of my dolls Kaboosky, though I am sure I never let anyone hear me say the name out loud. I used to pretend that my dolls were derby queens and smash them into each other. My parents could never figure out why the heads of so many of my dolls broke off. But that was the start of it."

6 WEEKS AND 2 DAYS BEFORE THE CHAMPIONSHIP BOUT

"Mom?" She is sitting with her back toward the door, and her hair is a different color from the last time I saw her, which was not all that long ago, maybe eight weeks. Now it's an even lighter blond, with highlight streaks in it. She's had it cut, so it's just above her shoulders rather than just below them. She turns her head, offering me a cheek to kiss. I kiss her, then come around the table and sit.

"Nina, darling. How are you? Glad you could make it." I know she is giving me shit for waiting five days to meet up with her.

"I'm okay. How are you?" I ask this with some urgency. Her message said it was a medical issue, though I know if she was seriously ill, I would have gotten another call.

"I'm fine. I have a few complaints, but at my age, who doesn't? And look at you? So many tattoos. You know you can't be buried in a Jewish cemetery. It's in Leviticus."

This is about par for the course, in terms of how my mother starts our conversations these days. She likes to confirm each of our places in the power relationship at the start of things. "There's dispute about what that passage means," I tell her.

"I just don't understand the appeal. You have such lovely skin. Why cover it and mark it all up?" I don't answer. I don't think she expects me to. We've been around this track before. "Do you want to get anything?" She hands me the menu.

"Your message said you wanted to talk to me about a medical issue?" She looks puzzled for a moment and then reaches across the table and takes my hand.

"Not about me. Oh, my god. You thought I meant about me? No. No. No. I told you. I'm fine; healthy as a horse. It's your father."

"My father?

"My ex-husband? You remember him? Balding? Vain? Cheap?"

"The guy I remember was coifed and fashionable, not to mention erudite, cultured, and generous. You're telling me someone else is my real father? Mom, were you fucking around?"

"Very funny."

"Why are you talking to me about dad's health?"

"Because he won't talk to you himself. Because I'm still his mouthpiece to you about anything important after all these years, like you don't know this. He knows if he calls you directly, you'll overreact."

"You guys are so lame. That's insane, don't you think? On both your parts."

"I also think he likes putting me in this position. It's some kind of long-term payback. I took you away from him, therefore I get to do his dirty work. Tit for tat."

So now I *am* panicked. "What's serious enough for him to ask you to surrogate to me?"

"Your father needs a kidney. He's on the list."

"What does that mean? He's on the list?"

"He's waiting for some schmo to die in a car wreck so he can get the guy's kidney. Or a schmo-ette, I suppose. The list is the national kidney transplant registry. I'm not sure what the actual requirements are."

"It can't be that bad."

"When was the last time you saw him?"

"I don't know. It's not that long. A few months, maybe. I talk to him on the phone every week."

"I'm sure he sounds fine on the phone. But his diabetes is out of control. He doesn't have anyone paying attention to him."

"I thought he was taking care of himself."

"You know this about him. You of all people."

"What do I know?"

"That he takes care of everything and everyone except himself. You've always benefitted from that."

"What's that supposed to mean?"

"You benefitted from his generosity. From his indulgence. He'd be broke, and he'd still take you out to dinners and shows. He'd still buy you expensive gifts."

"He was never broke."

"Shows how much you know."

"So, why'd you tell me when you divorced, he was never generous. Trying to get blood from a stone?"

"Don't be smart."

"Exactly how did I do it? Benefit from his generosity?" I was beginning to get pissed off at her, which is also exactly how our conversations often go these days. About five minutes in, she's saying stuff that makes me want to strangle her.

"Come on, Nina. He gave you whatever you wanted. I said no, you ran to him for yes. Nothing was off limits. He let you wrap him around your little finger."

"And what, you're still jealous of him? There's still a competition between you?"

"For you? Of course."

"It's time you got over it. What do you think I should do with this information?"

"Do? I don't know that there is anything to do. It's just how it is." She barely takes a breath before she says, "The smoked salmon eggs benedict is really quite good here. I had it just last week."

ELEVEN

NINA'S RECOVERY JOURNAL

My father gave me my first pair of skates. He gave me presents almost every time I spent the weekend with him. Divorced dad guilt. There are all these jokes about weekend fathers. I overheard my mother tell one to her friends years ago, something I'm sure she heard on TV, but she let her friends think she made up. It went like this. "When I first met my ex-husband, it was so romantic. I asked myself, 'Is this the guy I want to spend my life with?' I should have asked, 'Is this was the guy I want my children to spend every other weekend getting bribed by?'" If I could get you to hear cheesy music and a rim shot in this journal, I would. It was that kind of joke. Except when I heard her tell it, it just made me feel bad. And angry at her. I loved my dad. I didn't understand why she would be so mean about him.

But every other weekend I got a reprieve from my mother's anger – and from going to synagogue with her. You cannot imagine what a relief that was. In trade, I got working on the New York Times crossword puzzle sitting next to my father on his overstuffed couch in his cozy apartment, both of us in our pajamas. I got his "world's greatest pancakes" with real maple syrup on a TV tray in front of CBS Sunday Morning with Charles Osgood. I got presents, and hugs, and matinees at the theater, and ballet, and the "Significant Speakers" program at the Jewish Y. My father saw me in a completely different way than my mother did. He wanted different things for me.

For a while at least, especially when I was a young teenager, what he wanted and what I thought I wanted seemed like the same thing. He wanted me to experience the things he loved. To experiment. To have opinions. To talk and argue with verve. To have cultural literacy. To have fun. What I didn't realize was that he also wanted me to find my way to his version of normal. I wasn't supposed to go from getting roller skates to doing roller derby. I wasn't supposed to go from having friends *who were girls to having Girl Friends. And so, when the judgment started, when disapproval replaced encouragement, well, I can say with total confidence, that my father is the only <u>man</u> who ever broke my heart.*

6 WEEKS AND 2 DAYS BEFORE THE CHAMPIONSHIP BOUT

"Nice to see you ladies made it out to practice on time. Not like last night when a little rain seemed to keep half of you from getting here by our start time. I remind you that every minute we practice the more prepared we are to take on New York. If you think they're going to go lighter on you because you were rain-delayed or for any other reason, you're mistaken. They want to eat you alive. They're New York, and they feel there's a target on their backs, and they have something to prove. You slack off, don't push yourselves, you give them that much of an edge. I want you sharp as a razor blade, and that means every cylinder firing." I was going to point out the mixed metaphor but then thought better of it. Coach caught my eye, and then, as if he could see what was on my mind he said, "And don't piss me off. If it's raining Noah's flood, you get here on time. If it's snowing blizzards from Everest, you get here. Your momma's dying? You get here. Your girlfriend's ditching you? You get here. Not five minutes late, not one minute late. Not twelve seconds late. You get here. You got it?" Coach has jumped into crazy mode, we can all see that. He's salivating, he's so worked up. I get it that he wants this as much as we do, that it will make his coaching bones if we win this championship for him, but I just feel like all the rah-rah shit and scolding is too much. Or maybe it's true to say that one part of me thinks that. The other part is susceptible to it. I swear to god, as stupid as I think it is, there's a part of me that wants him to talk to us this way, not because I like being scolded or lumped in with the women who are more casual about their practice responsibilities than I am, but because it's the way we've all been told coaches talk to teams, and if he didn't talk like this to us maybe we'd suspect he didn't believe we could go all the way and win it. What he's saying, behind all the bullshit and bluster, is that we can get there.

We can win. With the right mindset, if we stay focused and hyped up and we bring our A games to the bout, we really can. We can be champions of the world.

After his tirade, coach takes off his sweatshirt. He's got himself in a lather. His face is red, and his armpits are soaked. But I notice he is already wearing what he calls his "lucky shirt," over his team uniform shirt: a Guns and Roses Needle-Skull tee shirt from their 1988 tour, at which time, I calculate backward, he was seven years old. "All right. Let's get warmed up," he says, fanning himself, looking to cool down his hot face. "How about we start with partner power drills."

Part of my see-saw reaction to Coach is because I came into the track tonight in no mood for bullshit. I just left my mother, who is guaranteed to make me crazy, and even though I know I shouldn't bring it into practice, or transfer my aggression to Coach, I say, loud enough for him to hear, "Who's this *we,* Kemosabe?"

He ignores me, which is good because I am just about keyed up enough that if he set me off, I think I could get in his face. The problem is, I'm not sure it's all about my mother. It might be the pressure of the championship coming up. Or it could be about what my mother told me about my father. Or it might be about whatever is going on with Rachel, who is on the ragged edge about something. She's started to see a shrink, though she refuses to discuss the direct cause of that, which also has me on edge. Or maybe it's something between me and Rachel that I'm too distracted to be paying attention to. I am not at all sure what that is, but even beyond the sudden need for therapy, I can tell there's something. I'm hoping she can wait to talk about it until after whatever is going on with my dad gets resolved, and until after the championship bout, however that turns out, win or lose. No. Can't think that way. After we win.

Then, for a moment, before I tune back into Coach's instruction, I think maybe, just maybe, I'm thinking my father is sick enough to die. I shake this thought off. I cannot process it right now. I distrust my mother's hyped-up anxiety, but something about the way she talked about this has given me the heebees. I promise myself I will call my dad later.

"Six two-minute sets of wheelbarrows in each direction." Coach is running down his practice schedule. "One pushing the other, no helping from the one in front." He changes it up every time, so we don't get bored or complacent, but it means keeping the order straight in my head and tonight, I admit, I am distracted. I just want to skate fast, hit hard, and push myself to a sweat. I know we'll be playing inter-squad games later. Maybe I can bulldoze one of the other girls and get some of this crazy out.

"Then six two-minute sets of pulling, no helping from the caboose. Then two sets of shopping carts, one hand on the small of the back of the front girl to steer. That's all. No other touching. When you're in front going into each turn, extend one leg in front of you. Let's look alive out there. You can't let up. This bout is for all the marbles. A year of national bragging rights. Coverage on TV. The whole shebang. What you ladies have been skating for your whole lives."

Which is not true for any of us, but I get his point. Unlike me, now a ten-year veteran of this sport, half of this team had never tied on a pair of skates until eighteen months ago. But we all want to win. I want to win. But not for any of his reasons. For me, it's personal. I want to be able to say to my mother, 'Look what I did, me and my tatted and pierced gay, trans, bi, and queer friends. Look what we accomplished.' And I don't give a damn if she gets it or not that it's as real as her crazy-ass religious practice. I just want to be able to say it.

6 WEEKS AND 2 DAYS BEFORE THE CHAMPIONSHIP BOUT

I come home from the practice after meeting with my mother and Rachel jumps on me. "How'd it go with your mother?" she asks. We haven't been doing all that much talking lately, which is my fault because I've been working out every night for the championship. Which I hope she understands.

I tell her, "I think life would be a lot simpler if you could just shake hands with your parents at eighteen, thank them for everything, get your medical records and inheritance, whatever it is, and be done with them."

"Isn't that what most kids do when they go off to college? That's my story, except the inheritance part. Or the thinking I have anything to thank them for part."

"If you decided you liked them after some set number of years away from them, like maybe five, you know, enough years to give you some perspective, you could have short reunions and get drunk and sing the old family songs, look at the photo albums, and pretend family life, like high school, wasn't torture. And then the next morning you could get up and fly home and not have to think about them again for another ten years."

"You said five."

"Five, ten, whatever. The medical thing is about my father. Apparently, he needs a kidney."

"Wait. Your mother, who has been divorced from your father for as long as I've been alive –"

"Longer."

"– was the messenger to tell you your father needs a kidney. Your parents win the most fucked-up-divorced-couple-of-the-century prize. They confuse me."

"Fucked up, yes. But I don't think they're all that confusing. They are in the relationship version of that kid's toy,

Chinese finger traps? The harder you try to pull them apart, the tighter they hold you. Once you realize that neither of them can let the other go, you have them solved. You just don't want to be the finger handcuffs."

"Which is you in this metaphor."

"You're being too literal, but yes, I suppose, now that you mention it." I head into the kitchen. I'm starving suddenly. I open the fridge. There's a beautiful salad with romaine, escarole, tomatoes, olives, cukes, and feta that Rachel has obviously slaved over. "This for me?"

"Yep. Your favorite stuff. There's a fresh tzatziki dressing in the measuring cup. And I cooked you some tuna. In the blue bowl."

"Wow. Thanks." She waits for me to take the salad and dressing and the fish out and put them on the counter. I'm hungry enough to want to eat it right out of the serving bowls, but I stop myself and get down two bowls and forks and serve us both. She scoots onto her stool at the counter. She pivots to follow me as I serve our food; I can tell she wants me to say more. When I slide in next to her on the other stool she asks, "So was this just an information session? A little whisper down the lane from daddy?"

"I'll call him later. I'm on parent Stratego overload."

"To continue the toys-and-games-of-childhood metaphors."

"When I was a kid, I thought I might want kids. I thought, I'm not kidding, I actually thought this, that I would do a way better job than my parents did.

"And now you've outgrown that pipedream?"

"I don't know. Maybe. I'm not sure."

"Oh. Oh. What a strange and revealing evening this is turning out to be. How come you've never mentioned this before?"

"Never came up. Never been with someone I wanted to parent with. Never felt so mortal. Take your pick."

"Are you saying you would or wouldn't want to parent with me?"

"I'm not saying anything. I'm just saying –"

Rachel cuts me off. "And mortal? Aren't kids the ultimate hedge against –"

"I think what my mother was saying is that if he doesn't get a kidney, my father will die."

5 WEEKS AND 4 DAYS BEFORE THE CHAMPIONSHIP BOUT

I'm thirty-one. A thirty-one-year-old body is not the same as a twenty-year-old body, but a thirty-one-year-old mind still thinks it's twenty. Some of my co-workers at the facility, the nurses and psychologists, tell me that a sixty-year-old mind still thinks it's twenty. Well, my male co-workers tell me that, anyway. Boys will be...whatever. On the plus side, there is nothing awkward about my sense of myself anymore. When I was in my late teens, I always felt I was about to spin off the edge of the world, fall into some abyss. This was physical, not emotional. Except when I was dancing, when the music gave my body clues about where to step and how to turn, there was a teetering quality to every step I took, as if my shoes were about to become untied and in the next moment one shoe would stomp on the laces of the other and send me sprawling. I wore Doc Martens well into my twenties not because I thought they were cool but because they made me feel grounded, weighted. Nothing else I put on my feet made me feel connected to the ground. When I was in college, I would watch women in my dorm head off to bars in high heels and think they were going to float off the earth. How could those tiny stilettos give them purchase? But that has passed for me. I know now it was not my shoes but my body. Like a colt learning to stand on its spindles, I learned. And then I got so I could do more than stand. I could run, canter, gallop. But my mother, she can always be counted on to make me feel like a wobbly foal again, like there is no gravity, like I am a novice Wallenda tight-rope-walking across a roaring Niagara without a net.

I'm outside of my father's place, pushing the buzzer for his apartment. Things were different with my dad, maybe no less weird, but different.

"Who is it? Hello?" He knows I'm coming. I called. I've talked to him on the phone twice this week to be sure he would be home, but he acts surprised to hear it's me.

"It's me. Who do you think? Buzz me up." The door buzzes open, and I head up the stairs to his place. He lives in a mid-twentieth century condo complex, a low-rise, three stories. This is a come-down from the rather elegant place he had in Manhattan when I was a kid and he was still practicing. He drilled into the jaws of a lot of well-known people, and he had a large practice, with four dentists and four hygienists working for him. When he got too shaky to work, he sold the Manhattan practice and moved down here, to be closer to me he said, though he didn't make much effort to spend time with me. Nor, I admit, did I try to spend much time with him. Maybe he secretly wanted to be closer to my mom, who moved down here after I went to college to take an administrative job at a Jewish Community Center. Like my dad, she's retired now with way too much time on her hands, but that's another story.

When he moved here, he got a gig supervising students in practicums and teaching at Drexel's dental school, and with the money from the sale of his practice and his condo in New York, and what he was making teaching here, he thought he was set. We saw each other, but it was intermittent. I knew Manhattan was getting too hard for him to manage; even if you are well fixed Manhattan is expensive combat, and I think he was thinking ahead about his economics. But the place he bought in Haddonfield was kind of a shock; practical and cheap compared to what he had been paying in New York between his mortgage, homeowner fees, and parking. It was about as generic a place as anyone could find to live. Nothing like the building he had been in, with its sculpted facade, faux Italian statuary, marble lobby, and liveried doorman. His new place could have been anywhere, in any suburb, anywhere in the United States. Here it's a quick jaunt to the supermarket, and he can take the high-speed subway into Philadelphia. But he rarely does either. He gets his food delivered, and his involvement with culture is that he has extended-service cable.

He has given up living the way he used to, engaged with the energy of the city and his surroundings. He's a virtual hermit here, but in our phone conversations, he swears he is happy.

His place is on the second floor, at the end of a long hall. He's standing outside his doorway watching for me to come off the elevator, but I appear at the top of the fire stairs, foregoing the one-story lift. He turns and watches me approach without the slightest bit of animation, and then at the last minute, he comes alive, as if someone had thrown a switch.

"Hi Sweetie," he says and throws his arms around me.

"Hi, Dad." Still standing in the hall, I ask him, "How are you?"

"Great. Couldn't be better. Come in, come in."

But I stand my ground. "Really?"

"Except for the being sick part. But that's old news. I have some new nerve damage. Neuropathy. I go in for dialysis three times a week like I have for a while now. The para-transit bus picks me up right out front. Well, four days a week. As of last week. And I shake a little. I'm a few pounds overweight, you can probably see that, and I can't seem to lose the extra weight. I'm told that's a function of age, not the diabetes. But aside from that, what else is new? I don't want to talk about my health. That's all the old farts in this building talk about. All in all, I'm as good as can be expected. I'm not unhappy or hurting." He shrugs, then turns to lead me in.

I still don't move. "Okay. Just so I understand."

He turns around just inside the door. "What do you want me to say, Sweetheart? Day-to-day, I don't notice it all that much. I go on with my life."

"It's just not going to get any better."

"No."

"And you need a transplant."

"No. Not yet. I'm a good way from that."

"But you will."

"Will you please come in here?"

I relent. When I'm standing in his kitchen he says, "Can we please talk about something else? 'How's your health' is the question that most bores the shit out of me, the most enervating topic of all. The minute one of my neighbors starts kvetching about her sciatica or palpitations, I make an excuse to run away." I notice the 'her.' He barely pauses for a breath. "I spend way too much time talking about it to doctors and insurance companies and pharmacists. Please. Tell me how you are. How's work? How's training going?" In our phone calls, I've told him about the upcoming championship bout.

I put my bag down on the counter. I've brought oranges and bananas. I can see that he has set out bagels and lox and vegetables. "You want to change the subject? Okay. Here's a subject. Why did you tell Mom to tell me your diabetes was getting worse and you might need a transplant, rather than just calling me yourself?"

"Is that what she told you? That I asked her to tell you? She's amazing, your mother. All these years, I still cannot predict how she will... I specifically asked her not to tell you."

"Oh. Familiar plot twist. Should have seen that coming."

"Yes. She twists everything. Always has. I didn't mean for her to..."

"You encourage her. You give her ideas, and you know she'll run with them. You're symbiotic, the two of you. Host and parasite. Torturer and victim. Only you keep switching who's who."

"That's not fair. No one's being tortured."

"Except for anyone who knows or cares for either of you, or who has a psyche."

"We still talk to each other. That's more than most long-time divorced couples can say about each other. We still care equally about you, no matter how that gets communicated."

This is supposed to shut me up on the topic of his health and his former marriage, a two-for-one gambit, but I am not in the mood to be handled today. "You need to tell me right now what the exact status of your illness is, and if I am going to be getting a call that you are being rushed to the hospital for emergency surgery any time soon. I have some things on my plate right now, and I don't want to be surprised by anything. You can understand that, right? I'm a little preoccupied and I would rather not have it sprung on me while I'm in practice for instance, that you're suddenly dying or even that you're not acting responsibly toward yourself. I'm not sure why this is such a hard thing to communicate, but it is unfair of you to pretend that everything is fine when it isn't."

"All right. I get it. You're worried about me. But there's nothing going on right now that's all that dire. Yes, I'm on the transplant list. I'm waiting to hear what's going to happen with that. They evaluated me. They'll make a determination. It's not in my hands. And no one can predict how long my kidneys will keep working. Meanwhile, I'm doing what the doctors say to do, taking my meds, getting my blood cleaned, trying to eat healthily. That's all there is right now."

Except it isn't. Somehow, he has sidestepped my need to really talk through what's going to happen in the future by lecturing me about the practicalities of the now, and he has made it seem like it's my overblown worry that's the real concern and not his illness. He's good at this kind of maneuver, and it makes me angry, but I don't know what else to say or do. He's an adult. If he wants to act like a jerk, I can let him know he's doing it, but I can't change him or force him to do anything unless I want to make him my ward or try to get him declared incompetent, or something like that. Which I'm not even sure is doable. By any measure, he's *compos mentis*.

When we're settled at his table for lunch, I tell him about how things stand with practice for the upcoming bout. "I have good days and bad. Sometimes I feel like I'm at the top of my game, but we had a practice the other day that really rattled me. I just couldn't get it together, and my play and my skating were crap, and Coach benched me. I was back on point at the next practice, but it scared me. How much longer am I going to be able to do this? I'm not a kid. I have to ask myself, realistically, if my skills are getting uneven. There's a top end agewise for players in almost every sport except golf, maybe. A lot of the women on the team are over ten years younger than I am. If they've got game and I'm off mine, they kick my ass. That's why it feels important to win this championship. If I'm going to lose my edge, I want to give this one my all before that happens."

"I've never liked that you do this, you know. I understand why it is important to you, or maybe I should say I understand that it is important. But why? It's just a game. A stupid sport. Weren't you the kid who used to sit on my couch with me and make fun of the behemoths on TV if we had to watch twenty minutes of pro football because some game ran long, and *Sixty Minutes* was delayed? And why is winning such a thing with you all the sudden? You never used to care about that. Wouldn't you get as much pleasure out of it even if the stakes weren't as high?"

"I'm not sure I can justify my extreme desire to win this, if that's what you're suggesting I do. I've never been a win-at-all-costs person, even though I was primed by you guys to do the best I could at whatever I did. But there's something about this team, this group of women, this moment, that I can't exactly explain. Winning this championship feels different, meaningful, maybe because of my age. I know that at some point playing this hard becomes physically less likely for me."

"You're not that old."

"To be playing in a sport that bangs you up as much as this one, I am. There are a couple of older players who skate with the team, but I'm the oldest on the first-string squad."

My father nods and takes this in, but he doesn't seem all that engaged with what I'm saying. I can't tell if talking about my physical abilities is painful for him considering how diminished his are, or if roller derby just isn't of interest to him because it seems so embarrassingly plebian, so rough and tumble, and so without the redeeming virtues of the highbrow versions of sport he once tried to interest me in – Ironman marathons, downhill skiing, even floor gymnastics that we tuned in to with a pilgrim's zeal every four years during the Summer Olympics. After eating in silence for a bit he says, "Seen anything good? Movies? Theater? Anything to recommend?"

"I haven't been out of the house for weeks except to go to practice or work," I tell him, and then he looks down at his plate and we are silent again. I know he hasn't been out either, so I skip the "how about you" question. We have exhausted the playlist for today; there is nothing we can talk about now that won't be just jabbering for jabbering's sake, and we both know it.

"How's Rachel?" he asks, breaking the silence. I'm surprised by the question since he has shown little interest in talking about our relationship in the past, and he has never met her or even seen a picture of her. I'm actually a little surprised he remembers her name.

"She's good. Working hard. We have our bumpy moments, but she's good for me. We're good for each other. I've never been with someone who loves me so much or unconditionally, so without reservation." I realize almost immediately that I have just condemned him, but I also realize what I'm saying is the truth. "It's nice."

"I hope it lasts," he says, but there's something under his hopefulness, some wariness, maybe, or an air of warning, which I assume means 'watch out, the ones who love us most hurt us most.'

"I'm trying to persuade her to apply to med school. I think she'd be a great doctor. She's kind and compassionate, someone who would truly care about her patients," I tell him, echoing the conversation I had with Rachel earlier. I tell him this because I want him to think well of her, but also because I think it's true, and there is part of me, I admit, that wishes she had a little more ambition. I don't believe she is likely to be happy long term being a massage therapist. But at the same moment I say this to my father, I know that I am doing the exact thing my parents have always done, pushing me to be something they want whether I want it or not. I'm glad Rachel is not sitting here to witness me saying this.

"Take it from someone who has spent a lot of time being in the care of the modern medical profession, there's no time for compassion. It's all about volume, volume, volume. You're lucky if you even get to see a doctor, or one with any real experience. I mostly see physician's assistants, medical students, interns, occasionally if I am in the hospital for something, a resident. Sometimes the lead doctor in the practice sticks his head in, but all the intake and follow-up is done by the physician's underlings, or by the intern teams under the underlings. There are no Dr. Welbys anymore."

"Who's Dr. Welby?"

"A TV doctor. Before your time. Very sanctimonious, very Waspy, very self-possessed. The kind of doctor who had all the time in the world for every patient and made house calls. Probably no one like him ever existed, but he was the idealized version of the doctor from my childhood. Even I don't remember house calls." He laughs at this. "When we got sick as kids, we got dragged to the doctor's office. Maybe back in your grandparents' era doctors came to you."

"You see specialists. I'm sure there are still some compassionate general practitioners."

"Maybe you're right. But having a doctor in the family would be nice," my father says. I'm struck by his casual inclusion of Rachel in the family.

"You're a doctor," I remind him.

"Dentist. Didn't go to med school."

"Doctor, dentist. You know what good health is about. Not that you take very good care of yourself. Isn't there a famous saying about doctors healing themselves?'"

"I thought we weren't going to talk about that anymore today."

"Fine. We don't have to talk about it. But you need to keep me in the loop if there are any changes. I mean it. I don't want any surprises, especially in the next few weeks. Are you hearing me, dad?" I realize how selfish this sounds, how far above his health I am putting my focus on the championship bout, but I can't help myself. It's how I feel. For me, as long as there are no crises, I am going to focus on training and winning. We finish our meal in virtual silence. At the door I say, "Do you want to come to the match? I can get you tickets, even send a car for you. You want to see your little girl kick some ass?'

"I'm not sure my heart could take seeing you get hit or knocked down."

"I'd like you to be there. I'm going to ask mom to come as well – but I'll get you tickets in separate sections. She told me she would never come to a match, but I think she gets it that this one is special. It's going to sell out, so if you're interested..."

"Let me think about it, okay?"

"Okay. Sure. I love you, Daddy. I want you to be healthy. I want you to take care of yourself."

"I love you too, Honey. But please, stop worrying. It doesn't do either of us any good."

When he leans in to kiss me, I notice that his breath smells odd, sweet and sour at the same time. I wonder if this is a symptom of something beyond the neglect of the one thing he was always most fastidious about. On the train, back across the bridge to Philly, I start crying. I don't know if I'm worried that he'll die, or just saddened by our inability to connect to each other anymore. Even though I try to stop them, the tears continue all the way through the ride and run down my face the whole way walking home from the subway.

FIFTEEN

SESSION NOTES RACHEL WILLIAMS

CONCLUSORY NOTES FOR SESSION ONE: Rachel presents as a healthy-looking young woman, with no obvious signs of physical distress, anorexia, or self-harm, though she exhibits a certain amount of nervous behavior. She makes intermittent but not consistent eye contact when talking. In our first session, we talked about her family, whom she describes as "cold and distant," and "unloving," with "an angry" and "disappointed" father, who "felt life cheated him out of something he felt he deserved," and a "passive and self-effacing mother." Rachel characterizes her parents as being "conservative" to the point of being harshly judgmental of her lifestyle, which she reports is as an "out lesbian" to her friends since about age fifteen, to her parents at age seventeen. She has "very little" current contact with her mother; her father is deceased. In our first session, she described her fears that her current girlfriend, a semi-professional roller-skater in a sport called roller derby, will leave her. Further sessions scheduled same time Tuesday afternoons for the next seven weeks.

PATIENT NAME: WILLIAMS, RACHEL SESSION # 2
DSM CODE: 300.02 Record # 447/17
DESCRIPTION: Generalized Anxiety Disorder
PRESENTING PROBLEM: Trouble sleeping with bruxism; anxiety about the future; fear of loss of primary relationship; self-doubt
REFERRING ENTITY: Self
Fonterra Healthcare HMO
SESSION: $175
CO-PAY: $40

5 WEEKS AND 2 DAYS BEFORE THE CHAMPIONSHIP BOUT

Dr. Gray starts with the usual formalities, cordial but mechanical. "Good to see you again, Rachel. Where do you want to pick up today? When we ended last time, you were talking about commitment. You worried that your girlfriend – Nina? Do I have her name right? – was not as committed to you as you are to her. You expressed some concern about your age difference which I think you said was eleven years. And you were talking about her obsession with ice-skating. Do you want to start there?" I am about to answer when she holds up a finger and flips a page in the folder on her lap, studying something in the folder again.

While she does her professional review, my eyes wander around her office. I didn't take enough notice of it when I was here last time. I wasn't sure if I wanted to start up with therapy again since I'd done a whole year of it in high school, but I'm resolved to see how it goes with this doctor who was recommended by my primary care physician. In high school, I went into therapy after I'd been brought to the principal by two freshman girls who found me crying inconsolably in the bathroom. I didn't want to tell her why I was so distraught – it was loneliness, at its simplest level – but she guessed that whatever it was, it was beyond her ability to handle as a school administrator. She sent me to see the counselor the school system had a contract with. Over a year's worth of talking gave me the confidence to come out to my parents. They dismissed my declaration that "I was a lesbian and attracted only to women" as something I'd better get over or I would be an outcast for the rest of my life. What brings me back into therapy now is how often I feel a little dulled, a little *attenuated*. That's a word Nina uses to describe herself when she feels out of it, like there's a film between her and the rest of the world. That's how I've been feeling lately. Off. Like there's a membrane of some sort that I'm looking and breathing through, and it feels womblike and enclosing, but not in the good, comforting, safe-and-secure-inside-your-mom way. It feels impenetrable. Imprisoning. I need help figuring out how to get Nina to see what I need from her, and that involves understanding what I'm feeling first.

Dr. Gray's office is homey, but perhaps a little too self-consciously so, too perfectly arranged to give the feeling of real warmth. There are pictures of kids on her desk, hers I assume, though who knows? When we talk, she sits on a chair across from me, not at her desk but in front of it, which is more intimate and less hierarchical, like we're friends having a chat in her living room, not doctor and patient, not limited by the clock or any monetary arrangement or insurance limitations. Her desk itself seems to be unnaturally well organized, stacks of paper in oak in-and-out boxes, pens standing neatly in a cup, various colors of Post-It notes in their own dedicated dispensers. There are knick-knacks around the office, stuffed animals and dolls, girls' toys, and action figures in military garb, boys' toys, (though Nina would dispute these gender-based assumptions) plus a few adult tabletop diversions, like metal flakes on a magnetic stand you can sculpt into shapes, and wooden mind-teaser puzzles. There's a polished metal fidget spinner on the coffee table. Some of those are probably of interest to her adolescent clients. Her website says, "psychological therapy for children, adolescents, and adults." Maybe some of her adolescent and adult patients need to hug the stuffed animals as they are talking to her, or bend the limbs of Barbie and Skipper, or pose GI Joe and his armed cohorts, or distract themselves with the dervishing tops. There are tissue boxes concealed in decorator-style containers made from the same dark wood as the desk set, strategically placed near each of the chairs in the room. I assume these are for tears and not colds, though I have never been in a psychologist's office as well outfitted as this one, so this is just my guess. The woman I saw in high school used a shabby, unused office in the school administration building, and we sat facing each other across a metal table. I wonder if people ever do feel sick here. I am feeling a little out of sorts and woozy myself waiting for her to finish studying her notes about me; my stomach is in knots, but my nose is not running. Yet.

The art on the wall of her office is all recognizable scenes. Forests and oceans, but none of the scenes are realistic. If I had to guess, I'd say faux impressionist, but I don't know anything about art. These look familiar like I should recognize them from seeing them before, but I can't say if I have or not. They're not famous pieces, the ones everyone, even me, would know, Van Gogh's *Starry Night* or Monet's *Waterlilies*. They're soothing, I suppose, colorful but not garish, not jarring, vaguely familiar, intended to not induce traumatic memories or evoke horrified reactions. Art as decor. My father once pronounced that, "the mark of true phonies is having pictures on their walls they don't even like, that don't look like anything you've ever seen before." He was anti-pretention, my father, maybe the one thing that was redeeming about him, even if he was all wrong about art and pretty much everything else, he had an opinion about. The art here feels like it has been chosen to be in a shrink's office. It doesn't seem like a reflection of anyone's personal taste, unless bland is what she was going for. Dr. Gray observes me looking at the art and writes something down. When she looks up at me again, I realize she is waiting for me to answer the question she asked before.

"We can start there, I guess," I say, answering her. "But it's roller-skating. Roller derby. Not ice-skating."

"Right. Sorry. Roller skating. It says that right here in my notes. Maybe I misspoke because I am not familiar with it."

I could tell her about the sport, but she is waiting for me to answer the question about Nina. "I think I was saying how she blows all her anxiety out with activity, and I keep everything in. We're like yin and yang, you know? We talk, but I sometimes wonder if there's something fundamentally different in our makeup that causes us to misunderstand each other, something that makes it so we really *can't* understand each other. Does that make sense?

"It's not an unfamiliar description."

"So, when I bump into that, I feel panic."

"Panic? Okay. Two things. First, tell me as precisely as you can what that feels like, and then, if you can, tell me why you think you respond that way, why you panic."

This is a lot to ask, but I jump in. "When we argue, and I feel like she is missing the point of what I am saying, for instance, or when I feel her getting pissed at me for not seeing what she thinks is an obvious point, I tense up. It feels like my throat is closing, or sometimes like my chest is clutching. That's what I feel, the physical part. I also feel hurt, stung. Or maybe crushed is a better way to say it. Not exactly physically squeezed, but deflated, like the air has gone out of me. Does that give you a sense of what it feels like? And why I panic I think, is because I'm reminded of all the things I could screw up that would make her quit me. If the argument is about us, about how we *are* when we're together, or how much time we are or aren't spending together, I get reminded of all the things ahead of me in line."

"Things you think are more important to her than you, you mean?"

"Yes."

"How long until the throat or chest part passes?"

"It depends. If she's there and she talks to me or holds me, sometimes it just goes away. If it's at night and she's sleeping, or she's not home and I'm just stewing or remembering some unresolved argument from earlier in the day when the chest thing happens, it can go on a while. I mean, if I'm alone and it's all going on in my head."

"If it goes on for a while, what is your major concern? Do think you're going to lose her?"

"It's more like, I stop being able to see the future."

"No one can see the future."

"No, I don't mean in a fortune telling way. I mean it's a blank. I can't tell if she's there or not. I'm sorry. Hearing myself say this out loud, it sounds so stupid. But when it happens, when I'm thinking about something like if we should plan a summer vacation together or maybe get a different apartment that's ours and not hers, that's when something grabs me by the throat or chest."

"Tell me about your apartment."

"Describe it, you mean?"

"That, yes, if that will help me understand. But more what makes you think about getting a different one."

"Nina and I met in a funny way. A friend dragged me to a roller derby bout. I was like, come on. Roller derby? You've got to be kidding. The whole thing seemed dumb, a bunch of women racing around in circles and banging into each other. But love is never where you expect to find it, is it? I was sitting in the stands, this was before the match even started, thinking about when I could leave gracefully, when the announcer introduced the teams, and there she was. I never felt anything like that before. Like I had been electro-shocked or hit with a lightning bolt. I had just broken up with someone, maybe a month or six weeks before. It hadn't been a very important relationship, and I knew it wasn't going to last, but it was a tough breakup all the same. Even though I knew we weren't right for each other, I was still nursing some heartbreak. It's hard to be left, you know? And she just dumped me one night, in a not very polite way, by hooking up at a bar with someone else and leaving with her. So, I was in the aftereffect of that. I wasn't looking to hook up with anyone, but when I saw Nina, I was just thunderstruck. At a break between bouts, I stood behind her team's bench, trying to get up the nerve to ask her if she would have a drink with me. It was like I was a teenager again, asking a girl out for the first time. Totally tongue-tied. She looked sexy as hell in her team uniform. Tough, but also something else. Intense. Then I saw one of her teammates point me out to her. I must have been so obvious. So, of course, I bolted back up into the stands. I couldn't believe what a geek I was being."

"How does this relate to how you're feeling about her apartment?"

"Okay, right. I'm getting to that. So, it ended up that I kind of enjoyed myself. I had fun with my friends, it was a mostly queer crowd, and I had the pleasure of watching Nina's team trounce the other team. But every time she fell, my heart clenched. And every time she scored, I was on my feet cheering. I didn't even know her name at that point, and I barely understood the game, but I was responding like that. It was just automatic. Then, that night, I had a dream she and I were shopping for apartments somewhere. That should tell you something about how intense this was for me. I was in let's-get-domestic mode after never speaking to her and only seeing her once, and I only learned her name after the match because I asked someone from her team I ran into in the women's room what her real name was. Her jersey said her derby name, which was Nina Sin Moan, which perfectly captures her high-brow-lowbrow self-image. In the dream, there were all these other skaters from her team who came with us apartment hunting, and I overheard them talking about us, arguing in whispers about whether I should move in with her. One skater said, 'She's notoriously unfaithful.' At first, I thought they were talking about me, but then I realized they were talking about her. Then one of them turned to me and said, 'You wouldn't be the first girl she's left, you know,' and another one said, 'I wouldn't date her. She's unreliable,' but another one said that stupid thing Woody Allen said, 'The heart wants what it wants,' but in the dream, I think someone made a dirty joke out of that and said, 'or your twat does.' Oh, Sorry."

"I've heard it before. Go on."

"Okay. So, then they were walking away from me and arguing about whose advice I should follow. One of them said 'Like she should listen to you about dating women. You're still doing men. Go fuck yourself.' These are all like lines from conversations I've had in real life with my friends about dating."

"Let's unpack all of that for a moment, though I want to return to what you were saying about the apartment, which you keep wandering away from – which might mean something, we'll see. But let me ask you this. Do you think she's likely to be unfaithful to you? You've been together quite a while now, right?

"I don't know. We've been together eleven months, but if I'm totally honest with myself, I guess I'd admit I don't know her

all that well. That's a hard thing to say after we've been together this long. This is the longest I've ever been with
someone, and I've never lived with anyone before. There's
something hidden about her. Some part of her she doesn't
share. Not with me, anyway."

"Okay. There's a lot here. Let's take it in order. First, just
so I understand, finish the story about how you met."

"So, like I said, I went home that night and I had that
dream, and I thought that was probably the end of it. You
know, just a passing fantasy and nothing more. But she put
an ad in the *City Paper* personal ads. You ever read them?
They have this "Missed Connections" column? People who saw
each other at bars or on the subway or whatever. She wrote a
little poem. People do things like write in rhyme to get attention in that column, but I don't think she expected me to ever
see it. It said, "To the woman who came to our bout last night,
wearing the back-band Phillies hat. You know I saw you behind our bench, to the right. I smiled, but you vanished.
Please call. I'm famished." She signed it with her derby name,
Nina Sin Moan."

"You have it memorized."

"You bet I do. It was the sexiest thing anyone ever wrote to
me."

"I can see why you'd feel that way."

"But I didn't see it. One of my friends, the one who dragged
me to the match that night, called me. She's addicted to stuff
like that. 'This is you, right?' she asked me. I didn't think it
could be, but I contacted her. I had to know."

"And the rest, as they say, is history?"

"We went from zero to sixty in two seconds flat. That's Nina.
She's all in. I was happy to just be carried along. Which I suppose tells you something about me."

Dr. Gray held my eyes for a minute and then wrote something down. Then she said, "Okay. So, the apartment."

"Yea. I was there every night for a few weeks, just stopping
back at my place to change my clothes and get my bills and
stuff. It was fantastic. I'd never been swept up like that. Then,
less than a month later, she asked me to move in."

"Fast."

"It was. Faster than I ever experienced. There was no thinking or considering or contemplating involved. I was in a swoon. It felt great. But the truth of the matter was, once I was there as her roommate or her live-in lover rather than as a visitor, I don't know, it felt different than I expected. It was a more of an adjustment than I thought. I was fitting myself into her place, her already well-grooved life, trying to make myself shape-shift into her space and schedule and routines. It really was her place, and she didn't give me much room to maneuver or make it mine."

"Meaning she made the rules?"

"Meaning she liked things a certain way. She had habits. I didn't know if anything I did in my whole life was a habit or was even something I decided to do as opposed to something I'd just fallen into. I guess, at first it seemed fine to fit myself into her patterns. I was enthralled. I wasn't even aware I was doing it. Until I was."

"You know these are issues that every couple experiences. If one person in the couple has a stronger personality or has more fixed ideas about how things should go. Or just owns or occupied the place the other one moves into, these things inevitably come up. I don't mean to minimize what they mean to you, but I want to say they often work out with time if you let them."

"The problem is, I feel like I'm still messing up. Getting things wrong. I feel like I get on her nerves or she feels I should have learned the ropes by now and I haven't. Except the ropes aren't always clear to me. Sometimes I think I'm doing the right thing and discover I'm not. Something has changed, or I misunderstood something, or I misinterpreted something. When that happens, I feel like I've been set up to piss her off. When I'm at my lowest, I feel like I'm just a failure at relationships and I should just wait for the other shoe to drop when she kicks me out. I'm primed to get dumped again. Does that make sense?"

"Let me ask you something. What would you change if you could change anything? What would you want Nina to do differently?"

"I don't know. Talk more about what she wants. Tell me what I need to do to please her. Ask me how I feel about things. Not assume. Not take my feelings for granted. Not be so moody."

"That's five things."

"Yeah. That's the problem. So, here's an example of the way I think about this. I go to practice with her sometimes now. Some days it's hard to watch. The coach really pushes them, especially now that they're competing for the championship. I told you about that, right? Her team is in the nationals and she's like a practice maniac. Anyway, her coach, he's like, 'Falls again, girls. Start clockwise. When you hear the whistle, everyone fall. Right knee, then up and sprint. No hands! At the second whistle, down on your left knee. Third time, both knees. Anyone shields with her hands, I'll add a lap. You newbies, you've gotta commit to this. You're gonna get roughed up. You can't take that, you can't do derby.' Stuff like that." I realize I am doing this in her coach's voice, performing it, but I can't stop myself. I glance at Dr. Gray, but she is showing nothing. I thought I might get a smile, but I don't, so I just continue in my own voice. "He's gruff, and they all take him with a grain of salt, but they all do what he says. It's the rules. I watch Nina during his instructions. She's completely secure with her skills. She knows she's not going to mess up. She's smart, strategic. And I'm fresh meat."

"Explain what that means, being fresh meat."

"That's what the roller girls call new players. I'm new at this. Relationships. Every little bump throws me. Aren't people supposed to sacrifice things for the people they love? Don't they make promises? Change their lives? Give things up? Do things for each other that are, I don't know, selfless?"

"You don't think Nina does selfless things for you?"

"I heard one of her teammates complaining about her. She was talking to one of the other girls, but she said it right in front of me and I had to wonder if she was trying to tell me something. She said, 'Nina? Oh, Honey. Open your eyes. Nina's the queen of not taking one for the team.' I feel like I'm always the one taking it for the team."

"Okay. I get it now."

"She knows my history. My parents were very...what's the word? Withholding? I need... I want assurances."

"Why don't you ask her for what you want?"

"Because then it's me asking, and her doing it because I asked, not because she thought of it or felt it."

"Okay. I want to get back to why you think a new apartment would solve your problems."

"Easy. Because then we'd both have to invent new routines. And we'd have to do that together."

"That's a very idealistic view. But what would happen if she imposed her order in a new place? She's likely to, you know, given how you describe her. She's a decider, and you're more compliant. So, let me ask you a few questions. Do you think it would be possible...or maybe I should say, are there ways you might further adjust to the current reality, or do you think it is only Nina who needs to change? Do you think you can get her to see your concerns, or do you think she is incapable of doing that?"

"I honestly don't know. I thought that was what you were going to tell me."

SEVENTEEN

NINA'S RECOVERY JOURNAL

I've been thinking about how I came to love derby. It started with ordinary roller skating, of course. When I was a kid, I skated first on these strap-on quads that fit over my shoes, and then graduated to actual roller skates. It was fun, I was confident at it, and I sometimes actually skated to school, though most of the kids in my junior high school thought I was weird. Roller skating was so out of fashion then. Then, when I was in high school, I started on roller blades. I was an early adopter. By the time I graduated from college, blades were all the rage and lots of people were using them to get around in cities. There was this great Dire Straits song, "Skateaway" that someone turned me on to, and for a while, I was okay with the taunts of "Rollergirl" from dudes who saw me breeze by. Then it stopped being okay after I heard it a zillion times. In college, I bought myself high-end blades, which were better transportation, much faster, and way smoother on streets. I rode them for about half a decade. Coming back to quads to do derby was an adjustment, but then I decided I didn't have to choose one over the other. It was like having two cars in my garage, an SUV and a sports car, different for different occasions, but not all that different in terms of how you drive them. What you do while driving, that's a whole 'nother story. So, I have been writing a bunch of silly poems about the difference. This is what you do when you ache all over your abdomen, know it's going to be months before you can skate again without strain or pain even for fun, and don't feel like getting out of bed anyway; this tablet sits easily on my knees and I am the queen of the one-finger poke-the-screen typists.

EIGHTEEN

NINA'S POEMS IN THE VOICES OF SKATE AND BLADE QUEENS

ONE
Brakeless inlines
for aggressive kids.
Built for speed and tricks and skids.

TWO
Putting the trucks side by side
gives a very stable glide.
Good for dancing, good for touring.
But compared to Inlines, a little boring.

THREE
Quads are best for indoor rings.
Inlines rock for outdoor things.

FOUR
Inlines groove for distance skates.
Good on rocks and sidewalk breaks.

FIVE
Quads are boss for "session" skating.
If you're into rinks, or slow rolls while dating.

SIX
Rink hockey's hot in many locations.
Quads are for sport, not recreation.

SEVEN
If you want to go fast, and mostly face forward
Go with inlines, you'll reap rewards.
Might just be me, I'm a style lord,

but I like tricks and arty moves more.

EIGHT
I feel like a roadster when I'm sportin' my quads.
I feel like a race car on my inline rods.
I see both sides. Others might not agree.
But single-row wheels set my devil dog free.

5 WEEKS BEFORE THE CHAMPIONSHIP BOUT

I get to practice today, and Coach seems like he is in a bad mood. He barks at us, "It's falls today, ladies. Twenty minutes, falls and rolls at the cones. Don't be dainty. You think you're not going to have to recover fast from face plants you need a new sport. Get comfortable with taking a dive."

Doing falls reminds me of the first time I took Rachel to a practice with me. She had already seen me skate in a match but skating in practice is different. I didn't want her to see me fall on my ass. She was kind of insistent about going and I didn't want her to see me do anything that made me feel like I was a weakling, or a failure, or a "girl" in the gender-horrific sense. I'm perfectly okay with girl-ness as long as it isn't, you know, girly. You'd think your instincts would help you stay upright, but they don't. They humiliate you. You have to learn to overcome them. But no one tells you how to do that. If you feel yourself start to fall, your instincts say, "stand up." If you do that, you throw your center of gravity up, and your weight is too high to stay balanced, and you go over on your ass.

"Come on you slackers, get low. Get low! If you think you're low enough, get lower. Bend those knees. Come on. You vets are looking like old ladies. Bend more. Bend. Bend! Bend your waist. Lower. If you feel you're losing your balance, get lower." All this stuff he's saying, it's like we're all fresh meat. He's freaked out about the championship, I get that, but it's like he's losing his grip. We need him rock steady. We need him on his best game.

But I follow the routine. I dive, fall, roll, and recover. The trick is to learn to fall on your knees and not go down with your legs out in front, or sit on the track like Raggedy Ann, legs akimbo, hands splayed out to your sides, fingers in the path of oncoming skaters like sausages waiting to be sliced, with no graceful way to pick yourself up. I hate not doing things well. Especially when I have an audience. I just hate it.

The thing is, Coach being weird today is not sitting well with me. I'm still all keyed up because of my visit with my father. There are so many tangled things about him and me. I can name them, or most of them. There are probably some hidden psychological ones I would need years of therapy to tease out, something I'll never do even though I probably should. The obvious ones, I know and understand, but knowing them never helps me have a conversation with him in any other way than I always have, with all his unchallenged copouts and silences. What I understand rarely helps me afterward when I'm processing my thoughts and thinking of all the things I should have said.

I know, for instance, that he infantilizes me even now, when I am thirty-one and have been living on my own and making my own choices for more than a dozen years. I can tell myself that it's ingrained daddy stuff for him, that he just wants to protect me from whatever he imagines is out there that will hurt me, but if I'm capable of seeing my friends and my relatives differently as they and I age, why isn't he? I'm not the little girl he was freaked out about roller skating down the ramp I built from the roof after he gave me my first pair of skates. I'm not the kid who habitually chose the wrong majors in college and ended up disappointed. I'm not the broken-hearted baby-dyke confused about the breakup with my first real girlfriend. But it's like he's blind to my adulthood, even when I am standing in front of him. And even though I can tell myself that, and tell myself that it's always been like that and maybe will always be like that, there's a part of me that wants it to be different, that wants him to be different, to stop seeing me as a kid and start seeing me as the grown-up I am. Or if he can't do that, then I want him to figure out a way to not let me see at every moment that he thinks I'm still fourteen even when I'm standing right in front of him. I mean, he can learn to do that, can't he? Or am I just barking up the wrong tree here? Is it too late to teach this old dog new tricks, to pile on the clichés? When I left his place after visiting him, I was thinking he's gonna die and he's never going to really get to know me. And as I was walking away, I got terribly sad, like I had lost him already. I don't know what the future holds for him health-wise. Maybe he miraculously gets better from his self-neglect and kidney failure and all the other problems that plague him like he's under attack from a swarm of killer insects. Maybe he bounces back, or he figures it all out, or he gets scared enough he's going to die that he makes some radical shift in his priorities and takes his health care and his self-care and whatever else he needs to, in hand. But leaving there, I could not shake the feeling that whatever fight I have in me to lend to his fight for survival, he's not interested in accepting. I feel like he's already decided to give up. Maybe I am wrong about this; maybe he just doesn't want to show me his fear. Maybe he sees me as the little girl I once was, and he wants to protect me from his anguish. But I look at his sallow skin and jaundiced eyes and his drooping skeletal form and I just want to shake him, rough him up, the same way when I want a good game on the oval I slam some girl on the opposing team extra hard, because that slam gets her riled, gets her wanting to fight me, and I'm at my best when I'm in the fray. Oh, Daddy. Why won't you fight for yourself? Why do I feel you have already conceded the battle, that you've already made up your mind to die?

TWENTY

SESSION NOTES RACHEL WILLIAMS

CONCLUSORY NOTES SESSION TWO: Session consisted of Rachel telling me the history of her relationship with her current girlfriend, Nina Gordon. Their relationship appears precarious to Rachel right now having to do with Rachel's feeling that Nina's attention is not on her but is elsewhere, on her athletic contest. This is a surface issue in my opinion, related to Rachel's general anxiety about herself, her self-worth, her place in the world. She worries her girlfriend will grow tired of her and leave her and needs reassurances, but I feel her problems stem from deeper emotional neglect issues that began in her childhood and continued through her adolescence.

PATIENT NAME: WILLIAMS, RACHELSESSION # 3
DSM CODE: 300.02Record # 447/26
DESCRIPTION: Generalized Anxiety Disorder
PRESENTING ISSUE(S): Trouble sleeping with bruxism; anxiety about the future; fear of loss of primary relationship; self-doubt
REFERRING ENTITY: Self
INSURANCE: Fonterra Healthcare HMO
SESSION: $175
CO-PAY: $40

4 WEEKS AND 2 DAYS BEFORE THE CHAMPIONSHIP BOUT

"How are you, Rachel? How did things go for you this week?"

"I'm okay, I guess. Nothing catastrophic has happened. Nina has been gone more than she's been home, so there hasn't been anything all that major going on between us. Her team is practicing for their championship bout with New York, so that's got about one hundred fifty percent of her attention right now. I don't think we've had a sit-down meal all week."

"A sit-down meal?"

"You know, a meal where she comes to the table – well, the counter in our place – and sits, and we have a chance to talk and relax."

"Okay. She eats and runs?"

"Eats and skates. If she eats at all. I went to watch her practice a couple of times. She wolfs down a power bar from the vending machine and some strange colored energy drink. That's her supper."

"Why do you go to watch her practice?"

"That's where I fell in love with her. Skating. You've got to understand. Nina is smart and she's capable of being kind and generous. She has an important job that she's great at. But if you ever saw her skate, you'd see that when she's racing around that oval, she's something else. She's a superhero. She's steely-eyed. She's pure form. I can't describe it.

"You're describing it very well. But I want to point something out to you."

"Okay."

"The question I asked you was 'How are you?' Your answer was all about Nina." There was nothing to say to this. She was right.

"Isn't talking about how Nina makes me feel talking about myself?"

She looks at me for a moment as if she expects me to say something else, but I have no idea what she wants. "Do you want me to tell you what happened after Nina and I met? Why I decided to move in with her?"

"Sure. If you want to do that."

We have another pause while I try to figure out if that's really what she wants me to do, and then I just go on. "The friend I went to that game with showed me the City Paper "Missed Connections" ad. I know I told you about this. I couldn't believe it. I called her, we went out, we had fun. She was a lot more than the thunderbolt from the derby course. She was smart. A killer Quizzo player. She knew what wine to order with what food, stuff I never paid attention to, or never learned, though I knew I should, because my parents thought wine with food meant Gallo in a jug, unlike Nina's parents who actually thought knowing things like what regions grapes came from was important. And about books. And opera. And ballet."

"She wowed you."

"Yes. At first, I thought there was no way she would stay interested in me, and then when she did, I thought maybe I should learn to skate, too, you know, so I could do it with her. So, I did what she would do, I researched. She told me early she was a switch hitter. When she first said it, I thought she meant she was bi, and I was disappointed. It's not like I don't have bi friends, I do. I just didn't want to be sharing her with anyone, certainly not some man, and I didn't want her to desire anyone but me. But I realized she was talking about liking both quads and blades. Those are types of skates. It took me a week to figure that out, if you can believe that. I read the specs for each type on the Internet. Learning about the skates was like falling into a deep rabbit hole, and like Alice, I just let myself go. I needed to get it. I wanted to get her."

"I can assure you that this is a common response to falling in love, trying to invest in your lover's interests. Sometimes this works out well, bonding people together, but I have treated people who feel like they lost themselves by diving so deeply into their lover's pool of interests." She says this like it's a great insight, but I feel like she is anticipating where my story is going, making conclusions before I give her all the evidence. I like her. She's easy-going. I don't want her to jump to generic conclusions. I truly feel I need help with what's going on in my life, and if I stop trusting her to listen to what I'm actually saying, I won't trust her help. When I am sure she is finished with her interruption, I lunge ahead, hoping for the best.

"After we had been dating for maybe a month, I decided to go watch her practice. I bought myself a pair of used quads after my little research project, and I practiced some in secret. I had lots of things to overcome. I think I might have gone roller-skating once as a kid, at a birthday party where all I did was moon over some girl who was so not interested in me. Or girls. I skated around and around after her as she skated around and around after some boy. Eventually, I saw them making out over where they sold food, a greasy smear of ketchup on her hair where he had touched her. An early heartbreak. So, the associations weren't great. And my physical skills weren't great. But every time I thought of Nina on the track, I don't know. I was completely turned on. I thought maybe I could reciprocate. It was crazy, I know."

"Turned on sexually?"

"Exactly. So, I was there, watching her practice, hiding my secret skates in my bag, thinking I could somehow join in, but then I realized something, and it scared me. Or maybe scared is the wrong word, but it made me see Nina in a different way, and I knew I should never have thought about skating with her. Practicing with those women, half of whom were in some version of derby gear, there was another vibe, something I felt alongside the athletics. All the women on that track were fierce. Probably not every one or all the time, not in their crappy jobs and not in their desperate marriages, the ones who were actually in those, and not in the workaday lives of the queer ones trying to figure out how to evolve some version of a new archetype, but on that track, executing their skills and stalls, they become one thing, a unit, pack hunters, tuned into the scent of their prey. They were lynx. Coyotes. Tigers."

Dr. Gray says, "Lions and tigers and bears, oh my.'" It's so out of character for her to make any kind of joking comment that I am startled.

"What?"

"Sorry. It just tickled me. When you said that about coyotes and tigers. I didn't mean to interrupt you."

I glance at my watch. Lots of time left I don't want to waste, so on I go. "It's totally exciting to watch, but if you're outside it, what can possibly compete with it? And that's when I understood. I didn't want to skate with Nina. I could never do what she does. It wasn't something you glom on to and try to do half-assed. It's the essential thing with her, an essential thing, the thing you love about someone, that defines them, that makes them, them. It makes you proud; it makes you want to be near them. It's like the girls I knew in college who fell in love with actors or rock musicians or poets whose personas seemed to be visible manifestation of something inside. It was like a light bulb went off. I took those quads back to the second-hand place and never told her about them. We moved in together two weeks later. The only problem was, I worried there was nothing about me that was anywhere near as attractive as that spark I saw in her every time she was on that track. What would keep her interested in me? What gets her hot about me? I'm a massage therapist who likes to read and cook and watch TV. I'm a homebody. I'm a nerd. I'm dull. What makes her stick around?"

4 WEEKS AND I DAY BEFORE THE CHAMPIONSHIP BOUT

When I get home from practice tonight, I feel depleted. I don't know if it was practice itself or the visit earlier today with my dad, my second in as many weeks. He needs to be doing things, taking a more proactive stance toward getting this operation, talking to his doctors more, pushing them to advocate for him to get moved up the transplant list. But our visit this morning didn't go well at all. He refuses to own up to how sick he is, and if I push him, he gets sulky and it goes downhill from there. He's a grownup, but he's acting like a baby. He needs a mommy, and I am not her. He makes me nuts.

At practice, Coach continues to be stressed. A woman playing pivot on my squad, Laura Angles Wilder, got dumped hard during warm-ups, and wrenched her knee. She'll be fine for the game, but she sat out drills and the intrasquad game today. We got our asses kicked. It wasn't her fault, but Coach snarled at her for falling and then glared at her the whole practice. Usually, the intrasquad games are close, which gives Coach confidence we're all playing up to snuff. But if one squad loses big, it makes him think there are weak links on the team, and he gets agitated. Somehow our loss became Laura's fault, even though she didn't play. His anxiety feeds everyone else's agitation and then the whole practice becomes a giant clusterfuck. During the second period of the intrasquad game, I fell hard too. I had just noticed Rachel watching in the stands – she must have come in during the break at the half when I was in the locker room because I didn't notice her – and she shrieked when I went down, which was not what I needed at that moment. I was fine, but then the rest of the women on the team wouldn't let up on me. "Ooh, better not fall, Nina, your girlfriend is all squeamish." "Don't dump out. Rachel's a squealer; she can't take it." And,

"Does she squeal like that in bed?" Trash talk. Of course, Rachel picked up on this. When my squadmates skated by her they said things like, "You can lick her wound later, honey," and made meowing noises or flicked their tongues at her between the V of their fingers and crap like that. They're all such shit-shovelers, those women, and as much as I love them, they drive me crazy. But the thing is, I got distracted. I lost my edge. The other squad skated through us like we were a package of rotten meat. Not even fresh.

When we got home, Rachel ran and got the liniment and the kinesiology tape and the heating pad and made me lie down on the couch so she could minister to me. By that point, I had shaken the fall off completely and didn't need any of that, but I know she was feeling guilty, so I let her have her way. "You're sure you're not Jewish?" I asked her. "What?" she said. "Atoning for your sins, real and imagined," I told her. Other than hurting for me, she hadn't done anything. She got all pathetic and hang-dog, apologizing for something I had caused. But even if I had been inclined, I was too tired to be annoyed about it. I know I might have given her shit if I had been feeling less beat. I just wanted to go to bed, but I knew she wanted to know about how it went with my dad. I pushed myself to rouse up and have a conversation with her.

"You know that awkward moment on your first date, or maybe after your first date, when you do the personal history? It felt a little like that. We talk like strangers. My parents are crazy," I say, avoiding the specifics of my pissed-off encounter with my dad. The truth is, I never know when to say things, or how much to tell her. When should I have told her how crazy my mother is? How passive-aggressive my father is? We're partners, and she needs to know these things, to know the details, but I can barely bring myself to say them. What is it? Do I not want to condemn them for what I know anyone with eyes can see? Or is it that I think she'll judge me for how insane they are? I just don't know.

Rachel says, "I've met your mother, so I have a good picture of her craziness. But you've never told me much about your father, and I've never met him, which I have to say, is strange given how long we've been together and how close he lives."

"I've told you lots about him. I've told you about how I saw him on weekends as a kid, how we did things."

"You don't tell as much as you think you do. I know his name, and now I know some details about his health, a few very pointed stories that prove what you want me to conclude about him, but nothing important. I only know where he lives because it's a place that, until two weeks ago, you avoided like the plague, not that anyone is ever all that eager to go to New Jersey. His address and phone number are in our book, but I know you almost never see him."

"I see him."

"Maybe once before these last couple of visits, since you've been with me."

"You're all the daddy I need," I tell her, but she gives me a dirty look. "My father and I, I don't know. I don't see him, and I don't talk about him because…he's hard. He has ideas about how I should live."

"He doesn't like that you're queer."

"He would never say that. He's a good liberal. He knows he should be okay with it. But he isn't. He doesn't want to face anything about the reality of my life. It's easier if he doesn't know all that much about me. He doesn't want to know."

"He knows about me, right?"

"Sure. He asked about you today. Just like the last time I saw him. I've shown him pictures of you on my phone, those cute ones from when we saw Monnette Sudler at Warmdaddy's."

"That's something, I guess."

"I don't know. He wants it to be neat. He wants to say I'm gay and have an end to it. He's never expressed any interest in meeting any of my girlfriends. He's never asked to meet you. It would be too real. He knows you exist. He knows your name. He knows we live together. But he doesn't have any deeper interest. The more abstract you are for him, the better." I can see she's hurt by this. I change the subject back to me. "Did I ever tell you he once told me I looked like a dyke."

"You're kidding."

"It was a long time ago. Before I came out to him. He thought he was making a joke. He had never thought I was, but as soon as the words left his mouth and he saw the look on my face, he knew."

"He took it back."

"Apologized but not retracted. He was freaked out."

"So, you stopped talking about it?"

"Yes. No. I just stopped telling him things. That's the point. That's why he doesn't know much about you. I stopped telling him. It's not all that hard to talk to someone without telling them anything. You can tell people about all kinds of things that distract them from the important stuff."

"Do you do that with me?" she asks me. I give her a fishy look, but it isn't an answer. Then she lets it go. "He's been retired for a long time, right?"

"From his dental practice, yes. Disabled. Diabetes and the kidney thing. He was still teaching part-time up to about a year ago. He stopped right before I met you."

"What was it like having a dentist for a dad?"

"What does being a dentist have to do with how he was as a dad?"

"Does that mean you don't want to tell me?"

"He saw patients. He had a big office. I went there to visit him every once in a while. It was clean and white. He had a white doctor's smock which he didn't wear home. He wasn't a sadist, as far as I can tell. Dentists have that reputation, you know. Like the guy in *Little Shop of Horrors*."

Rachel starts to sing "I am Your Dentist," from the musical version of *Little Shop of Horrors*. Unlike me, Rachel did not grow up in a family where someone starts singing at the drop of a hat in response to, well, anything that suggests a song, so I assume she has picked this up from me. She knows it amuses me. She sings the lyrics about how dentists enjoy inflicting pain on patients with a manic look in her eyes.

I tell her, "Please stop," but I'm laughing.

"That's an okay thing to do with your life," she says, suddenly serious. "Helping people."

"I never thought much about that. I did make him wash his hands in front of me whenever I went to his apartment after he and my mom got divorced, or if I came to his office. There was something about the idea that he put his hands in other people's mouths that creeped me out, but even that wasn't all that big a deal. I asked him once if he liked putting his fingers in other people's mouths. He said, "It's better than being a proctologist and putting them into other people's **tuchuses**." That was his kind of answer, inappropriate for a thirteen-year-old, but some proof we were beyond petty father-daughter stuff and could tell each other dirty jokes and have our little secrets together. I knew he was treating me like a grown up when he said stuff like that, so I liked it."

"I think I would have died if my father ever included me in some kind of dirty joke at that age. Well, with my father, at any age."

"The truth is, he was always really gentle. That's what his patients told me if I was visiting him and sitting in the waiting room when they came out of the procedure rooms. 'He's very gentle,' as if telling me that was something I needed to be re-assured about. I guess they assumed I knew the reputation of dentists. Sometimes I heard people moan in pain, but I never assumed it was him hurting anyone. It was just his job. I didn't think beyond that until I was older. He's still alive, so he wasn't eaten by a plant like the sadist in that movie, who deserved what he got. I don't think he ever used nitrous as a recreational drug. Drug highs are not his style. He's strictly a gin and tonic man. Was. He's not taking decent care of him-self, that's clear to me, but he's not stupid enough to be drinking. I'm pretty sure. I hope."

4 WEEKS BEFORE THE CHAMPIONSHIP BOUT

It's 4:30 in the afternoon and I am at home. My last client was at 2:00, so I bolted when her session was over. I've been edgy all day. I don't know if it's all of the tension in the house from the upcoming championship or something else, something I'm generating. She's practicing hard and half the time she comes home grumpy, dehydrated, and hungry, not in the mood to talk about anything serious, not even in the mood for sex. I feed her, carbs and protein. She eats like she's starving. Usually, she recovers enough to veg in front of the TV, but sometimes she just takes herself to bed. Our lack of engagement is one source of my anxiety. I'm talking to Dr. Gray about it. Those conversations are going fine, though I sometimes feel like they're a little behind what's going on in the moment. I want to be dealing with problems that feel immediate, but we're always talking about the past. I assume that after all the talking I'll come to understand something new about myself. Maybe I'll have a better idea how to ask for what I want, and how to silence my doubts about myself, or at least make them feel less intrusive. I want to stop doing the same things over and over.

I start to get ingredients out of the cabinets and fridge for dinner. Food preparation is the kind of ritual activity that distracts me when I get stuck in an unsolvable loop. I take out peppers, onions, carrots, and zucchini to chop, and some chicken to marinate for Nina. Since practice started, we often eat different meals. Pasta is most often the base because Nina wants the carbs. I'll have vegetarian stir fry on mine, but she'll want heavy protein, beef or chicken. Even though I don't eat meat, I like to cook for her. It's what she likes, so I cook it.

Nina comes in. She tosses her briefcase on the counter and heads down the hall to change. "No practice tonight?" I call after her, wanting to be sure.

"Coach is drilling Marianne's squad. Night off for me. I can use it. I'm tired."

After we eat, we're silent for a while. She takes my hand and gives it a squeeze. "Thanks for dinner. I know you don't love cooking meat."

"It's okay. I don't mind."

I think about how I want to bring up a topic we have sort of talked about a few times and then aborted, having kids. Aborted is the wrong word. Discontinued. I should probably put it off, but I don't want to. I know she'll resist. Or she'll make jokes. I was going to bring it up again last night after she got home from practice, but she made it clear she was too tired for anything serious. She said, "I don't want to talk about work or how practice went today or my father or politics or our relationship or anything heavy. Just let's talk about nothing, about nonsense. Stupid stuff you overheard on the bus or something someone in your office did." I showed her some cute animal videos on my phone. Cowardly.

But tonight, I'm determined. I back into the subject. "Remember the other day when we were talking hypothetically about having kids? We never finished that conversation."

"When was that?"

"We were talking about parents and the future and it came up and then you got me off the subject."

"I got you off the subject? How did I do that?"

"I don't know. We switched to talking about our relationship, and then we followed that path."

"Okay."

"So, I'd like to finish that subject."

"What subject?"

"Don't make this hard, Nina. You know what subject. Kids. Babies."

"I think I remember now. We were talking about my father."

"Yes. And your mother. And how they were as parents."

"But you want to talk about us having kids now."

"Right."

"Okay. So, without talking about them, remind me, how did kids come up?"

"You said you were never with someone you wanted to parent with. I asked if that meant you did or didn't want to parent with me."

"Okay. It's coming back."

"It's a worthwhile topic for two people who live together to chew on." I can't tell if she's stalling or if she wants me to drop it, but I'm not in the mood to let it go. I say, "We can start back where we were, talking about your father, talking about the past. Not his being sick. What he was like for you growing up. Or is that off limits right now?"

"No. That's okay, I guess."

"So, what was he like? As a dad? What was his deal?" I realize that if we're going to have any kind of conversation about this it's going to be in fits and starts, a mashup of stuff about her parents and mine, desires and ambivalence, things we want, things we can imagine for ourselves, and things we can't. I decide to just go with the flow.

"There was no deal. He just wanted me a certain way. He didn't know what to do when I turned out not to be the way he wanted."

"Is that why you don't like to see him now? Because of that? You don't even want to spend holidays with him or anything?"

"I don't get the thing about the holidays. Do you know anyone who loves being obligated to go see their family on certain specific days?"

"They're times everyone sees family. It's a custom. Maybe we do family days so that when everyone goes back to work, we all have the same things to complain about."

"Seeing him Thanksgiving or Christmas would be plenty. But what would happen is, if I opened the door, he'd want a key. He'd want a regular dinner reservation every Tuesday. He'd want to be in my life. And then there would be all the stuff I don't want to talk about right now to deal with."

"It might make things easier."

"What would?"

"Deciding we'd see him every Thanksgiving. Not every Tuesday. Or we could travel. Take him and his grandchildren someplace new every year. Hawaii maybe."

"Wow. Can't stop you when you get on a track. We've gone from abstract talk about maybe babies to traveling with our actual children? I'm not someone who sees herself as a breeder. And just for the record, there is no way I'm spending any major holidays with either of my crazy parents. Holidays with them were always the worst, with the who-gets-who-when custody arrangements and all the feelings that came with that."

"In my fantasy, we'd be together and there'd be no custody discussion."

"I'm not even addressing how either of them would be as grandparents. That's a whole other crazy train. Spending holidays with either of them would just be reliving the worst moments of my childhood when they fought tooth and nail over who would or wouldn't have me for the week between Christmas and New Year or for the long Thanksgiving weekend, or who would have to take me because of who was headed off someplace with their new special friend. One of them was always on the way to a place where I was never invited."

"Okay. Okay. We could do the opposite, leave our kids with one of them so we can go skiing in Biarritz or swimming in the Caribbean."

"I am feeling the extreme need to change the subject," she tells me. "Let's put this in the don't-want-to-talk-about-it-to-night category, too, okay?"

"Sure. Let me rub your feet." Her feet are always sore now from the beating they take, torqueing on turns around the track. I take them in my hands and apply pressure to the bottoms. She moans. "That's so nice."

"I can see myself doing this to you in a cabana on a beach in Tortola."

"Or you would have to rub cocoa butter into my stretch marks in our hotel room before I put on the muumuu I would wear before I'd let anyone see me that way."

"I could do the stretch-marks part. I would be happy to."

"Okay. Too specific now. Can we please back up?"

"Sure. But just so you know, I want to spend Thanksgiving with you. Every year. Wherever."

"But not other times."

"No. Only Thanksgiving. Maybe Flag Day."

"How about Groundhog Day? I take Groundhog Day very seriously. Ever since I saw that movie."

"I'll bet your father's grandchildren will love that movie. As will their grandfather if he doesn't already."

"Because being stuck in an endless loop is kind of his style."

I know Nina is signaling she wants this conversation to end, but I'm not ready. "Okay. I know you don't want to talk about it, but I need to ask you and then I'll shut up, and please don't blow me off about this. Is there any chance you're serious about this?"

"About what?"

"That you might want kids."

"Speaking of being in an endless loop." Nina puffs out her cheeks and then blows the air out. "I don't know. I think about it sometimes. What do you mean by serious? Do you mean thinking about it soon serious? Or theoretically serious? Or –"

"I guess I was a little stunned by your saying it at all. I just assumed you'd never...I don't know what to do with it."

"Are you?"

"Am I what?"

"Serious. Is this something we need to seriously talk about? Is this a deal breaker for you, if I say I never will? Are we moving to some new stage of our –"

I interrupt her. "Because if you are serious, I guess I have to say, I would be delighted. I thought this was most likely off the table for you. And I would be all right with that, I guess, if I knew. I just want to know. I guess I always assumed you didn't want kids. I can't imagine you'd like anything about it. The restriction. The way it changes your body. The time required. Being at home. I can't imagine you'd like having someone so dependent on you."

Then all the sudden, I feel the conversation shift. Something I have said has thrown her. She's annoyed. Or maybe she has just run out of steam talking about this. She says,

"I'm not sure you know everything about what I'd like. But I think it's you who wouldn't like it. Sharing me with someone else."

"That's a mean thing to say. I've lived with you for eleven months. I think I know what you like. I'm a fast study. I think I know you at least well enough to have an opinion about it."

"I don't tell you everything. I don't tell you lots of stuff, in fact."

"This just gets thicker. Are you being mean to me to end the conversation? Because if you don't want to talk about this –"

"I'm not being mean, Rachel. I'm not hiding things. Some things just never come up. Some things, I don't know, I just don't say."

"This is not where I was expecting this conversation to go. I thought we were sharing our lives."

"Are we? It's all decided? Now and forever? I don't think those things are –"

"Tell me now."

"What?"

"Tell me everything you can think of you've never told me before. About everything you can think of that someone in love with you should know about you."

"You're pissed off, Rach. Let's please do this when you're not."

"I'm not pissed. I was having an important talk with the woman I love about our future. I think you're the one who's pissed. I'm just at sea. I thought we were...I wanted to believe we could...I don't want to put this off."

All of a sudden I feel like I have trapped myself. I don't want to have the conversation, but I can't seem to let it go, either. Then Nina says, "Alright. You want to do this? Let's go into the bedroom where I can turn out the lights."

"What? Why?"

"We don't have to get into bed together. But if I'm going to tell you secrets or embarrass myself, or just tell you things that are hard to say, I want to have the option to do it in the dark, so I don't have to watch how you're reacting. I'm sorry.

Maybe I'm being a coward. But if you want me to talk, and you want me to tell you whatever comes into my mind to, I need a little insulation."

"Insulation? From me? From telling me things?"

"Yes. Maybe. I don't know. Please just do this."

Nina gets up and takes my hand and tows me into the bedroom. I'm not so much resisting as trying to anchor myself to the muddy bottom of a lake she wants to stand in but whose depth I cannot gauge and do not trust. It might be slimy down there, icky with mud. I move like I am being dragged through the muck. When we get to the bedroom, I stop inside the doorway. There are no windows in our bedroom; it's an interior room. I turn on the overhead light. Nina moves past me like she is in a trance. When she arrives at her side of the bed, she turns and looks at me. "Sit down. I'm going to sit here, on the bed. You sit there." She points to our reading chair.

"What next?" I ask her.

"Please turn off the lights. It'll be better."

"I want to see you. If you're going to tell me things I've never known before, I want to see your face. Let me turn out the overhead and leave a lamp on. Or I can get up into that fixture and unscrew half the bulbs." We have a ceiling fixture that has a half-dozen low wattage champagne bulbs in it.

"As long as we make it as dim in here as it can be. I don't want to watch you while I'm doing this."

I stand on the bed and unscrew the bulbs, but the room is not as dark as she needs it to be. She ends up turning off the overhead light. She leaves a small desk lamp on, but drapes it with one of her black camisoles, which gives the room a haunted glow, murky as fog at dusk.

"Is that dark enough? You know this is strange, don't you?"

"Indulge me."

I sit in the reading chair. She sits on the bed, the glow of the lamp behind her making it hard to see her facial expressions, exactly the way she wants it. "Okay," she says. "I'm just talking here. Whatever pops into my head, okay? I'm not prepared for this. It's not going to be organized."

"Doesn't matter. Just talk."

"What if it's mostly stuff you don't say out loud, you just assume, except you shouldn't. You know what I mean?"

"I'm just gonna listen, okay? Don't ask me to respond right now. You talk."

"Okay. Here goes. What I like, by Nina Gordon." She takes and deep breath. "I like sports. Soccer and hockey. I like when women play hardcore sports."

"Obvious."

"Shh. Don't say anything or I'll lose my nerve."

"Okay"

"I like this city. I feel safe here. Comfortable. I like it better than Manhattan or anywhere else I've ever lived or visited. It's easy to live here. Everything's close, stores, transportation. I like this apartment. I like that it feels like me and smells like us. I like that when you moved in here you fit yourself in. You didn't ask me to change much. I'm not sure I would have liked it – liked you – as well if it felt like an invasion."

"Wow. Thanks for saying that. I appreciate it. I think I knew it, but I appreciate you saying it. I sensed you'd bolt if I crowded you. Or you'd kick me out."

"Okay, I guess I can't keep you from commenting, but keep it to a minimum, okay?"

"Sorry, sorry, sorry."

"About feeling crowded, I don't like crowded, except in the jam."

"Mm-hmm."

"I like books. As objects and as art. I like novels with involved plots. I like words that taste like food in my mouth, that you want to hold on to and savor before you let them go to do whatever it is words do to make us gasp or cry. Or give you sustenance. Nourishment. I like words that sound like what they mean. Priapic. Synesthesia. Integument."

"Onomatopoeia"

"Shush. I love the first-generation feminist poets, Adrienne Rich, and Anne Sexton and Denise Levertov, Diane Wakowski because they were searching, because they defined me with better words than I could find for myself. You should read them."

"You should read them aloud to me sometime. You know I would love that."

"I like meat. You already know this. I like the way it feels when I'm chewing it, the way it smells while it cooks, the way it floods my mouth with saliva when I'm eating it."

"Ugh. Ok. We'll agree to disagree on that one."

"I like fried foods. I like white bread. I like diet soda. I like candy and cake. I like almost everything that's supposed to be bad for you. What doesn't kill you makes you stronger, right? I like stronger."

"That's such bullshit, and you know it. Some things are actually harmful to your –"

"I like hard weather. I like scratchy clothes. I like cloth that abrades my skin like wool or canvas. I like jewelry that looks like restraints but is worn like a flag. I like puzzles and tricks."

"And riddles. You like riddles. Nina, I feel like you're not –"

"I like complicated. I like the idea that things are unpredictable. Out of my control. But maybe I like that in the abstract more than I like it in reality. I feel like sex is the perfect place for the unpredictable. I like to be taken out of myself."

"I like to take you out of yourself."

"I think most of the things I think are secrets have to do with sex. Is that the same with most people? I know some people are great at talking about everything. I'm not one of them."

"Is this what you need to say to me? Is this why you want me to turn out the lights?"

"It'll be better. Can we turn them all off now?"

Even though I want to look at her, I let Nina turn off the lights. I don't know what she's going to say. I just know that our relationship hinges on her saying the right things in this moment. And it's not just the content, but the feeling of it, the tone. She takes a long time before she starts, then she plunges in and it's like a dam has broken. It's like she has to talk about sex, or she will never be able to talk about anything else. This is the cliff. She takes a deep breath. She leaps.

"Okay. Here goes. I like it when my lover finds the softest part of the inside of my neck and bites, just a little too painfully. I like to put on loud rock and roll and get myself off when no one is around. I like to oil up my hands and put one, two, three, four, five fingers inside myself, reclaiming what is mine by inhabiting myself, starting slowly with each digit until I am firmly in, overcoming the resistance until I am near wrist deep inside. Or when I am with a lover, I like the smell of her underside on my face. And I like the feeling of being known by my own smell. I like the way a tongue can be delicate as a butterfly kiss or abrasive as a file on the inside of me. I like filling my mouth with the exquisite female liquids of sex and sharing them. I like to be made to wait for pleasure. I like punishing my lover for coming before me. I like being forgiven for the same transgression. I like discovering black and blue marks in the shape of fingers on my arms, where my lover has held me. I like the hurt in the back of my neck the next morning after I have bent my head back bringing my lover to orgasm. I like being stretched to the limit of my skin's elasticity. I like to be fucked out of sleep. I like to be taken from behind. I like to lose my breath. I like to be pinched, spanked, startled, stretched, turned, tickled, taken. I like to pinch, spank, startle, stretch, turn, tickle, and take. I like being touched so gently it is like a cloud has moved across my body and left only the shadow of rain. I like taking inventory of all the acts I have committed and have been committed upon me. I like seeing the visible flush on my skin, and its deeper invisible echoes. Those marks are my lover's signature on my body, tiny wounds. I like licking my wounds. And I like licking my lover's wounds. I like the way every orgasm I have ever experienced, my own or my lover's, is different, but I like best the ones that start in my feet and rocket up my body. I like the way sex takes me out of my head, out of my day, out of my life. I like that I feel connected to something eternal when I come, something manifest, something joyful, something holy. I like being the giver and the receiver of joy."

I sit in the dark, totally silent. And then I stand up, turn on the lamp under her black camisole so there is once again a tiny bit of light in the room. I cross the room to her and take her by the shoulders and stand her up. I walk her to the center of the room and when she is standing there, I start to sing. I have not planned this, it is just what comes out. What I sing makes sense to me and is simultaneously about as totally nonsensical as it can be. I sing her that song by Melanie Safka about bicycles and roller-skate keys, which is also about the overwhelming desire not to be alone. I start off a little shaky, I'm not that great a singer, but the further I get into the song the stronger my voice gets. I know I am singing for my life, for my love, for everything that matters between us.

When I finish, she takes my hand and leads me back to the bed and sits me down. She sits next to me. After a few moments, we reach for each other. We fall into an embrace and make out for a long time, kissing and touching each other. It doesn't start as sex, but it's sexy, and it's tender, and it's loving. Then it turns into sex, and we are ravenous for each other. When we finish, we lay next to each other in the dark room for a while. I have no idea what time it is. There are no windows in the room; there is no way to gauge the time by what is outside of this box. I imagine it has gotten completely dark outside, the kind of dark that happens in the city after everyone goes to bed and all the TV's and lamps are turned off. A kind of misty dark, lit only by lights from apartment windows, dimmed storefronts, and streetlights, lights that rub the hard edges of the night soft. We drift into sleep.

When the phone rings, Nina reaches for it out of instinct, presses it to her ear. I know immediately, even as groggy as I am, that it's mistake. Why does she pick up the phone in the middle of the night when she lets it go to the answering machine the rest of the time?

"Hello?"

Out of the tiny earpiece of the phone I hear, "Nina? It's your mother."

I know instantly that something is up. No one gets late-night phone calls unless it is a disaster, an illness, a death. I sit bolt upright. She says, "Mom? What's wrong?"

Her mother does not beat around the bush. I hear her say, "Your father's in the hospital. It's just a precaution right now, but they've admitted him." I scoot over closer to her to listen.

"Why? What happened?" Nina asks.

"There was some kind of emergency. An episode. He was taken to the hospital in an ambulance. One of his neighbors heard him hit the floor. 'He hit hard,' she said, and knocked some things down along the way. Thank God, they're all so nosey over there. She went upstairs and couldn't get any response from him when she knocked."

"Who told you all of this?"

"The hospital called me. They told me what she told them. She followed the ambulance. I'm still his emergency contact if you can believe that. They found a card in his wallet. It must be twenty-years-old, something he's never taken out of there. It probably has our old address on it, like we're still living together. I'm headed over to the hospital right now. Cherry Hill Regional. He's in emergency, but they're going to move him to a room as soon as one is ready. I think he needs a kidney. His are failing. The nurse who called told me they are doing tests to see how dire his renal status is. Those were her words. I'm sure if it's bad we'll have to fight to have him moved up on the list."

"For a transplant."

"Right."

"Is that our job? Your job? Doesn't he have a doctor who advocates –"

Nina's mother interrupts. "I don't know. What I do know is that there are never enough kidneys. When I talked to him last month about this, he told me not to get ahead of myself, but if we're the ones who will have to make decisions, there are a lot of considerations." Even without the phone pressed to my ear, I can hear Nina's mother is crying. She's not concealing her sobs. Nina is crying, too. I sit up now, move closer to her, put my arms around her. I hear Nina's mother say, "I have his medical power of attorney, you know."

"You do? Still? I'm surprised," Nina says. "Better you than me."

Her mother says, "I don't want to have to make any decisions for him without your consent, Honey," she says. I can't imagine the conversation in which Nina's father asked his ex-wife to do this for him. Then I realize he probably didn't ask. Nina is right. They're both crazy.

"Is it a certainty he needs a kidney?"

"Pretty much. Sooner or later."

"And if he doesn't get one, he'll die?"

Her mother snaps into information-dispensing mode. "He was at about 87% negative function when we talked about it last week. He can still be on dialysis for a while, but not for long." I can tell that Nina and her mother are about to start a conversation that might last a while. I excuse myself and get out of bed. I stand close enough to hear her mother's voice through the phone. I'm eavesdropping, relieved that I am not in the conversation about what's to come.

Nina says, "But that's the truth of what you're telling me, right? He needs a transplant, or he'll die."

"Yes. He can't go on like this forever. It's time to get tested. They think there's a better than average chance."

"A better than average chance of what? That I'll have kidney problems? I don't drink. I don't have diabetes. I don't each much sugar. I watch my carbs. I never smoked.

"Not that. To see about candidacy."

"Are you suggesting –"

"If it's a family member, he can avoid going on the list."

"You're asking me to get tested to see if I can donate a kidney to him?"

Standing next to our bed, listening, I'm thinking why did you answer the phone? We were in the middle of something. I want to be hugging Nina now.

There is a long silence. Then her mother says, "Nina?"

"I'm thirty-one years old."

"So? What does that have to do with anything?"

"I have to think about this, mom."

"If your father needs a kidney and you're a suitable candidate, what's to think about?"

TWENTY-FOUR

NINA'S RECOVERY JOURNAL

I know my father's eyes are brown, but when I see him in my head his eyes are always blue. I don't know where this comes from, but I have a hunch. When I was little, when he and my mother were still together, still living in our beautiful house in Kew Gardens, it was his job to put me to bed most nights. My mother, who usually cooked and cleaned up the kitchen, would kiss me goodnight after she finished her domestic work and she would settle on the couch to read or watch TV or whatever she was doing that evening. My father and I would march up the stairs hand in hand, and after I was in my PJ's and had brushed my teeth and washed my hands and face, I'd jump into bed, clamp my eyes shut, and wait for him to sit next to me. He would say, "Before I can tuck you in, I have to be sure you're my Nina and not some other kid pretending to be my Nina, so open your eyes. Prove to me your eyes are blue." Then he'd sing a song about how his baby has blue eyes.

The lyrics are evocative, the reverie of someone far away from the person they love, imagining that person across time and distance, imagining being together again. It's a love song, but I didn't understand that then. I thought it was about my father and me, about him going away and then coming home. It's not that he did that much; he didn't travel for work, maybe to a professional conference once a year at most, but that's what I thought. When he finished singing, I'd pop my eyes open and say, "But daddy. I have brown eyes. And so, do you." He'd lean in close, so close I couldn't even focus on him, and he would put his hand on my forehead and gaze into my eyes and say, "Oh. So, you do. So, you do." He always said it the same way, the words and the cadence, full of surprise and amazement. Then he would say, "I must have picked the wrong song," and he would sing a verse about a brown eyed girl. I didn't know if these were real songs or if he had made them up. Years later I realized he was vamping on Elton John or Van Morrison or Willie Nelson, sometimes getting the lyrics right, sometimes making a mashup. When I asked him about it, he said he didn't remember ever singing about the color of my eyes. I wanted him to. Those songs comforted me. It was something between us that no one else got from him. He sang me other songs too, but none were as memorable as those. It's funny. Thinking about it now, he never sang me any songs by women. Maybe he knew he couldn't pull off Grace Slick or Janis Joplin, but Kim Carnes' "Bette Davis Eyes" or Crystal Gayle's "Don't It Make Your Brown Eyes Blue" – he could have nailed those.

The problem is, the day of the operation, lying there before they came to take me into the operating theater, I couldn't remember which color eyes he had. I wanted to see them up close to be sure, and I was kind of panicking, singing the refrains from all the eye songs in my head, trying to figure out which was the right color. I was sure if I couldn't remember his eyes something terrible would happen and I would never see him again.

The reality of the situation was beyond me. I'm not someone who panics. What the fuck was going on? I could feel my heart thumping against my chest. I tried to calm myself. I knew he was already being prepped for his operation, the same as I was. Seeing him wasn't possible. They had already started my IV, "To relax you before the full dose of anesthesia" the nurse told me. But it didn't quiet my anxiety. I was sure my father would die, and I'd never know which color was the right one. I kept trying to remember what his eyes looked like when he leaned down toward me all those years ago. The nurse could tell I was agitated. I tried to tell her I just wanted to ask him what color his eyes were. I knew I wasn't making sense. She told me, "Everything will be fine. It'll all be over soon." I said I didn't want it to be over. She adjusted my surgical cap and tucked in my hair. I wanted to tell him I would be brave like I was as a kid when he thought I was fearless. Then I heard his voice in my head singing about eyes and colors, and I was gone.

4 WEEKS BEFORE THE CHAMPIONSHIP BOUT

When we get to the hospital there is chaos. No one knows where Nina's father is. He had been in the Emergency Room, everyone agreed on that, but no one seems to be able to say where he has gone or been sent after that. One nurse suggests he might be in ultrasound or getting another test, but ultrasound is in another wing of the building and the ER docs would have needed to call "transportation" to take him there or bring him back, and they don't have a record of that. The head intake person in the ER says Nina's dad is "probably going to his room," but what room that is "hasn't hit the system yet." Nina's mother, not the most tactful person on the planet, to begin with, is unhinged. She says she "could walk the halls and look in every room faster than their computers can figure anything out." That is the least snarky thing she says about the ER staff, the hospital, the intake clerk, or the nurses. After that, the intake clerk moves from her desk in the ER to an inside office, where she can see through an interior window if anyone comes in but does not have to deal with Nina's mom. The problem is that Nina's mom does not get the hint. She stands in the middle of the ER waiting room making speeches to the walking wounded and their waiting families assembled there as if she was performing soliloquies on stage, "I have never been treated so rudely by anyone in all my life" is her theme. That the clerk is black, and Nina's mom is white doesn't help the situation, or encourage any real sympathy from the people waiting for treatment. Finally, a supervisor appears, all apologies, though there is nothing to apologize for, and he sends us to the sixth floor, where Mr. Gordon is in renal intensive care.

Nina's mother marches off toward the elevators without so much as a thank you to the supervisor. Everyone in the waiting room follows her with their eyes as she exits, glad, I am sure, that she is not their spouse or mother.

Mr. Gordon, when we find him after a full swing around the horseshoe-shaped hall, peeking into the rooms of every patient bivouacked there, is in a room so full of machines that there is no room for the three of us to stand. I am not unhappy to be consigned to the renal floor waiting area, where there is a small sitting area, with a basket of Waverly Wafers and a coffee and tea vending machine. The tea is caffeinated, probably the only time in my adult life I have been happy about that, and I drink two cups before I run out of quarters.

While I wait, I replay in my head the conversation Nina and I had in our bedroom before the shit with her father hit the fan, trying to decide if we solved anything or if there would be any immediate change in our relationship because of her revelations. I want to believe that the conversation, despite its strange twists and turns, is a positive step toward solving some of our issues. My issues, I guess. I wonder how I will tell Dr. Gray about the conversation, which leads me to think about how I'm running out of time with her, since the insurance only approved eight sessions. I open my bank's mobile app on my phone to see how much I have in savings and calculate if there is any way I can afford to continue seeing her on my own after my insurance ends. My thoughts aren't running in a linear fashion. They're jumping from the conversation about having babies, to the conversation about what Nina likes, to the part about what she likes when we have sex, to thinking about singing to her, to images of us having sex. But I keep coming back to her mother's call shattering whatever we were onto last night. It feels personal, that call. Intentional. I know that's crazy. Nina's father didn't get sick last night to piss me off, and Nina's mother didn't interrupt our night of intimacy to diminish me. The anger I'm feeling is not rational. But Nina and I were in the middle of something important and now I worry we'll get so thoroughly sidetracked that we'll never get back to it. My head feels like a stone flipped sidearm across the water, skipping from being civil to Nina's mother to being angry with myself for my selfishness, to being attentive to Nina and her needs, to being confused about what our talk tonight will come to. Nina and her mother have both snapped into efficiency mode, though they do efficient differently. I watch Nina's forced smile and I recognize her professional demeanor, the same one she uses to talk to insurance companies and bureaucrats. She is getting things done. Nina's mother wants to get things done, but she is so snide you can watch the nursing and medical professionals arch up their backs like cornered cats. She is not helping. I watch all of this with the distance of an outsider. Nina has yet to allow me to respond to her as if I'm part of her family, and this, I worry, is significant. If I'm not able to talk to Nina soon, like that tossed stone, inertia will soon rob me of my forward motion, and I will sink.

3 WEEKS AND 6 DAYS BEFORE THE CHAMPIONSHIP BOUT

It is well after noon before we get home, and Nina is a zombie. She is missing a day of work; I listen as she tells her boss the abbreviated version of the events of the last twenty-four hours. When she hangs up, she shuts the ringer off on the phone, ditches her clothes and climbs into bed. I follow her. She's snoring in under a minute. I can't sleep. I've had as little sleep as she has, but my brain is on overload and is still bouncing around from thing to thing to thing. I am dreading, for instance, the call she will need to make to her coach tonight. She will be missing practice. I know what he'll say. I have heard him say to the team, only half kidding, that "death or near-death experiences are the only excuse for missing practice now." He means a member of the team's death. This excuse does not extend to children, parents, or loved ones. He couldn't care less about them. Or worse, she could decide not to miss practice, even though she is in no condition to skate, let alone be in a serious intramural jam with her teammates. I worry that if she goes, she'll get hurt, or worse, that she will haul off and hurt someone else to release her anger and her frustration. I know she won't want to hear any of this from me. There's nothing I can offer that will not piss her off. I consider pretending to be asleep when she leaves for practice to keep myself from telling her what I know I should say. I'm such a coward about this; she is so cranked up that it seems to me that there is no way I will avoid her anger if I venture anything. But because we have just gotten started sharing stuff we've avoided for months, I don't know what will happen if I tell her how concerned I am about her. Perhaps she'll see it as evidence of how much I care, but she could as easily see it as an intrusion into places in her family life where I have yet to be invited. Not knowing how she'll respond to anything I say or do right now, I realize how off the rails we really are.

When we left the hospital, she and her mother were barely being civil. They had an argument in her father's room – right in front of him, in fact, though he was out of it – about Nina getting tested as a kidney donor. I had just ducked out into the hall and only heard it in bits and pieces. Nina's mother insisted that Nina get tested. I couldn't tell what they were saying, only that whatever her mother said pissed Nina off. Perhaps it's the same kind of pissed off I worry she'll aim at me if I intrude, blowing up to release pressure but maybe not meaning anything terrible in the rational light of day. But it could be something more, a real disagreement. Is Nina thinking about giving her father a kidney? Is her mother asking her for that? If we were married or engaged or had an official relationship I could chime in here as an interested party and assert myself. As far as her mother is concerned, I am not important enough to consult or to have a say. I worry that Nina's opinion is not too far off from that.

She is sleeping next to me, snoring lightly, shifting around every couple of seconds. She is not relaxed. I feel for her. I wish there was something to do. I wish she would let me share her pain over this.

TWENTY-SEVEN

NINA'S RECOVERY JOURNAL

I am thinking about the day my father went into the hospital, the day his kidneys really failed, and we ended up heading toward the operation.

Rachel and I had been talking, something we had put off for too long, about ourselves, our dreams, our relationship, and our future. Then we made love and were sleeping in each other's arms. We were awakened by mother's call, and I was freaked about what was going on with my dad. We charged off to the hospital. In the chaos after that, the things we started talking about were put aside. Earlier that night she had been singing to me, which is funny when you think about it, like we were characters in an opera and could only express our feelings through arias, except she was singing a pop song– not even a current pop song but one she must have known from when she was a kid, though I have to wonder how she came across it. I suppose some songs are ubiquitous; they seep in everywhere, like a cross-generational slime. I'm sure neither of her parents sang that song to her as a lullaby. But she knew all the words and while she was singing, I was thinking what a lovely voice she had and how I needed to encourage her to sing to me more often because it was sexy and sweet and I was really digging it. I meant to tell her after she finished but we started kissing and one thing led to another and I got distracted. Then, after my mother's call, I forgot. The next day when we got home from the hospital, we both walked around the house in a kind of daze, getting ready to sleep – brushing teeth and getting out of our clothes – and again she was humming something. I was about to tell her she needed to sing more often, but I didn't want to interrupt her, so I let her go on. I was trying to figure out what she was humming. It was something I knew, but I couldn't quite get it. Just now I realized what it was. She was humming Regina Spektor's "Samson," a breakup song.

3 WEEKS AND 4 DAYS BEFORE THE CHAMPIONSHIP BOUT

Last night, at practice, I slammed into Kia, a woman on my team who was practicing as a blocker on the opposing practice squad. I hit her so hard that I stopped skating and helped her up, which pissed Coach off at me double, once for the hit and once for acting like a human being afterward. He benched me, and even as I threw my helmet at the wall, pissed in equal measure at him and myself, I knew he was right. Afterward, I apologized to Kia. She shook it off, but I knew she was hurting. I did not intend to hit her that hard. It wasn't personal. I just wasn't present in my body at all in that moment. I was thinking about my father in the hospital. Usually, I can get out of my head when I practice. Last night it was impossible. I'm still dog tired. Rachel put me to bed when we got home the morning after he was admitted. We had waited all night and into the next day for information, drinking bad coffee and eating from vending machines. I tossed and turned, and she told me later I was talking in my sleep and snoring and making sudden movements. She said I was shaking the whole time I slept. It occurs to me now that that must mean she did not sleep. I'm sure she was as tired as I was. I know she wasn't happy when I got up and went to practice, but she didn't say anything. I need to tell her how much I appreciate her being there for me. I hope she knows.

Meanwhile, as tired as I was, I was skating with fury on the track last night, acting out the rage burning through me. I know when I get like this I revert to the behavior of a six-year-old who gets punished for something she thinks is unjust, then takes out her anger at the injustice on the doors she slams on the way to her room where she has been exiled as punishment. The door slamming proves the point to her parents, or whoever sent her to her room, that she needs to cool down, but it doesn't change anything for the six-year-old. In my rational brain, I know Rachel didn't force me to have a conversation I would have preferred to avoid. I know that my father did not end up in the hospital that night just to spite me. And I know my mother did not call me at the worst moment because she is helpless or can't function or make decisions without me. None of it had anything to do with me. But together these things have derailed me, derailed me when I need to be thinking about my game and my team and my strategies for winning, when I need all my focus on that single thing to be my best in the championship.

The first words my mother tells me when I sit down with her at the cafe are "I'm not telling you what you have to do here," but if she isn't going to try to persuade me of something she already knows I don't want to do, then what am I doing here? We could have just as easily talked on the phone. I have seen my father twice since his admission to renal intensive care, the night and day after he was admitted and then this morning after another night of bad sleep after my terrible behavior at practice. I had to go back to work today, but I'm seeing my mother at lunch between patients. I'm hoping this isn't going to be a worst-case-scenario strategy session. This is a tactic my mother uses all the time, inviting me to lunch so she can work on me. I suppose I have to cop to the fact I enable her by continuing to accept her invitations. I have high confidence I'm right about what's coming. She believes, and I have provided her with enough evidence over the years to convince her that her belief is accurate, that I am more biddable face-to-face than over the phone.

But this time, I have thought through my motivations and I have agreed to be here willingly. I need to hear her arguments. I have my own feelings, and I have heard Rachel on this subject for two nights now, though she doesn't think I am listening to her. But I am not any closer to deciding than I was the night my father ended up in the hospital and my mother started haranguing me to take the compatibility tests.

His stay so far in the hospital has been a journey from one depressing revelation to another. It turned out when the real kidney docs got ahold of him yesterday, after the overnight interns and the morning-rounds residents had done all the workups, that his kidney failure was the least of his immediate problems. He has an infection, not uncommon among dialysis patients, that caused him to spike a fever. That's why he collapsed. He was also dehydrated. The doctors predicted that several days of IV antibiotics and forcing fluids will get him back to his baseline, which the head of his "team" told me "is not a good starting place, believe me," as if I wouldn't, "but at least that will give us some idea whether he can bounce back enough for us to take the next step." My mother blanched at hearing that, another moment in which I recognized that, despite their long estrangement, she was still in love with this man she hasn't lived with for over twenty years. "Secondary infection is a big worry," the doctor told us. "The fact that we are keeping him is some indication of how serious we think this is. If his numbers were better, we'd send him home with oral meds, but he needs watching for a few days at least. When he's stable, we can begin to look ahead."

At the restaurant, the urgency with which my mother presents the need for a transplant feels premature, but it has the effect of making me face the fact we need to have a plan for that eventuality, which I know but haven't wanted to admit to myself. At some point, he is going to need a kidney, or he will die. It makes me want to scream in his face, "Why didn't you take care of yourself? Why have you done this to yourself?" Like that would help anything.

My mother tells me again the first step is to get myself tested. "It's no longer necessary that the donor be an exact match in blood type, though as his daughter, you're likely to be the best candidate. The closer the blood match," she tells me even before the waitress has delivered menus, "the fewer the potential complications." I know she is quoting something she read somewhere. This is not something any of my father's doctors have said because I was present for all of the conversations with them. "World's greatest unlicensed diagnostician," I think to myself, a sobriquet I got from him about her. "There are some other physical factors and psycho-logical issues that have to line up, but I'm sure they will. And if a family member donates, he doesn't have to go on the list."

Becoming my father's donor would complicate my life, but what it means for me does not enter into my mother's think-ing. As far as she's concerned, there is no excuse not to do it. That doesn't mean I have to do it; I have plenty of reservations, though admitting those reservations to my mother is nearly impossible. She would just shrug them off. What legitimate reason could I possibly have to be that selfish? She hasn't said any of this yet, I'm having a one-sided conversation in my head as I listen to her rattle on about the procedure itself, but it doesn't matter. I'm already feeling guilty for even thinking about refusing. That's what she does to me. I know my mother wants us to get a jump on this. She wants to know what she will have to do as his medical decider when the time comes. She will conceive of her job as supporting me in our recovery – 'our' because that's how she'll think about it, even if it is me who gives up an organ to him – and supporting my father in whatever crazy way this all plays out. I wonder if they could end up living together again. I can conceive of it but hardly imagine it, given their last attempt at long-term cohabitation. Being an invalid might make it different since he would be under her control instead of trying to assert some independ-ence of his own. Which would be torture for him and would secretly delight her evilest motivations and stoke her belief in her saintly necessity. Or if, in the far less likely situation that someone else is the better donor, she will still make assump-tions about the role I should serve.

Looking at her as she eats her salad, I wonder if there is any chance that she could become his donor. Then I think about being the caretaker for both of my recovering parents and I shudder. If that ever happened, I know she would revel in her martyrdom and would expect me to compensate for what she is giving up by giving up more.

"Are you cold, honey?" my mother asks me?

If it turned out that she was the better donor, I'm not sure she still wouldn't try to persuade me to donate anyway because of whatever factors she thinks really matter, her age or her overall fitness, or her long-term feelings of ambivalence about him. They have been divorced for years; she has zero legal obligation. Which means nothing. She would do it if there was no other option, I know she would. I wonder if she might want to do it anyway, despite trying to persuade me that it's my obligation. She is just crazy enough, self-involved enough, charitable enough, calculating enough, or some combination of motives that make no sense except to her, to offer herself as that kind angel. Or martyr. Or ex-wife still in love with a man who, for over twenty years, she has ridiculed to her only child and derided to anyone else who asked her about her past.

It is impossible to make sense of this to anyone who does not know these two people. They can't live together; they were singularly incompatible as a married couple. And they were the loves of each other's lives. How else to explain a codependency so elaborately structured and still so often angry and destructive that they cannot refuse each other's involvement but are incapable of cohabiting? They somehow believe that they exist on this earth as the exclusive keeper of feelings for the other, as if no one else could duplicate their emotional bond. All of this runs through my head before I respond to my mother's description of my father's current circumstance. I remind myself that the conclusions I have already drawn might not, in fact, be the result of an actual conversation.

"I want you to talk to the transplant team at the hospital," my mother says. I have not touched my salad, though I have been holding my coffee cup like it's a life-raft. I know I'm wracked from bad sleeping and angry skating, and the burden of dealing with a family crisis in the middle of trying to prepare for the championship bout, but having to plod through the conversation I have already had with myself and her avatar in my head seems so far beyond the call of duty I almost bolt. During the last few weeks of practice, before we had our interrupted talk, Rachel has been trying to be the perfect partner, making sure I eat right and drink plenty of water, preparing her signature meals for me, massaging my shoulders in the bath, massaging my feet in bed. I think about her now, wondering if my mother was ever as good to my father as Rachel has been to me. And the other night, how she took charge of our sex life, delivering on all the desires I expressed to her in the dark. She has been nothing if not attentive. But nothing she has done has been able to remove this dislocating weariness. And here is my mother nattering on. Despite the fact I know I have not actually had this conversation with her before, it feels like *deja vu*. I want my mother to shut up.

Talking feels useless now. The weight I feel is not going to be lifted by a good practice or a hot shower or a perfect meal or an exquisite fuck or a perfect night's sleep. Nothing my mother can say – nothing I can imagine – will alter the feeling that the walls are closing in, or the unshakable dread that whatever I do, everything will end horribly. Because underneath everything is the fear that no matter what, my father will die.

"I know you are in the middle of practicing for your big game," my mother says, "but maybe, and let me finish before you bite my head off, you should step away from that for now. Your father needs help, and he's stubborn about everything if it comes from me, so it's going to have to be you who is the voice of reason. Given how things are going right now, he needs someone to help him good make decisions, to talk him out of his worst impulses. I'm counting on you to help him focus, and you can't be distracted by some meaningless hockey game."

"It's not hockey, which you know, and talking that way only pisses me off. If you want me on your side, you need to stop doing that. If you want me to have a reasonable discussion with you about what we need to do next, you need to respect what I am doing now and stop treating me like my life isn't important."

"I'm sorry, Nina, but nothing you're doing with your life is important. All right, your work, which, I get it, you think helps kids, and maybe really does, but which I think has negligible effects and is beneath your skills and talents."

My mother looks at me when she says this like she is daring me to dispute it. I feel my chest tighten. I know I need to restrain myself. I cannot tell if her cruelty is intentional or oblivious. It could be either. After I moment holding it, I take a breath. "Fortunately, your opinion is not the opinion of the parents whose kids' mobility I can improve and whose lives get better because of what I do. It is also not the opinion of the agency I work for or the doctors who refer those kids or the state that funds their care. But I'm curious. When did you become an expert on physical therapy and its uses and impacts? Oh wait, I forgot. You're an expert on everything medical. You know what, fuck you and your poisonous opinions." I stare back at her with the same look she has just used on me. "You are really shitty at this."

She barely pauses to absorb my anger before she answers. "No one is good at it, dear." Then she plows on. "You can't argue there's anything important about your so-called sport, which as far as I can tell is brutal and mindless and involves about as much grace or athleticism as snow shoveling. Not to mention being dangerous. You are facing the life or death of one of your parents. I'm sure it's a big inconvenience but let me tell you something. This is not about you."

"What are you talking about? You have no idea what I think or feel, since you never ask."

"I don't care either way what you're thinking or feeling. You have a duty to your parents, and if you don't want to accept that there is a biblical requirement you honor that, then think about the personal duty you owe to the people who bore you, raised you, provided you with every necessity and comfort, who saw you were educated, paid for your first apartment, paid for college, paid for your professional training, and who have always put you first before themselves."

I am always blindsided by my mother's inserting her religious beliefs with such ferocity into our conversations. I do not share her devotion. My Jewishness is something I rely on for cultural identity and ignore between the times she reminds me how important it is to her. I am at a loss about how to respond to this, other than to just call it all bullshit. All the rest, her recitation of their parental "gifts," is her standard guilt-tripping which, like some rusty old Victorian-era train engine, pretty much can't pull the load of crap she is trying to lay on me up the hill of my susceptibility anymore. Too much milk makes the baby go blind, as they say.

"If I'm going to do anything, Mother, I'm going to do it because I want to and I think it is the best thing to do, not because you have brow-beaten me into it or because I have some artificial sense of duty to you. Let me remind you that lots of people who need kidneys don't have family and can't find donors and wait patiently for the outcome of the regulated consideration process. Daddy has not asked me to get myself tested. In fact, when we talked about it briefly a while ago, he said just the opposite. He's opposed to it. I'm not sure what his feelings are about a transplant would be now, no matter the source because he hasn't been in much of a condition for another conversation about that, but it's a conversation that needs to take place between us without you hovering in the background. He may have different feelings about the importance of the things I do with my life. He may have strong negative feelings about going through surgery. He may just want to continue the regimen he is on now for as long as he can. I'm not willing to guess what he wants. He's an adult. He is sentient. He has rights."

"I think your father is an ass, but I agree he's not stupid. He knows that if he's going to live any longer, he's going to need a transplant." Then her usual closing gambit, cutting off the conversation, as if having the last word makes her right. "I have said everything I want to say on the subject. You know what you need to do. You want to play games about it, fine, but you need to come around to the fact that if you are the best match and you do not give your father a kidney, you will have killed him. Sorry to be blunt, but that is the truth of the matter." She pauses for a moment to see if I will say anything. Sometimes I do, just so she doesn't get the satisfaction of having the final say. Today, I just take a deep breath and shake my head. I am too exhausted to deliver a comeback. After a moment she says, "Eat your salad. You look terrible."

TWENTY-NINE

SESSION NOTES RACHEL WILLIAMS

CONCLUSORY NOTES SESSION THREE: We have been talking about Rachel's family the last few sessions, but Rachel's girlfriend's father is sick, and somehow, I'm not sure how yet, this has had a severe impact on Rachel. I know this because she called to give me a heads-up, she might need to reschedule our session, something I usually refuse to do, but Rachel's phone call was nearly hysterical. Turns out, she is coming in at her regular time, but she has told me that this is what she wants to talk about today.

PATIENT NAME: WILLIAMS, RACHEL SESSION # 4
DSM CODE: 300.02 Record # 447/26
DESCRIPTION: Generalized Anxiety Disorder
PRESENTING ISSUE(S): Trouble sleeping with bruxism; anxiety about the future; fear of loss of primary relationship; self-doubt
REFERRING ENTITY: Self
INSURANCE: Fonterra Healthcare HMO
SESSION: $175
CO-PAY: $40

3 WEEKS AND 2 DAYS BEFORE THE CHAMPIONSHIP BOUT

"I'm sorry about my panic on the phone the other day. Family crisis." I start when I sit down.

"Tell me about it."

"Nina's dad had a dialysis crisis. He collapsed in his apartment and needed to be rushed to the hospital for emergency treatment. He has an infection, or had, I think they're ahead of it now, which Nina says is not uncommon for people on dialysis. He's probably going to need a kidney."

"I see."

"He's stable for now. But it's bad. He's diminished. He looks like he's starving. His skin is the color of cement and his eyes are all rummy. Is that the right word? Or do I mean runny? They're yellowish and bloodshot and sort of wet at the corners."

"Rheumy. Right idea, wrong pronunciation. It just means red and wet."

"Yeah. The call that he was in the hospital came just after a conversation Nina and I were having about our future. I think it was about our future. Maybe it was just about sex. There was a lot of talk about sex during it, but I think the sex talk was about something bigger than sex. I felt like it was. Having sex was where the talk about the future went, telling each other what we like to do to each other that we hadn't said because we had things we never said to each other but assumed we knew. So, it might have been about getting to know each other better for the future. That's how want to interpret it."

Dr. Gray writes something down and then says, "So let me back you up a minute here. You were having a conversation about your future, and it morphed into a conversation about intimacy? And then you had sex. That sounds reasonable. But let me ask you, did it cover any of the things we have been talking about for the past few weeks? The things you're inse-cure about? Did she make any promises to you, or seem to come to any better understanding of your needs and desires?"

"That's the thing. It felt like we had cleared the air, like we could get to that, like maybe the next thing we would do is define things, maybe name them, like calling ourselves part-ners and saying we intend to move forward together and work on our relationship. That was before her mother's call. Her mother's call and her father going to the hospital derailed that."

"You can't blame her mother."

"Her mother has a knack for picking the worst times and places to insert herself into Nina's life. Okay, not picking. That's not fair. But it's uncanny. We had just gone to sleep after some really nice lovemaking. A little break from her fam-ily would have been really nice.

"Yeah, that's not always how things go."

"Her father has been in the hospital a few days, but noth-ing has been decided medically about what he can and cannot handle given the shape he's in, and her mother has all but accused Nina of being a murderer if she doesn't give her father her kidney. I'm pretty sure that given that, Nina is not going to be thinking about my needs for a while."

"Wait a minute. Back up. Her mother wants her to give her father a kidney? Have they been through the evaluation pro-cess yet?"

"No. That's the thing. Nina came home from having lunch with her mother today all conflicted, and she hasn't really talked about her feelings at all, or what she's going to do about her father. She is practicing and stewing. It's been three days of sheer madness. We were at the hospital and then we were exhausted, and then she went to work and back to the hospi-tal the next day, and then she was like stoic Nina, off to practice, which both her mother and I told her she should skip, and then home and exhausted again, and then she met her mother for lunch today and her mother said that stuff to her. Every conversation she has with her mother makes it worse. She's a total wreck."

"I assume the 'she' in that sentence refers to Nina and not her mother, who is probably a total wreck too, given what you have told me about her."

"You'll forgive me if I don't have much sympathy for her mother. Nina's the only wreck I'm interested in. Her mother is awful to me so fuck her. Now here I am. And here's what's eating me up. She hasn't talked to me about any of this. Not in any meaningful way. I've been there the whole time, but the most she lets me do is cook for her or massage her feet. Why won't she talk to me? That's what I am always worried about with her, that there will always be something in the way of her opening up. I don't want her to be giving that man a kidney, no matter how decent a guy he is or how much she loves him. That's horrible to say. But it's the truth. But she hasn't asked, and I don't think I can say it until she does. I want to have her total commitment to me. I feel like I've made it to her. I love her. Does any of this make sense to you?"

"I'm not sure I believe there such a thing as 'total commitment' in humans, and I'm not sure you mean those words literally either, but I understand what you're saying. She's putting something ahead of you, and she's not consulting you, and that adds up to something that feels like you don't matter to her, or matter less than others matter. Is that a fair restatement of the problem?"

"Yeah. When you say it like that, it makes me feel shabby."

"Let's stay off blame for a minute. You have a legitimate desire here. You want the woman you love, who seems to want to be your partner much of the time, to act like she wants to be your partner all the time, to take you into her confidence and make decisions in concert with you. Okay. This is all of a piece with what you have been saying from the beginning of our sessions."

I sink back into her sofa. I guess I've wondered since Dr. Gray and I started talking if she was really hearing me, and even if my desires were legit. I feel for the first time that maybe she thinks they are. "Why don't you believe in total commitment?"

"Explaining that would take time I'd rather focus on you. Suffice it to say that I'm not sure that total commitment is as important as total willingness to be upfront about the things couples don't have mutual feelings about. You can live with people who see the world and even behave differently from you, if it's not a surprise, as long as it's something you agree to accept, or you have mechanisms to deal with those differences. That's the short answer. Take me out for a drink sometime and I'll give you the long answer."

"You'd do that?"

She laughs. "No. Let's focus on what mechanisms you need to develop to calm yourself down so you can exist in this relationship until you work things through, or, failing that, that you know why you are leaving it."

"I don't want to leave it. I want her to..." but I can't say out loud what I really want. I want her to love me enough to do what I ask her to do, not give up any part of herself to anyone else.

3 WEEKS AND 2 DAYS BEFORE THE CHAMPIONSHIP BOUT

My father's improvement in the days after his collapse – as the antibiotics caught up with his infection and dialysis and hydration made him look less like a zombie – causes him to be both jovial and grumpy. Jovial enough to want visitors who, despite the grumpy side, have stopped by to see him and bring him flowers and fruit. My mother's a regular. A few people from his apartment complex have come to see him, including the woman who heard him fall. Her interest seems more than casual, which amazes me because he's not a great candidate for long term involvement, but what do I know about geriatric romance. If that's what it is. Even Rachel stopped by to see him, yesterday after work. I tried to discourage her, feeling it was a weird way to get to know your girlfriend's father, but she insisted. I asked her if she wanted me to be there. She told me she'd rather see him on her own. I didn't resist; I didn't want to take any time away from practicing. I was a little stung by her refusal to have me accompany her, and a lot relieved. It's hard enough for me to see him on my own or with my mother hovering without berating him about what a dumbass he's been about his health. I didn't want Rachel to see me badgering him, though he deserves badgering and worse. I hoped she would find a gentle way to tell him the same things; she's good at that.

When I get home after practice, she tells me he didn't try to test her knowledge of opera or 1940's movies, which I warned her he might. She says they had a reasonable conversation during which she told him he needed to think about taking better care of himself in the future. He got her to talk about her parents, something she has only done in dribs and drabs with me. Not that I've asked her all that many questions, I admit. She makes her family sound irrelevant, so I don't ask about them. When we first got together and we had the where-did-you-come-from-who-are-your-parents conversation, she backed me off. But my father got her talking. It's one of his great skills. He convinces total strangers to reveal their life stories. I think it was part of his dentist persona to come on as everyone's buddy. He put his patients at ease. I assume, since my parents are a sore spot with me, that everyone's parents are a topic better left unexplored.

Today when I see him, he tells me things about Rachel I didn't know, as if he was angling to fix us up and her biography might convince me of her worthiness. There's a lot I didn't know about her, like how badly her coming out to her parents had gone. It's curious how much sympathy he generated for her without the slightest acknowledgment that he and I never had a real conversation about my sexual orientation, pre-or-post coming out, or that he once shamed me for desiring women over men. To Rachel, he seems completely comfortable having a gay daughter. The first thing he tells me today when I arrive is "I love your girlfriend," and he scolds me for hiding her. Whatever.

The grumpy part of my father's post-collapse behavior is his rejection of the idea that anyone he knows should consider giving him a kidney. "I know your mother wants you to do this, but I don't want you to," he tells me. "Please wait until the infection clears up before we worry about next steps. I don't think it's urgent right now." When I point out that 87% negative function is a scream for urgency he says, "I've been at that number for months. There's no way to predict I won't stay there for many more months, years even. I've had lots of conversations with my doctors about this. If I don't get worse, continuing to get dialysis will get me through. If I crash, I'll do what I need to do. Please don't volunteer to do anything rash." He wants that to be the end of the conversation.

If I ask him the questions any rational person would ask like, "Wouldn't you rather have at least one healthy kidney so you can get back to an active existence and not be tethered to these machines three or four times a week?" he cuts me off. "Not thinking about stuff like that now." Or, "I'm getting enough pressure from your mother. I don't need it from you, too." Grumpy.

Waiting outside his room while he gets a sponge bath, I hear him giving a nurse a hard time. "I'm not a child," he barks. "I don't need your help with that."

"What was that about?" I ask him when she's done and she has carried off his dirty linens, washcloth, and towels.

"I can wash my own private parts," he tells me. "Been doing it for years."

"You don't like having a young woman play with your dick?" I'm being cute.

He snaps, "I don't need that from you. It's hard enough that I'm reminded about my infirmities every time I take a piss without some nurse reminding me what I can't do anymore."

"She was just giving you...." A bath, I start to say, but he looks dejected so shut up.

I never think of my father as a sexual being – who does about their own parents? The realization that sex is off the table for him catches me up short. I want to hug him, to tell him it is okay, that it doesn't diminish him, but I'm not sure it's true. If it was me, would I be any less angry? Sexual pleasure is wedded to who I am, who we all are. What can I say that wouldn't sound false or make him feel worse? Pretend he's exaggerating? Insist it isn't that bad? There is an awkward moment between us, and then I take the easy way out. I use his favorite tactic on him. I change the subject.

"Do you want some juice or ice cream? I could get it for you."

"No. I'm fine," he says, though I know he isn't. We sit in silence after that, and I realize after a while he's crying. "Daddy?" How long has it been since I called him that?

"I'm tired, Honey. These drugs make me groggy. They make me feel like I can't control my emotions. I'm sorry I barked at you. Look at me, all weepy over nothing. What's changed from five-minutes ago that I'm suddenly a waterworks? You don't need to stay. I should rest. If you go now, I won't worry you'll think I'm boring company."

"I'm not thinking that."

"Whatever you're thinking."

"I'm thinking I want you to get better so you can come to the championships. I really want you to see this team play. We're really good. And I'm the star, Daddy. I'm not bragging. I really am. My picture will be on the front page of the program. I want you to be proud of me." He hasn't been to a bout in two years, and the last time he came it was reluctantly. He has many of the same reactions Rachel has. He doesn't like to see me fall or get stomped by the opposing team's blockers.

"I'm proud of you. Not just for this. For all the good things you do at your job and for caring about me and your mother and for being a good person. I'll tell you what. If they let me out of this prison in time, I promise I'll come to your bout."

I'm not sure he'll be out in time, but I'm pleased he says he's willing to come. "You'll be home by the weekend if you're stable. Your doctors told me. These days the insurance companies don't let anyone stay in the hospital if they can possibly send them home."

"We'll see if they keep their word. They are so dishonest here. They told me there'd be chocolate pudding last night. There wasn't."

"Right. No credibility. Shameless liars!"

"They're lying about how bad off I am."

"I believe you could convince yourself of that."

"Yeah, well, they'll get theirs. I'm contemplating lawsuits. And a jailbreak."

"I'll break you out if they try to keep you one second longer than they said. Maybe I could leave a revolver in the privy." This is a standard reference between us, to the escape of Billy the Kid from the Lincoln County Courthouse in April of 1881. One of Billy's buddies left him a gun in the outhouse and Billy used it to kill a deputy when the sheriff was at dinner. We know about this because one of my dad's favorite movies, Sam Peckinpah's *Pat Garrett and Billy the Kid*, includes that scene. Billy then goes on to shoot the sheriff, Robert Ollinger, with his own shotgun. Legend has it, and historians swear it's only legend, the sheriff loaded the gun with eighteen silver dimes to terrorize Billy into behaving. Billy was not particularly susceptible to threats of this kind.

In his best drawl, my father says, "The son-of-a-bitch sheriff will buy it double-barrel. When it happens, you can dig out the change." This is also lifted from the movie. Kris Kristofferson played Billy.

I kiss him on the forehead, glad to see a glimmer of pluck in the gray ghost who has stolen my father's body. The exchange has perked him up too. As I am leaving, I think he's such a good con man that he can con himself into acting like he's not a sick and forlorn old man. He's so good that for a moment he's almost conned me.

THIRTY-TWO

SESSION NOTES RACHEL WILLIAMS

CONCLUSORY NOTES SESSION FOUR: Based on the session just completed, I think we are making some headway in getting to the root of Rachel's feelings of insecurity and self-doubt. She worries she is not interesting enough for her rather extroverted and (from her description) perhaps intimidating and domineering girlfriend.

PATIENT NAME: WILLIAMS, RACHEL SESSION # 5
DSM CODE: 300.02 Record # 447/26
DESCRIPTION: Generalized Anxiety Disorder
PRESENTING ISSUE(S): Trouble sleeping with bruxism; anxiety about the future; fear of loss of primary relationship; self-doubt
REFERRING ENTITY: Self
INSURANCE: Fonterra Healthcare HMO
SESSION: $175
CO-PAY: $40

THIRTY-THREE: Rachel with Dr. Gray, Session Five

2 WEEKS AND 2 DAYS BEFORE THE CHAMPIONSHIP BOUT

"It was so strange," I tell her. "I rarely remember my dreams, but this one was so vivid it just stuck with me. And it was so different from my normal. If I remember dreams at all they're usually violent or scary. But this one was absurd. I was the color commentator at Nina's championship match against the team from New York. The guy calling the play by play was named Butchy Trucks."

Dr. Gray motions me to keep going, but I see her surprise when I break into character voices.

"'All right. All right. All right. You can feel the excitement building tonight. Welcome to the East Coast National Championship Jam. If you are just joining us, we are live on Derby Television Network Dot Com for this all-important regional championship matchup. We are mere seconds from the line-up for the first skate of this highly anticipated bout. I'm your announcer, Butchy Trucks, with the call – being joined today by the lovely Rachel Righteous with color commentary. Rachel.'" And then he hands me a microphone so I can do the commentary. I know that's not how it happens – commentators each have their own microphones – but that's how it happens in my dream. I protest.

"What? No. I don't do commentary. I'm just a fan. I just come here to watch my girlfriend. I don't have anything to say."

"'These teams have seen some legendary players on their rosters over the years. Any insights into their strategy for today, Rachel?'" I am having fun doing as close an approximation to the voice in my dream as I can.

"Um...Nina thinks the bouts are better when the teams are well matched."

"'You've got to admit that there is a definite expectation of blood being spilled in this very competitive bout, Rachel. In this first jam, the rivalries being played out on the track go back about a decade to when these clubs were formed. Given the bloody and pugnacious history of these opponents, tell us what you think the outcome will be.'"

"Oh, I..."

"'Okay, okay, okay. Here we go. They're lining up for the jam. And there's the whistle. They're off and skating. Ooh. Right away. Turn one. A big pileup. A full-fledged yard sale. But now the jammers are up and battling. Who will emerge as lead? They're both trying to get around a double thick wall of blockers. It's a barn burner, Rachel, a barn burner. There's a setback. Nina goes down hard. That's a penalty.'"

"Nina? What? Was Nina in that jam?" I'm calling her name in my sleep. "Nina? Nina?"

"'Oh. Another tough crash between turns three and four as these two teams, whose bad blood is legendary, battle each other and the clock.'"

"That's when I woke up." I look at Dr. Gray. I am pretty sure she has no idea what to make of all of this, or how to relate it to what we've been talking about, but for a moment, at least, I feel like I have entered Nina's world to an altogether new degree. Not trying to share her world as a skater, but instead having a purpose, albeit a goofy one: broadcasting from the sidelines.

Dr. Gray shakes her head at me. "I'm not all that sure the way we remember dreams is interpretively useful. I could say that the dream is about your desire to have a function in Nina's world you don't currently think you have, but there is no way to verify that's what you were thinking when you were dreaming. It could be purely associative, in the way many dreams are. Most psychologists who study dreams and dreaming, if you read the literature, think dream memory is unreliable, and some think dreams are a chemical response that occurs moments before waking. In my practice, I tend to discount dream interpretation and even dream description except to maybe get patients talking. But you're already talking, and we know what the issues are for you, and how you feel. You articulate them very well without the overlay of anything as fanciful as a dream structure. So, the question is, and this is where I think we could focus our current time, what do you want to do about the feeling that Nina is not attuned to your needs? Do you want to talk about tools for talking to her about it? Do you want to consider if you can stay with her? Because, of course, that is the extreme choice, to leave when the situation is imperfect if you feel it is not likely to change. We could try to create a kind of table of positive and negative reasons for you and Nina to go on, and add them up, and then try to balance them against the hopefulness you feel about her changing and your love for her, which I know is strong. You only have a few more sessions insurance will cover, and we should try to make it the most useful to you especially if you can't afford to continue with me on your own. I know that sounds a little direct, but I'm just facing the fiscal realities you also must face."

I feel myself recoil at the idea that Nina and I would break up. "I'm not leaving her. And she hasn't made any moves to heave me out the door. I just want to feel better about the way we are together."

"Then let's start with a list of things you can broach with her, to get her to talk to you about how you feel. You might want to consider some joint sessions, not necessarily with me, but with someone who can help facilitate the conversation that has been difficult to have at home. It sometimes helps to say things aloud in front of a third party. It makes them more real somehow. An old therapist's trick."

"You're not that old," I say, but the joke falls flat. It occurs to me that I might have just blown her sympathy, but she just goes on. "Let's start with the most important thing you need to tell her you don't think she understands."

2 WEEKS BEFORE THE CHAMPIONSHIP BOUT

There might be nowhere less welcoming or conducive to the belief that healing will occur than doctors' offices on the premises of hospitals. It amazes me that no one gets how creepy they are, I mean how creepy the whole atmosphere is. I work in a freestanding medical building, and it's bad, but not nearly as bad. There are human touches in my building, attempts to make it feel less medical, less about the efficient delivery of care and more about something else: anonymous comfort perhaps, or the consolation of the familiar. These features are designed into the planted sitting areas, the wall art, the lighting in our building. But the modern hospital feels entirely corporate to me, with the plaques on the donor wall and rah-rah inspirational advertising posters that tell you your life is worth the medicine the hospital can provide. Maybe I'm just weird, but this ambiance makes me think they're hiding something, that someone has just died but now everything is cleaned up, nothing is dire, nothing is remiss, everything is fine.

I'm sitting in the waiting area for the Nephrology Department, under a sign that says "Ask About Our New Clinical Trials," reading a brochure they have given me with my paperwork that lists the virtues of being a kidney donor. At the top of the list is 'honor in your community.' I laugh out loud and the other people in the waiting room, patients and donors I assume, look up and scowl at me. I am rescued from further humiliation by a woman in scrubs who calls my name.

"Nina Gordon? Please follow me," she says. I gather up my forms and follow her. She leads me into the office of Dr. Wolfe, the transplant team psychologist. In a moment, a woman in a gray business pantsuit under a blue hospital coat comes in. "Please, sit down," she says. I have been standing, looking at the graphics of kidneys on the wall. There's a talking kidney with speech bubbles meant to explain the transplant to kids; it's the organ detached from a body, which has grown tiny arms and legs and has a face on its belly, an image I know I can't unsee and will haunt me forever. Dr. Wolfe sits at her desk. "You have all your paperwork?"

I hand it to her. She looks it over. "You've worked your way through all the materials we sent you?

"Yep," I tell her. "An astonishingly thrilling read."

Dr. Wolfe does not smile. Instead, she launches into a speech I know she has given dozens if not hundreds of times. "My job here is twofold. First, making sure you understand what this decision entails and then assessing whether you're a good donor candidate. There will be a medical evaluation later, but this step is no less important. Shall we begin?"

"You betcha," I say, not sure why I am being so obstreperous.

"Why do you want to donate your kidney to Mr. Gordon?"

"Tax write off on my Federal return. I get one for the value of my organs, right?" She just scowls at me. Okay, I think. Better answer her straight because she doesn't seem likely to get me at all. "Other than that, he's my father?"

This gets her to look up at me for the first time. "Is that the whole reason?"

"I wouldn't do this for a stranger."

"No? Lots of people do, you know."

"Yeah, I read that on the Internet. I don't believe much I read on the Internet."

"It surprises you."

"It seems like a big sacrifice to make for someone you don't know."

"For most donors, after recovery, it's no sacrifice at all. And many people get satisfaction out of giving the gift of life to another person."

"Honor in your community," I say.

I look at Dr. Wolfe. She is totally blank. "What?"

"It's all the stuff that can go wrong before recovery that would give me pause."

"Is it the physical risk that troubles you?"

"Partly. Although it's funny to hear myself say it."

"Why is that?"

"I have some experience with physical risk."

"You want to tell me about that?"

"Not particularly." There's a long pause after this as she looks me up and down.

"All right. Why don't I take you through the standard issues and if we need to talk about anything, we can stop and explore. Is that all right?"

"Sure."

"There are things you need to know before you commit to this. I'll go through them in chronological order starting with what you have to do before, during and after the procedure."

"During?"

"Well, for you, there's not a lot you need to do during. That part is mostly us. But it's just so you know what's going to happen."

"Too bad. I think I could do my own incision. Did you see that movie about the guy who had to cut off his own arm to get free when he got trapped in a slot canyon in Utah while hiking? James Franco played him? Gory but great."

She doesn't even crack a smile. We would never be friends, this one and me. Although I have to say I admire her game face. I have my own version of the game face, though I tend to put it on when I'm, you know, actually playing a game. After a long pause, the good headshrinker says, "So, beforehand, there are things like stopping smoking and stopping birth control pills if you take them, and switching to low calorie and low-fat meals. The diet changes will continue after you donate, since your body will have a slightly harder time digesting both fats and carbs because it will be processing with only half the kidney power as before. And it's never a bad idea for us gals to cut down on those things as we age anyway."

"Yes. Us gals sure do need to watch our figures." I decide not to make a joke about the idea of "kidney power," though one occurs to me. Dr. Wolfe takes a long time before she says anything else. She doesn't seem to know what to make of my responses.

"Is there something you're nervous about?"

"Nervous? I wouldn't say that. Why?"

"Your answers seem glib and half serious. Sometimes people joke to cope with the anxiety of this decision."

"I haven't made a decision."

"Okay."

"Do I need to be serious to donate my kidney? Okay. Serious. I'll try to do that."

Another long pause, and then she asks, "How's your diet?" she asks.

"A mix of crappy and guilty. Wine, red meat, salt, fats, and indulgence followed by a few days of repentant kale. Then back off the wagon."

"You look like you're in terrific shape. You must exercise."

"Are you flirting with me, Dr. Wolfe?" When she scowls again, I say, "I'm just...active."

She recovers and says, "Active is good. You'll probably have to curtail some activities for a while, but you know what the kidney docs say."

"No, I really don't."

"The healthier you are with two, the healthier you'll be with one."

"Is that what they say?" In my mind, I see myself getting up from the chair, and slamming into Dr. Wolfe with all my might, with the same body check that might get me a penalty in a bout if I did it on skates. I'm not usually a blocker; I'm a born jammer, but if I was on a revenge mission, say, for a bad check someone gave to one of my teammates, I wouldn't hesitate to take the offender out with a slam that lifted her off her feet and landed her on her ass. That's what I feel like I should do to Dr. Wolfe.

"I only have a few more questions, maybe a page," she says after flipping through the papers on her desk in front of her, as if she has never seen them before and needs to check how much more there is to go. Then there is another long pause. I wonder if she can sense I'm doing everything I can to not punch her in the nose and bolt. Finally, she asks, "Have you written a will?" I haven't and I tell her so. "You will need to do that. And instructions on what to do if there's an emergency, problem, or crisis."

"How often does that happen?"

"For the donor? Almost never. It is less serious for you than it will be for your father, shorter in duration and with fewer surgical steps. I've never heard of a problem occurring in this hospital, but things do happen. This is major surgery, Nina. If you were to have a stroke on the table or stop breathing long enough to have brain damage, what would you want us to do?"

"After you sawed out my kidney and heart and anything else you can harvest for the good of someone else? Dump the rest in the garbage."

"It's good to have a sense of humor about everything, but there are serious –"

I interrupt her. "I get it. I need advance directives. I need a will."

"Okay. I know what you do for a living. What do you do in your spare time?"

I wonder for a moment if she is asking me about my sex life, and then I shake that thought off. "I'm a semi-professional athlete."

"Really? What kind of sport do you play?"

"Roller derby. I'm a jammer on the Philadelphia Freedoms." I land heavily on the *doms*.

"What's a jammer?"

"If roller derby was football, the jammer would be the ball. It's my job to outrace the opposing jammer, get through a pack of blockers to get around the track, and then keep passing them to score points. The more times you pass your opponents, the more points you score. That's the gist. But I think what you're asking is if the sport's dangerous, and I guess I'd have to say yes to that question. I'm in the fray. I get hit sometimes. It's physical."

"I see," she says, then pauses to write something down.

"Have you ever seen roller derby?" I was sure I already knew the answer.

"Not live. I started a movie about it on TV once. *Whipped?* Something like that. It was bad. I turned it off."

"That movie is called *Whip It*." I thought of how hot I was for Ellen Page when I saw it and started to say, "And didn't you just want to tongue fuck Bliss for like hours?" Bliss is the name of Ellen's character. I stopped myself at 'want to.' I was getting awfully tired of her condescension. She looked at me, waiting for me to finish the thought, but I shook my head. "You should come to see the *Freedoms* sometime. It's a great night out. You could bring your...let me not presume...which way do you go?"

"Sports aren't my thing."

"I'm surprised. What is your thing?"

"Oh, I don't know. Theater. The symphony."

"Me too. I just heard the Orchestra perform Bruckner." She shoots, she scores, to borrow a metaphor from a lesser sport. But Dr. Wolfe doesn't even flinch, which, I admit, annoys me and amps up my desire to punch her again. So secure in her insular life, I can't seem to rattle her.

"So, let's be straight with each other here, Nina."

"As if."

"Beg pardon?"

I decide I don't want to go where that comment would lead, so I follow her road. "I'm going to have to give this up, right? That's what you're gonna tell me?

"Is it strenuous?"

"Two hours of continuous action. It's a full body contact sport. As hard-hitting as football."

"Is it dangerous? Can you be injured?"

"That's the fun of it, taking and dodging the risk of that."

"I see."

"So, yeah, let's be straight with each other, Doc. I need to know how this will change my life."

"For most people, nothing changes. After time, you can resume...you can do everything you did before your donation. One kidney does the work of two. But a full body contact sport..."

"You know, I think you should come see me compete. It'd be great knowing you were in the stands."

"How old are you?"

"Thirty-one."

"Do you speed when you drive?"

"Are you kidding? Doesn't everyone, unless you're Canadian?"

"Do you like to get drunk when you drink?"

I nod. "Not falling down drunk, but I am a gal who appreciates getting a good buzz on now and then. Not that I drink all that much anymore. And almost never since we started training for the playoff bout. But when I do." She is scaring me. I think she's going to run down the entire list of my vices.

"Ok, so here's the thing. There's a risk profile. Not everyone subscribes to it, since it is more anecdotal than statistical, but without being overly scientific, the behaviors you're describing put you at a higher risk for post-donation difficulties. Most people can live perfectly well with only one kidney. But if there is an increased risk you could injure the kidney you have left, your donor profile changes."

I start to sing. "You've got to change your evil ways, baby."

"Yes."

"Or I could take my chances."

"If we accept you and you take chances, you're statistically more likely to cause yourself irreparable harm. If I believed that was likely, it would be unethical for me to recommend you go forward with this."

"Someone's studied this? There's stats?"

"Have you **ever seen a mortality chart? They were invented by the insurance industry a hundred years ago to predict how long people would live. No insurance company I've ever heard of has gone out of business from missing their guess.**"

"And you're the decider."

"I will present my evaluation to the transplant team. Most of the time, the post-operative life of the donor doesn't factor in. For you..."

"I get it."

"The question you have to answer for yourself before you answer it for me is whether you are willing to give up your athletic career?"

"It's not a career. I do it for love. It's one of the few things I love."

"Perhaps you could find another hobby."

"It's more than that. It saves me. It keeps me sane. It gives me something. I found myself...never mind."

"Nina, why are you doing this? You don't have to, you know."

"Straight up? I don't know exactly. When I skate, and I sacrifice myself, take out another team's blocker or trip up the opposing jammer and I draw a penalty, I understand the reasons. It's a game. There are rules. Violating them is part of the game, a calculated risk that the reward is greater than sacrifice. I don't do it very often but when it needs to be done, I do. And it's the same for the players on the opposite side. We're all playing with the same strategy. But with this, there are so many things to consider and I can't sort them all out intellectually. So, it comes down to a feeling. And my feeling is that my mother may be right. I might owe my parents something that this is the right way to repay. Even though my father says I shouldn't, and my mother, who hasn't lived with him in a hundred years but is still crazy in love with him, says I should, underneath, there's something else. I just have to. It's as simple as that. I can't not. Do you understand? I am not a freak in the jam. But sometimes it's your turn to make a hard play. I'm tough. I do what has to be done."

"I think I get it."

"I just don't know if I can give it up."

"You need to think about it. But not too long. Your father is nearing full renal failure. Once he gets there, time's up."

Riding home on the subway, I think about what I'll tell Rachel about my conversation with Dr. Wolfe. I know I won't tell her everything. I sure can't tell her about the last part, where Dr. Wolfe told me what I would have to sacrifice. That would be the whole story for her. I suppose it should be for me as well. But somehow, it just isn't.

THIRTY-FIVE

NINA'S RECOVERY JOURNAL

I have this strange dream memory. Maybe it isn't a memory, maybe it's something else, something I thought up later and just feels like a memory. I remember thinking about slamming into Dr. Wolfe in a jam when we were talking in her office the day she did my transplant interview. So, this might be something I called up because of that, now that I am on the other side of this operation, in recovery as she would have called it. But it isn't recovery if the thing you lost can't be recovered. My kidney is gone. Maybe that's what I am supposed to realize from this. Maybe I'm telling myself something. Or maybe it's just a random set of images I'm trying to build into something sensible. Are dreams ever reliable sources for metaphors? I have no idea. Anyway, this is the dream.

I'm riding home on the subway, standing as I usually do, leaning against the doors opposite the ones that open at all the stations between where I get on and where I get off. These days, I never sit on the subway. Too wired commuting between places, coming down from what I've been doing or amped up because of what I'm headed toward. Either way, I'm off in my head. Maybe I don't sit down because I am afraid I'd fall asleep and miss my stop. That happened a few times when I was in college after putting in an all-nighter studying or partying, and I got pissed off at myself when it did. So, I'm standing against the door, and the train is lurching back and forth as it speeds between stations. Suddenly I'm thinking about Dr. Wolfe and imagining what it would be like to be in a jam with her, only I am not wearing derby clothes. I'm wearing the kind of pads a hockey goalie wears. And I'm not on quads; I'm on ice skates. Dr. Wolfe is on the ice opposite me and we are skating toward each other as fast as we can. I am gritting my teeth, but she's babbling on about the risks of our collision and how we should stop before we slam into each other. About ten feet from me she stops and stands facing me. But I don't stop. I speed up. And then I slam into her full force. I see her body shatter. Her helmet flies off. Her teeth are shooting out of her mouth. Her arms fly up and she splits in two. And I am smiling with a 'take that, bitch' grin on my face. Then I'm holding my stick aloft and celebrating, and I just keep going, like there is nothing in the way, like there's an endless river of ice for me to speed along, like there's no way I'm ever going to slow down.

Of course, I'm aware that this is a metaphor for my anger at her for telling me I can't do something. It's about me on the roof again after my parents turn their backs. It's about Picabo Street or Lindsay Vonn slamming down the mountain after the doctors tell them they'll never ski again. It's about all the girls who get up and kick ass when the world says to stop.

2 WEEKS BEFORE THE CHAMPIONSHIP BOUT

I come in the door still steamed up from the conversation with Dr. Wolfe. "Rachel, I'm home," I sing as I come through the door, imitating that irritating jingle from the nineties sitcom that goes 'Hi honey, I'm home.'" Rachel comes out of the bedroom. She's just home from work, and she's showered and is half changed into sweats. I have never quite understood how she can stand touching people's bodies all day. Adult strangers. I know she has some regular clients, and some people who never get weird on her. People she knows and likes. But some of the stuff she's told me makes her job seem icky. Guys who come on to her. Guys who think it's okay to lie on the table naked before she comes into the massage room instead of covering up. Guys who try to wiggle their towels off their asses when she is working on their legs, so their penises show. Yeah, it's always guys. Or maybe she only tells me about the guys. Now there's a thought I've never had before.

"Hi, Sweetie," she says as I plant my bag on the kitchen counter and my ass on the counter chair. I am exhausted. "Your mother called," she says before I can tell her to give me just a few minutes before she gives me any bad news. I groan. I see her face fall. I didn't mean to lay my crappy mood on her, but she switches gears and lights back up.

"I keep thinking about this dream I had the other night. I've been meaning to tell you about it. You wanna hear it?"

"What did she want?" I ask before I can stop myself. I am so not interested in my mother's shit right now I could scream but can't overcome the impulse to ask. I could just as easily put it off ten minutes.

"She didn't say. I was wrecked after work. I had an extra client. Unscheduled. My hands hurt."

I wait for her to say more. When she realizes she says, "She doesn't like to tell me anything unless she can make a *big megillah* out of it. She really doesn't like to talk to me."

"'Big megillah?' Them-there's fighting words in her language."

"I got that from you."

"What was the dream?

"I dreamt I was doing color commentary at a jam. The championship."

"I don't think you'd be the most impartial –"

"That's what I told him."

"Him who?"

"Butchy Trucks. The play-by-play guy."

"Butchy Trucks. That's funny. Did you make that up? Trucks are the names of the wheels and Butchy –"

"I know that. I made it up in my dream. Call your mother back."

"When I get to it. I'm not in the mood." I watch her head drop. She feels scolded, which isn't what I meant, so I say, "How'd we do? The team. In your dream."

She looks me right in the eye. "You got stomped in the first jam."

"Fuck you." The minute it is out of my mouth, I regret it. Rachel turns to head back down the hall, then she wheels around on me.

"What is your problem? It was a dream."

"I don't have a problem."

"You have all kinds of problems."

"I'm sorry I said, 'fuck you.'"

I want Rachel to understand my issues with my mother, and I feel like I've made them clear to her, but she misses something essential about how hard it is for me to deal with her. I want her to be on my side. "With my mother, it's always *something*. She never just wants to talk. There's always some huge crisis, something that can't wait, that always can."

"You let her get to you. You could just decide not to."

"Maybe I could in some alternate universe. In this one, she just does. It's like the Labradors we watch in the park, that pair the woman with the purple Adidas walks. Those two dogs seem to really love each other. I've watched them play in the dog run. They're soul mates, bunkmates, best friends, and rowdy chase buddies. When one barks, the other one hunkers down into a defensive position, ready to attack, if attack is necessary. The bark might have been at a bird or a leaf scudding by, or some other dog chasing a tennis ball, but it's stimulus-response. This causes that. The dog who didn't bark is on alert, ready to fight. It's been going on so long, it's ingrained. I'm the dog who hunkers down."

"It's instinct."

"Right."

"Not the dogs. I'm talking about your mother. Her desire to mother you. To keep mothering you. The thing you hate."

"I'm thirty-one. It's time for her to knock it off."

"I think for her it'll only get knocked off if you get knocked up."

"I'll get right on that."

"Really?"

"No. Anyway, you'd be a way better baby-momma."

"You know I'd be happy to, but it won't count for her unless it's her bloodline."

"Yeah, well, whip out your dick. Let's get to work."

"Seriously?"

"Give me a break, Rachel."

"Cause if you want to, I know where I can get us some amazeballs spermatozoas."

I know she's joking with me about it so I'll stay in the conversation, but I can't resist. "Did you just say 'amazeballs spermatozoas'"?

"What would you call them?"

"I think spermatozoa is one of those collective nouns that don't pluralize with the addition of an s."

"I researched it. Them. It. After we talked about kids the other day. Just in case."

My involuntary response is to clench up. I can't explain it. It's sweet but impossibly impractical at the same time. I recoil at the thought of what being pregnant will do to my balance on skates. I know this is a huge leap, but there I am in my head with a hugely distended belly. I shake the image away. Better to stay with the joke. "In that case, yes, please. Fill'er up."

In her best Kmart announcer-in-her dreams voice, Rachel says, "We have a special on the turkey baster and spermatozoa together, the full insemination kit. Comes with a Mantovani CD, a rose, and a box of Whitman Chocolates.

"Eww. I need better chocolate than Whitman's. Green and Black's Organic dark at least. But eww."

Rachel doubles down. "Or for those of you who aren't proportion queens, we have hypodermic needle sized infusers. Big ol' shot' o sperm or little bitty shot. Shots correspond to infuser size. No warranties expressed or implied, and size, of course, does not matter."

"Infuser size? Double eww. And size so does. I've seen you with the elephant dong you love so much. And you never use the soft silicon Pee Wee Herman vibe that – what was her name? Your last girlfriend? – gave you. So thoughtful."

"What about the sperm donor's genetic characteristics? Predispositions? Intelligence? Kindness? Athletic abilities? Stature? Style? Look? Artistic skills? Musical talent? Would you want it to be someone you know or a stranger? We should make some lists."

"Choice or Prime? Chevy or Cadillac? Camry or Lexus? Orchestra or balcony? Nordic or tawny? Blue eyes or brown? Wouldn't getting knocked up just make it worse?"

"What?"

"My mother's mothering. Wouldn't she want to start, you know, grandmothering?"

"It's different. There's no comparison. One trumps the other. There's some weird transference thing that happens. It's chemical. Grandmothering turns on, mothering turns off. Grandmothers are all good. You should know that. Fairy grandmother?"

"That's godmother."

"Whatever."

"You are so talking out of your ass."

I tackle her. I can't tell if I'm acting out of lust for her or if I am in total avoidance mode about calling my mother. I have her out of her sweats in a half a minute and my doctor-visiting clothes are in a ball at my feet and we are mouth to pussy like we are teenagers discovering sex and have exploded out of our caution to do this for the first time. When we are finished, we hold on to each other for dear life. It is the best we have done together since the conversation my mother interrupted.

"Where were you this afternoon?" she asks me.

I tell her about Dr. Wolfe, all the way through the part of the conversation where she told me that if I was healthy with two, I'd be gangbusters with one. "She kept saying things in this qualified way that did not make me feel very reassured. 'Assuming there are no medical reasons which prevent you from making this donation, what about the other people in your life?' Stuff like that. That tone. Then she asked me, 'Do you have a husband?'"

"What'd you tell her?"

"I was in full snark mode at that point. I said, 'Golly. Do I need one?'"

"You didn't."

"I did. Then she was all, 'I'm sorry. Have I misspoken?'"

"What'd you say?"

"I told her I'm queer. To which she said, 'You're gay,' like in this insistent way. To which I said, 'You say tomato.'"

"How could she know what to say? I think you're too hard on straights like her. You can't ask them to know our nomenclature."

"You're absolutely right. I was hard on her. But she was asking me all these personal questions, writing down the history of my life. I had a right. She finally relented and said, 'Queer. Okay. Do you have a...partner,' and then kind of buried her nose in her forms."

"What did you say to that?"

"I told her yes. Then she wanted to know if our relationship was 'formalized?' That was the word she used, as if what it meant to have kidney transplant would be different either way. I told her we weren't married, if that was what she was asking, but I wanted to be sure you had decision-making power and not my mother. She said that the only way to ensure that was to get married. If we stay unmarried, I could assign you my medical power of attorney, but it's challengeable by a blood relative."

"Let's do that," she says, serious and responsible. Then, "I'd marry you in a heartbeat, you know. I'd love to be married to you. I think. Probably."

"You don't sound sure." She gives me a peck on the cheek and then rolls me over and starts massaging my back. I realize that Rachel has just sort of proposed to me or accepted my implicit proposal, but I blow by it. "She asked me what I call you. I know she was just looking for me to give her an easy way to talk about you in the future, you know, 'your partner' or 'your companion' but like you said, I just couldn't resist making it hard for her. In my best little-girl voice I said, 'I call her Honey-kins.' She didn't know if I was kidding or serious. Then I let her off the hook and said, 'I call her Rachel.' There was another break in the action like she had to figure out the best way to handle me. Then she asked, 'Does Rachel know you're considering giving a kidney to Mr. Gordon?' I felt I had to tell her the truth about this one, so I said, 'She knows, and she doesn't approve.' That's the truth, isn't it?"

Rachel stops stroking me. I crane my neck to look up at her, but she turns her face away, avoiding my eyes. "It is. I don't." After a moment, I lay my head back down.

I feel Rachel shift her weight, and then her hands are back on me. "What else did you talk about?"

"I think we kept talking about you after that. She wanted some practical information like your address and phone number and what you did for a living, stuff like that. I think she's planning to hit on you if I die. She's okay, for an older straight lady if you would ever be interested in that. Not your physical type, I don't think, but I'm sure she makes a ton of money. and would set you up in a really nice place. Sturdy legs, too. The rest of her was kind of too covered up to make a considered judgment."

"What did you tell her?"

"About what you did for a living? I told her you were a juggler with Cirque du Soleil."

"Shut up."

"That's close to what she said. She was so impressed I took even greater pleasure shooting her down hard about that. Then I told her the truth that you were a fireman. Firewoman. Which got us talking about sex."

"Your favorite subject."

"I told her 'I love talking dirty.' She wanted to warn me I wouldn't be able to resume sexual activity until my stitches were out and I felt healthy enough for sexual activity. She said the words sexual activity six or seven times. She said she was trying to give me all the info so I could make an 'informed decision.'"

"What does that mean? No sex? For how long?"

"She said, 'Your body tells you when you're ready. I said, 'You're talking about like penetration and active banging?' and she went into professional jargon mode. I think I had her rattled. 'I suppose these questions are presumptively heteronormative,' she said. Can you believe that? I mean this lady was up on all the latest verbal crack, right? So, I said, 'But tell me. Can we still do gentle girly stuff like with fingers and tongues before we go wild off the reservation and return to pounding each other senseless with our giant dildos and vibes and stuff?' She knew at that point she had offended me. 'The point of these restrictions is that sex can put a strain on your newly insulted body. Insult being the term of art for a body that has been surgically...assaulted.' Made me wonder if she has ever experienced a really good orgasm in her life. You'd think with like fifty percent of the American population not doing vanilla sex and gay marriage being legal that someone in her position would figure out how to talk to us like we're specific. I told her I'd make it easy for her and say I understood that I needed to take it easy before I returned to pounding you with my strap-on – or having you bang me."

"Sometimes I am glad I am not in the room with you when you get like this. No. Not sometimes. All the time. Maybe as a fly on the wall, so I could see the expressions. But not in person."

I roll over and face her. "Come on, Rach. This is all hard enough without douchebags like her getting stupid on you." Rachel does not respond to this. Then I say, "She asked if I had someone to take care of me after, if I decide to, you know."

"I'm not okay with it and this is not permission, but if it happened, I'd take care of you."

"I know. I do." We kiss, and then I tell Rachel about what I was thinking about in the waiting room before Dr. Wolfe called me in. "I was thinking about the first time I was on skates. My father bought me a pair of white, strap-on roller skates, quads, though I don't think anyone used that word then since I don't think most parents were letting kids skate on in-lines back then. They were just skates. I was at the dining room table doing my times tables. My mom was sitting next to me like she always did at homework time. My parents were still together then, though I suppose if I had been more astute, I would have seen that they were already in combat mode. But I was a kid; what did I know? Anyway, he comes in with this box and he unwraps it and holds the skates up and shows them to me and my mother. 'Helen, look what I got for Nina,' he says. My mother is out of her seat going ballistic before I can even focus on what she's screaming about. 'You want her to kill herself? Why would you get her those?' He answers in his earnest dad way that he got them because every kid loves them. He loved them when he was a kid, and he thinks I'm the kind of kid who might love them too. My mother tells him she didn't love them when she was a kid, and she remembers her friends who skated always having skinned knees and bruised chins and elbows. This feels to me at the time like all their conversations; it doesn't strike me as being in any way different than their arguments about whether I'll like some vegetable she's cooked or if some shirt is appropriate for school. Then she drops the big bomb. None of my friends skate, she tells him. She says, 'Skating is old fashioned,' as if that will end the conversation. Her real worry is I'll be a laughingstock, an outcast, as if I'm not already the weirdest kid in second-grade. But while they're having it out, I'm on the floor putting the skates on. When I get the stakes laced up, I'm out the door, down the driveway, shouting back over my shoulder, 'Daddy. Daddy. Watch me. Take my picture. Take my picture. Here I go.' It's that picture on the shelf over there. Come to think of it, my mother hauled me out of that house shortly after that. Maybe that was the straw that broke the camel's back. I'll ask my dad when I see him."

"You want me to come along?"

"He's your new best friend."

"I like him. I get why you like him. I see how you're like him."

"I'm not liking him so much right now."

"You'll get over that."

"I have to talk to him about this transplant thing. He's not going to like what I've decided."

"Wait. You decided? I thought you were still considering it."

"I decided to get the medical tests. That's only the first step. There's a long way between getting those tests and letting them carve out my guts with a scalpel."

"We're going to talk some more before you make an actual decision, right?"

"Sure," I promise her, but I'm not sure I'll keep the promise. If I decide to do it and she objects, what do I do? He's my father, and like I told Dr. Wolfe, sometimes you take one for the team.

"There's a lot of steps between getting tested and becoming an actual donor. But I have to know if I'm a candidate. You get that, right? That I have to know?"

I WEEK AND 6 DAYS BEFORE THE CHAMPIONSHIP BOUT

We're practicing every day now, and on the weekends it's day-times instead of evenings. We started at nine this morning. I get off at two-thirty and head to my father's place. I know I stink, I'm wearing the sweats I threw on over the underwear I skated in, but I didn't want to delay for a shower. I'm guessing we're in for a long session. My mother told him I went for the initial interview with the transplant team. He was pissed.

He's at home now. They sent him home yesterday, satisfied that he can resume his routine of taking the para-transit bus to the dialysis center and fend for himself at home. My mother drove him back from the hospital, went food shopping for him, got him settled. Another example of their crazy connection. Or hers, I guess. I'm not sure how he felt about her invading his space like that. And given how negligent he is about taking care of himself, I'm not so sure he will fend for himself. I keep thinking about him collapsing again, only this time with no nosey neighbor to hear him fall. What then? But as Rachel keeps reminding me, he is not a child. Except in all the ways he is.

I'm not in the door two seconds when my father is all over me. "You may not do this. I forbid you."

"You forbid me? What do you think I am, seven? We're pretty far past you telling me what I can and cannot do."

"I told the hospital not to test you. I told the surgeons and the nephrology docs. I told them I would not accept a kidney from you."

"They don't honor the patient's wishes over there. Remember the incident with the pudding they promised?"

"Nina, I don't want you doing this."

"You'll die without a kidney."

"You don't know that. I'm still on the cadaver transplant list."

"And you are not likely to get one. You have three strikes. Old. Diabetic. Neglectful."

"You know I'm not a religious man, so I asked your mother to pray for someone with an organ donor stamp on his driver's license to wrap himself around a pole."

"Without mashing up his kidneys in the process."

He smiles, changing his tactic. "Kidney and mash. That old British working-class delicacy. Yes. Without doing that."

"You think we should let you die waiting to get a kidney from some asshole who misses his guess speeding through a yellow light? You think we shouldn't be thinking about this at least? What mom says about you is true. You'd ignore this until it was too late."

"Don't sacrifice anything for me, please, Nina. Don't sacrifice anything you love for me. If the situation was reversed, I'm not sure I would be willing to do the same for you. Or for anyone. That's who I am. I love you, but I'm selfish. Nothing I did in my life cost me anything near what this will cost you. Don't make me die ashamed of myself for that."

"First of all, you're not going to die. Let's take that off the table right now. And second, aside from the fact that that is one of the most hurtful things you have ever said, it's a bald fucking lie. You would cut off your arm for me and I know it. Making yourself seem like an asshole is a terrible tactic. I already know exactly how much of asshole you are. You wouldn't think I would love you as much as I do, given what I know, but that's my strange psychology. I'm someone who thrives on the pain other people cause me. So, shut the fuck up about not getting tested. As I have already told Rachel, there's a long road between getting tested and going through their screening process and getting this done. Let's at least go through the steps and see what the results are, okay? Then we can make decisions that really piss each other off." I realized my father is crying. "God damn it, Dad. What is this about?"

"I don't deserve you. I've been a horrible father. You make me ashamed of myself."

"Yeah, that was my goal here, to make you confess that. Can we drop all this maudlin crap for five minutes? You were the father I wanted. And loved. Still love. Now tell me what you're reading, or what sports you've been following on TV. Tell me what you're thinking about. Tell me if there's anything I can get you, what you've been binge-watching if there's anything I should dive into after my tournament is over. Tell me anything that is not about what is going on inside of your body or inside the scariest places in either of our heads."

"I'm pretty hooked on *Orange is the New Black*," he says.

This is the last thing I can imagine him liking, and I crack up. "See, I knew you'd come around about lesbians."

"I think the reason I never got into porn was because there weren't any stories. There were stupid setups, leading to sex that never looked like real sex to me. All posed for the camera, not even remotely how real sex looks."

I start to say, "I think there's some more realistic..." but I stop, thinking better of it.

"Even watching the girl-on-girl sex, which I admit was a turn-on, got boring real fast because there was no character development, no plot. But those women prisoners, with their isolation and needs, their fucked-up lives, bad haircuts, and thwarted desires, them I can get into."

"Their desires are hardly thwarted. There's more pussy on that series than on *The L Word*."

"What's that?"

"It's on Showtime. About lesbians. Binge it after you finish binging *Orange*."

"I only have HBO."

"So, splurge a little. You're hoarding your money now?"

"I have to ask, is your life as crazy as that? Are you, I don't know, confused? Do you go back and forth?"

"You mean like Piper with Alex and Larry? No. I'm old fashioned. I'm a one-partner-at-a-time gal. You've met Rachel. She's terrific. And I don't do men. Never have. You've known this for a long time."

He's silent for a while. I'm sure there's nowhere else to go with this conversation that wouldn't mortify him. He's trying so hard to be cool with me, I know, and it's sweet how hard he's working at it, at being on my side. He wants to persuade me he understands my life well enough that he can say no to my being the donor if it comes to that. If I had never forgiven him before for what I believed he felt about my sexual orientation, as he called it, I have to now. Except, except, except. He always has an agenda, and it is almost always about as clear as mud. Is all his objection a kind of misdirection? I can't help but think so. No one wants to face the prospect of dying, even if to live you have to ask someone else to take on your pain. Had this selfish Grinch suddenly grown a heart? Or is he playing me so he doesn't feel as bad as I know he will if I give up my kidney for him? Or is he addled in some way? How would I tell?

Riding home on the subway, I am having conversations with myself about everything that has happened this afternoon. I know there is something else behind my father's objections. I know he knows my mother wants me to donate the kidney to him, and he wants to oppose anything my mother wants. Rachel is right about their relationship; it's super fucked up. And try as I might to keep their craziness out of my decision-making process, I have to say that my mother's point of view seems a lot more rational than his for one simple reason. If he doesn't get a transplant, he dies. My mother, for all her disdain for him on a day-to-day, practical, quotidian life-level, does not want him dead. She loves him. I get this. Love is not the same as being able to live together, or even as liking each other. When you first get together, when it is all passion and hot sex and exploring the world of the other, you each ignore things -- the ways your new love is self-indulgent, the inordinate amount of care she pays to things that are not significant to you. You ignore the amount of self-involvement your new partner exhibits. You ignore bad habits and physical tells, you ignore the hairs in the sink and the dirty underwear balled up in the corner and the uncovered food in the fridge and the toothpaste splatters and the gargle spits on the bathroom mirror and everything else that invades and kills you later. You ignore it because it's easy to ignore. Love has clouded your eyes, pulled the wool down over you. It's like you're wearing a hangman's hood only you believe you aren't because love has filled your eyes with rainbows and stars. Everyone's on his and her best behavior. And maybe, even though you are not trying to hide things, the truth about certain ways you act never becomes visible until the shit hits the fan, when there are hard decisions to make about careers, where to settle down and live, how to raise your kids, how many times a week you're going to make love, whose money is going to get spent on what, and how much of your budget is going to buy that new TV or car or kitchen or whatever the hell it is that one of you wants and the other couldn't give a shit about. It's easy not to see the authoritarian streak in a person until kids come along. I think about Rachel's mother, and how unaware Rachel thinks she was about her father's lack of empathy, until Rachel was in the picture and was messing up his peace and quiet and the order he imposed on his wife that she didn't even recognize was his idea until having a kid challenged it. Then he blamed her mother because he thought it was her job to control her "damn kid" as if he had nothing to do with it, and later he blamed Rachel because she was energetic and happy and wanted what every kid who craves loving parents and doesn't have them wants; she wanted them to act in ways that made her life feel more comfortable, their innate behaviors be damned. He wanted quiet and he wanted order and he wanted normal. How would Rachel's mother have known his unspoken requirements until questions came up? Which mirrors how it was for my parents. Two smart, needy people, who loved the same operas and the same books, who thought they saw the world through the same lens, suddenly discovered that they had very specific ideas about what their daughter should be like, and how she should be raised, and those ideas were as different as they could possibly be. Their tug of war over their daughter was the same as the U.S. and Russia fighting a surrogate war in Afghanistan in the 1980s. With the same lingering results for their child as there were for the occupied country. Internal unrest. Contradictory impulses. Lashing out. Desire for disconnection. Unabashed tribalism. I embody all those things.

What I want is at war with what I know would be best for me. What is best for him is at war with what he wants for me. What my mother wants is at war with what he wants. We are bound together in a dance we can neither ignore nor avoid, with potentially fatal consequences for two of the three dancers. And still, we dance.

THIRTY-EIGHT

SESSION NOTES RACHEL WILLIAMS

CONCLUSORY NOTES SESSION FIVE: We are continuing to talk about Rachel's relationship with her family and her insecurities about her girlfriend, Nina. She reported a strange dream in great detail. It was about roller derby, the girlfriend's sport, but I think it revealed something deeper about what Rachel fears. In her dream, she was at one of Nina's games (matches?) acting as a kind of sportscaster, but she couldn't do the job because she got focused on her girlfriend getting hurt. This reflects her core issues. She has all this doubt, but she is unable to detach herself sufficiently from the immediacy of the situations in her life to objectively consider how to overcome them, or what her next or long-term actions should be, and this is the source of her pain.

PATIENT NAME: WILLIAMS, RACHEL SESSION # 6
DSM CODE: 300.02 Record # 447/26
DESCRIPTION: Generalized Anxiety Disorder
PRESENTING ISSUE(S): Trouble sleeping, bruxism; anxiety about the future; fear of loss of primary relationship; self-doubt
REFERRING ENTITY: Self
INSURANCE: Fonterra Healthcare HMO
SESSION: $175
CO-PAY: $40

I WEEK AND 2 DAYS BEFORE THE CHAMPIONSHIP BOUT

Sometimes talking to a therapist feels like it's going nowhere. I felt this with my therapist in high school, and I sometimes feel it now. I'm talking, answering questions, not straying too from the subject at hand, not going off on wild tangents, but I look up at the doctor and I do not know why I am saying what I am saying or how it can possibly help ease my anxiety or make me feel better about the things that have brought me here. We've been at this for five weeks. I know I only have a few more sessions that my insurance will pay for. I don't want them to put me on some anxiety drug or Prozac, but I'm guessing that's what will happen if something doesn't click for me. If we get to the end of the sessions I'm allotted and the doctor asks if I'm doing better or able to handle things on my own and I say 'no' or 'I don't know' what's the alternative but to try to chill me out chemically? And it would probably work. But is that what I want to happen? I feel like there are things I want to figure out, decisions I want to make, and I want to make them clear-headedly, not under the influence. I know a ton of people on serotonin drugs; half the people in my office are on them. More than half probably. They're not zombies. They are rational and they must feel they are doing better than they would do without the drugs. But I'm not depressed – not unless I think about never having kids or never being accepted as Nina's partner by her mom. Dr. Gray thinks continuing to talk about my parents will help me see how my own needs got created. Maybe there is something I haven't understood yet, but I'm beginning to feel like talking about my own family is beside the point. Understanding Nina is the point, and how to convince her to pay more attention to me. Or the right kind of attention. I know she's not the one in therapy. I am. Maybe what I want is for Dr. Gray to just go ahead and tell me what to do, to solve something for me.

Today we are talking about what tools I have to help myself out of my funk. I tell her about reading, about rejecting my parents' religion and reading about other faiths. She asks what tools I used to relate to my parents after I came out to them.

"Unlike Nina's crazy parents, mine were simply dull, petty, and venal. I suppose in their way they still loved me even though they thought I was an abomination. They gave me very little in the way of self-help tools. My high school counselor gave me a book on Transcendental Meditation. I read about what to do, though I never went to a formal session and no one ever gave me a mantra. I used some ideas I found in the book. I felt better. Calmer. Meditating helped me find a center, a way of facing things, which made my life easier. Then I read about Buddhism and I tried to put the precepts of Buddhism into practice, wisdom, kindness, patience, generosity, forgiveness, and compassion, but the truth is, I'm pretty lousy at it. Well, maybe not lousy, just inconsistent. I can neither forgive as deeply as I need to nor embrace as broadly as I should. I'm selfish. I want things I should be able to give up, according to the teachings I've read. The teachings I studied require that you open your heart to all humanity and to see sacrifice as ennobling and spiritually enriching. And I hoped I could learn to cleanse my spirit, learn to reduce my ego and embrace the world. But so far in practice, like when something like this kidney thing comes up, I realize I'm still a total failure at it. I do not want to see Nina hurting, even for an instant. And I don't want her to do anything that would diminish her. I want to protect her from the harm this world inflicts on us. I do not want her less than whole. As much as I worry that she will leave me, I do not want Nina to give away a single piece of herself to anyone else. I want all of her all to myself."

"That's a pretty clear feeling. I assume she knows that?"

"I think she does. I've said it. But I don't think it's going to matter."

"Doesn't she risk hurting herself playing her sport?"

"Sure. But it's different. She could get injured, break a leg or something. It happens. But she'd come back from that. If she does this, there's no coming back. She's done. If she skates, she risks hurting herself in a way that could threaten her life."

"Is she that reckless?"

"I once heard Picabo Street's mother tell a reporter that for the first fourteen years of her daughter's life she saw her primary job as keeping Picabo alive. She was a daredevil. There are pictures of her climbing up on her family garage in Idaho. Her mother was being interviewed at the winter Olympics in 1998, one of those 'up close and personal' things. Nina was fifteen in 1998. Picabo was Nina's hero. Picabo was coming back from a devastating injury and no one expected her to win her races that year, but she did. Every interview was about how tough she was. And that's what Nina heard. She wanted to be tough, too. It wasn't about winning. Not then. It was about being as bad as the boys. It was about never showing fear. Right after her father gave her that first pair of skates, she built a ramp so she could launch herself onto the driveway. She told me this story on our first date. She dragged these old plywood sheets out of her garage. When her father realized what she was planning he came running out of the house screaming for her to stop. She told me he had visions of her torpedoing into the street in front of a car. But it was all she could do to wait until he had gone to work so she could try it again."

"What you're describing seems to me to be a kind of selfishness that would be hard to want to be bound to. Are you sure you do?"

"How do you tell yourself not to love someone?"

"I don't have an answer to that. Maybe there isn't an answer. Maybe you need to consider if that's the right question."

We talk for a while longer, and then the session comes to a close. Heading home I wonder if I am missing something, if the questions pressing on me have already been answered. If they have answers. I leave the building and head for home. I feel anxious like there's a lot looming. Nina's bout. Evan's illness. If her team loses, she'll be a basket case. If Evan declines, she'll feel she has to do something. What will she want from me? What will I be able to do? Nothing feels resolved.

6 DAYS BEFORE THE CHAMPIONSHIP BOUT

"You signed the papers? It's all decided?"

"In case there's an emergency. I wanted to have it done before this week. I'm practicing every night. It's a distraction. I need to focus."

"I thought we would talk about this."

"There's nothing to talk about."

"I think there's plenty to talk about. Like why? Why take the risk for him? You know he won't take care of himself afterward. I've been to his apartment. He's already backsliding."

"He's my father."

"And I'm your girlfriend. I'm really trying here. I'm trying to buffer you from your family a little by taking up some of the slack. I know how important this match is for you. But I'm also trying to be realistic about what I see there. This is a bad idea. He's a terrible candidate for transplant. You know it. He knows it. I think even the doctors know it. But since you're a family member, they won't stop you."

"You think they should discourage me from trying to save my father's life?"

"We live together. I hope we'll get married someday. Soon. Don't I even get a vote? A perfunctory conversation?"

"I don't need a conversation. I already know how you'd vote."

"They'll make you stop skating. They told you that, right? And I Googled it. There aren't many post-recovery restrictions. Most places consider kidney transplants routine surgery if you accept that any time a doctor cuts you open and takes an organ out it could possibly be routine. But every website, every hospital, every nephrology practice, every single one, says the same thing. The single restriction for the rest of your life? No full body contact sports."

"I know.

"What will you do if you can't do derby?"

"I'll do something else."

"Like what? What? What would that be? You going to take up knitting? Stamp collecting? It won't be the same. You won't be the same. Nothing will be the same." She is crying. "We won't be the same."

I want to comfort her, but I can't. I want to tell her everything will be all right, that we will be all right, that we'll figure it out, that it's just new territory. I want to remind her I'm thirty-one years old and that while there are women still doing derby who are twice my age, not many of them are playing at the competitive level; I will have to face the fact of my age when it inevitably diminishes me and things change. But the words do not come. I know we aren't talking about derby, and I'm not prepared to talk about all the rest of it, my parents' mortality, or my own. I let her cry for a minute before I put my arms around her.

"Will you take care of me after? If it comes to that? If there's an operation?" I know this isn't what she wants to hear me ask, but I need to make sure she will. I have no one else. I can't imagine my mother taking care of me, and of course, if she devotes herself to anyone's care it will be my father's, crazy as that is. I'm not surprised when Rachel gives me a raft of shit for asking.

"Sure. Maybe we can all move into your father's place. I can play nursemaid to that Dr. Frankenstein monster, too."

"Rachel, come on," I say. And then she unloads, double barrel.

"When are you going to choose me, Nina? When does it start to matter to you how I feel? What I want? When?" Then she is weeping in my arms again. When she is cried out there is nothing to do but go on, to dinner, to bed, to the next day and the day after that. In the days ahead, I have the championship bout to practice for and then play, and the final medical exams and blood work for the transplant, to be ready if it comes to that. I have talked to my father every day, and every day he tells me to just let him die. He pleads with me over and over not sacrifice myself for him. But I know I have already stopped thinking of it as sacrificing anything. I see it as returning a small part of myself to him, the man who, for all his flaws and missteps, gave me my first skates, and stayed far enough out of my way so that I could learn who I should be, whether he approves of the woman who emerged from that girl or not. How, I ask him, and now I ask Rachel, can I do any less in return than prepare to give him a small piece of myself if I am called to?

THE MORNING OF THE CHAMPIONSHIP BOUT

Today, I take a holiday from work to do all the tasks I'm assigned to make the bout tonight successful. This is the burden of a do-it-yourself organization. When there's a fire, everyone's a firefighter.

My job is to help set up the rink. There are a lot of little things to do. Each team gets an area. I start by setting up chairs where the players rest between skates. There is a sound system to set up, and though I'm not responsible for wiring it, I help hump the cases in from the truck, and once everything is set up, I have to marshal the team to go around the hall and make sure people can hear the announcers' squawk everywhere. To do that, everyone scatters into the stands and signals thumbs up when the sound is clear in all the far reaches.

There's the scoreboard and the slave scoreboard (that's what it's called) to set up. These items are all rentals the team has had trucked in from somewhere in New York State. The scoreboard is custom-made for derby and shows the match time and the score and some other info like time left in each jam, the jam score, and the overall score.

There's the distribution of the new team jerseys which have been washed after they were worn for a few practice sessions, with each team member's derby name stenciled on the back, and there are the freshly washed leggings and shorts that complete the uniform.

The New York team, the *Broadway*, arrived last night, and some of them are here warming up and practicing, getting a feel of the room, the speed of the track, and the general vibe of the place. When we go on the road, I'm always the first person at the arena where the bout will take place. I want to get the lay of the land, the corners of the arena where bright lights will shine in my eyes, where flashy distractions are likely to pop up. The *Broadway* women skating right now could be mistaken for our teammates, dressed in practice garb, taking it slow, not pushing. That's for later. Final warm-ups are an hour before the match. For now, just some easy glides around the rink, testing the place out, soaking in the atmosphere and aura.

I work hard to stay on task, to not watch our opponents skate. I want to be skating too, or at least studying them from the sidelines like they were the textbooks I used to pore over to get good grades back in college. We've faced this team a few times before, this year and last, and we're well-matched, but there are a few newcomers I'd like to get a look at. I'm keeping my eyes half peeled for them while I finish the set up. Across the room, outside of the ring itself, I see our volunteers setting up the tee shirt table and a membership kiosk where we'll sell *Freedoms* logo gear and distribute information about joining the team. Later there will be food vendors selling sausage sandwiches and cheese steaks and pizza and Cokes and beer from the windows at the back of the arena, but right now there are some guys washing the counters and restocking the ketchup packets and sugar and Sweet' N Low baskets. I notice these guys are paying more attention to the women skating than to their work. Men watching women instead of working, what a shock.

Rachel has promised to meet me here this afternoon after she gets off from work but before the excitement starts. She is taking a turn at the tee shirt table. Everyone in this league is always hustling to raise money. As much as I love the fact that the players are part owners, it would be nice if the league had some dough, and the teams had some cushion. Forget about the players being paid real salaries. That seems eons off. But just being able to hire people hourly to do setups for the major bouts, and maybe having enough to offer team members some help with the medical insurance costs and equipment would be great. As it is, we all rely on our work health insurance or Obamacare for coverage. As long as that lasts. The only medical stuff the team pays for are the few hours a week the chiropractor comes to practice. He'll be here tonight, too. During and after a hard bout, someone always needs him.

Pretty much all the kids who are skating in our junior teams are also here today helping. Fresh meat. Except at this point in the year, they all know the drill. One of the team managers called them "spoiled meat" last week when they all whined at having to have work assignments during the bout. We recruit in the fall, and by now all those former newbies have skated in undercard bouts, even the ones who aren't all that good. We charge fresh meat to join the team. It's a training fee and is slightly higher than the annual team membership. If they're not having a good time or getting better, they don't get invited to the next higher level at the end of the season. Most of the stinkers and slackers and Sunday drivers have already dropped out by the time the season ends. The ones who've hung around are either good enough to move up or motivated to want to work to get better, which is sometimes enough reason to keep them. Many of them do get better. Desire can turn some soft dough into tough cookies if you give them enough time to harden up. I watch the activity around the arena. Banners going up boosting the team. Bunting is unfurled on the judging and timekeeping tables. Computers are set up to control the scoreboard.

When I finish my tasks, I don't need to be here, but it feels good to set an example for the newbies. It's a team, and if you take that seriously, you show up for everything. I know I would be useless at work if I was there today. I'd be biting people's heads off. I'm too keyed up to focus on other people's problems today. Which is why I have ignored my mother's calls for the past two days. I assume she's not calling with good news. I also know ignoring her will catch up with me eventually. I know my father is in rapid decline. His kidneys are failing, and his spirit is worse.

I haven't told either of my parents or Rachel I have gotten the approval to donate. I still need to decide if I'm willing to do it. Rachel's freak-out when I told her I was going through the testing process was enough to make me want to never tell her. But that's going to seem like minor hysterics compared to what will come if I decide to donate. She'll feel betrayed. She told me as much. The question is whether she'll get over it.

Once everything is set up, there's a long break. I'm heading home to nap if I can. And then it's on.

THE DAY OF THE CHAMPIONSHIP BOUT

I pick up the clipboard with the list of appointments at the desk of the facility and see that Mr. Wertime, the guy with the burned back, is on my roster. I haven't seen him for a while. He told me the last time he was in he was running low on money. When I greet him in the waiting room, I extend my hand for a shake, but he pulls me into a quick hug. "I'm glad to see you," he says as he squeezes me. Ugh. I really don't like it when clients do things like that, but I don't react. I'm going to see him nearly naked in a moment or two, and his affection seems spontaneous, so I let it go.

"How are you doing?" I ask him as we head down the hall toward the massage rooms.

"Quite well," he tells me. I'm a little surprised at his tone, light and enthusiastic, not what I expected. Not that he has ever been morose. He's one of my most damaged clients but has always been one of the more upbeat ones.

"It's good to see you, too. I thought you were through coming."

"You know, I think my reasons for stopping were foolish. You said you had done all you could for me, that there was no further therapeutic improvement likely, and I should consider whether it was worthwhile to continue. I decided I should stop. I convinced myself it was too expensive, a waste of money. I hope you aren't offended by that." Before I can say I'm not, he goes on. "After a while, I realized that whether massage had therapeutic value or not, I missed it. I missed your touch, and I missed the routine, and I missed believing that you were helping me heal. You said there was no therapeutic value, but you were wrong. My back is scarred. It's deeply damaged. That's not going to change. Massage helps me feel better. Helps me feel more human. So, here I am. I hope that doesn't sound stupid."

"It sounds fine," I say, not sure what else to say. I busy myself getting my massage oil ready, turning on the warmer, laying out towels. I want to say, "I hope I don't disappoint you," but I don't. "I'm going to step out now so you can get ready. There are towels on the table. I'll give you a moment before I come back in."

"What I'm trying to say is, it's not awful."

"What isn't?"

"Having to live with this. I thought it was going to be awful. I thought no one would ever want to touch me or see me naked again. But that's not what I'm experiencing. I have a new boyfriend. He's not the least bit put off by the scars on my back. Like you weren't. When you were treating me. You gave me hope."

Now I wish I had let him hug me a little longer in the hall. There's an awkward moment while we stand facing each other, and I just smile at him, then I leave the room. In the hall outside the massage room, I burst into tears. What am I crying for? Everyone's pain? All the times there are no good choices? Nina's likely choice to sacrifice herself for her father despite what I feel about it. My own selfishness? One of the chiropractors who works in the facility happens to come out of his office at that moment and sees me bawling and asks if everything is all right. What can tell him? The world constantly surprises me and is amazingly fucked up at the same time. That's what I'm feeling. Everything is hard. Everything. A lot more doesn't make sense to me than does. But I don't know who I am crying for, I really don't. "I'm fine," I tell him. "A client just said something very sweet to me."

"And that's the reason for the waterworks? There are so many things I don't understand," he says, echoing what I am thinking. He walks away shaking his head.

"Right," I think. "So many things."

LATE AFTERNOON THE DAY OF THE CHAMPIONSHIP BOUT

When I arrive back at the rink in the late afternoon, there's already a crowd outside waiting to get in. Fans of the New York team have come down in a caravan of cars following a bus the team chartered for some of their supporters and owners, and there are a lot of them in the parking lot, tailgating. There are grills set up and I can smell meat cooking, brats and burgers, and there are open coolers filled with sodas and wine and beer. This is one way that the fans of this women's game resemble male fans of football: they eat meat before the game. None of Rachel's grilled veggies and tofu wraps for these screamers. They want to see blood on the boards as much as they want to see bloody meat on the grill. I'm with them on this.

I thread my way through the cars, past the New York fans, who are playing loud, New York-centric women's rock and roll through their car stereos, *War on Women*, *Downtown Boys*, *Speedy Ortiz*, *Diet Cig*, *Vagabond*, *Snail Mail*, and *Soccer Mommy*. I knew none of these bands before this year's team came together and the younger women turned me on to their music. There are a few Philly bands the kids on the *Freedoms* like, like *Gang* with Amanda Damron and Jaclyn McGraw, though I think they might have broken up. Before I got into these rockers, the women I listened to were a generation older, like I was. It was mostly music I listened to when I was fourteen. I was all in on the timeline that included Tori Amos, Alanis Morrissett and Courtney Love on one end, and *The Breeders* and Liz Phar on the other. And, I have to admit, I liked a lot of guy bands of the head-banging variety for warmups and speed practice. But rock is not the only thing I listen to. A lot of my friends listen to the same things over and over. I listen to classical at work and at home, opera and Broadway musicals at home and on the subway. I don't have a genre. Music works for me in different ways, and I want different soundtracks for different moods. I have my father to thank for this. He loved everything, from jazz to gospel, from Senegalese street singers to Viennese choirboys. I realize as I think this that my father is in my head today and I need to shut him out, for the evening at least. I hope he is doing okay.

As I breeze through the parking lot and into the arena, I pass the line where people are waiting to get their tickets scanned and head to their seats. I know it will be a circus inside the building, with vendors and boosters and food sellers. There are programs with my picture on the cover, but no one recognizes me walking past. I have my hoodie up and a baseball hat pulled way down under that, and my sunglasses on, pretty well disguised. Derby is not a household-name/facial-recognition sport yet, though a lot of the women on the team hope it will be. Being that kind of star would be invasive and awful, but it would also be kind of cool to feel what male sports figures have felt all these years, getting the adulation they get. Still, I suppose if I want to be recognized here, I could drop the hood and lose the glasses. Would someone make the association between the face on the program and the person walking by? I guess I hope they would, but I keep up my incognito approach. I'm just as happy to sneak in. There are individual women stars in some sports, tennis players, gymnasts, and figure skaters, and maybe one or two on dominant Olympic teams where all the members of the team became stars, but to have a league sport where individual players have that kind of recognition would be amazing. Maybe I'm flattering myself that it would be me people wanted autographs from, the lead jammer, but at this moment, on the Philly team, I guess I would say who else? But I also like that I can be an observer and not have to share myself that way.

As I make my way through, I realize as much as they will try to rattle me later, I'm glad the New York fans are here. It will make the whole thing better. The more noise, the jumpier the crowd, the easier it is to get hyped up on it. If the arena is full to the rafters and there's racket the whole time, all our adrenalin will rise. The more jazzed the crowd is, the more they're in the bout, the more exciting it will be.

Once inside the arena, I notice that the smells are even more intense than those outside. There are a lot of cooking smells, grilled brats and roasted peppers from the concession stand kitchens, and fried onions for steak sandwiches. They're making my mouth water because they're all things I have not been eating for weeks. I'll binge tomorrow after we win. I am down to my lowest weight since I was eighteen, and I'm as muscle-bound as I have ever been. My calves and thighs are rock hard, and even my upper arms, which get the least play in derby of any part of my anatomy, are tight. I'm ready. The whole team is ready.

Inside the building, there's a lot of noise. Music is playing over the PA system as the fans wander in the hallways and up and down the stairs and aisles in the stands. As I pass the tunnels out to the stands, I see that the seats are filling up. There are vendors inside working the crowd, people selling tee shirts from past tournaments, and shirts with last year's New York and Philly logos. There are official shirts, shorts, and hats with this year's insignias on them being sold at the official booths, but as a team, we decided not to block women who want to earn a few bucks by selling last year's gear. There's still some attempt to honor the do-it-yourself culture that built this sport, even as we also need to honor the fact that we are now a legal entity with contracts and obligations, and we need to raise and make money to stay in existence.

I'm not carrying much, just a light gym bag, as I duck into the locker room. I left clean underwear here yesterday just in case, but I showered and changed before I left home. I changed the trucks on my skates last week to a set I broke in in practice but aren't too worn to give me any problems. New trucks are sometimes slippery and tend to skid a little, so breaking them in enough to take the slide off them is the way to go. My uniform was cleaned and pressed by the team, so what's in my locker is my other stuff, protective gear, helmet, knee, ankle, wrist, and elbow pads, extra socks, and toiletries.

When I come into the locker room there is a pulse of energy. The women on the team are pumped up. When we're all geared up and ready to practice, Coach comes in and gives us his pep talk. We are gathered in the open space between the locker area and the showers and, looking at my teammates, I feel the charge coming off us.

"Ladies," Coach begins, "we are here. We have made it to this moment. We are drilled and ready, and now all we must do is go out there and execute. You know what you have in you, how deep you can dig, and you are going to have to dig that deep to keep this New York team from winning. You know that they're good. But you need to know something else. They want this win as much as you do, maybe more. They're determined. They see themselves as having something at stake, defending their championship berth. Call it pride. Call it smugness. Call it vanity. Call it arrogance. Whatever you want to call it, they have it in spades. It will not be easy to take it away from them. It will mean you will need to be scrappy, to be down and dirty with them every minute, to match their skill and energy on every jam. But you have the stuff. I have watched you for the past three months become the team I have always wanted to coach, a team of winners. You are the best players I have ever seen, and you work together better than any team I have ever coached or witnessed, and that includes your opponents today. They are a good team. A battle-tested team. But you are better. Trust me when I say this. You are better. Now all you have to do is go out there and prove that to them; they're the only people in this building that don't believe it. Because everyone rooting for you knows you can. And every one of us, from the assistant coaches to the players on the junior squads who have been watching you work out knows you can.

"I am not going to say anything like 'whatever happens out there, you were the best.' There is nothing that's going to make you or me happy other than winning this championship. You think any coach in any sport says to his team, whatever happens out there today in the championship game, the biggest game of your lives, it's okay? Just getting here is honor enough? Bullshit. I want you to win. I want you to crush those women who are skating against you. I want you to throw away every grain of sympathy and kindness in your heart and turn relentless. You have to bring your killer instincts to every minute of this bout. Do not let up for one second. Do not slack off for even a moment. Only when you are finished, and they are sitting vanquished on their bench, and you have won that trophy and skated it twice around this arena, holding it high over your heads, can you afford to be gracious. Then and only then. Until then, you are at war. No quarter given. No prisoners taken. Skate like your lives depend on it. You are gladiators in the Roman forum of your lives. It's kill or be killed. That is how I want you to think. And if you do, and if you play like you know you can, at the highest RPM you have ever played, then you will win."

There is a long silence after the game speech. I am not sure any of us has heard Coach string this many sentences together the entire time we've known him. He has rehearsed this speech, or if not, he is channeling some superior sports orator because I can feel it working. However pumped these women were before he started, something new has happened during the time he's been speaking. We are bound now, in some inexorable way. We must not, cannot, will not fail. That is the feeling we skate out onto the rink with. It is time to warm up, to get loose for the bout. It's time to get deep into the zone.

I look around at the women who are geared up around me. Slowly, heads lift, eyes make contact, smiles break out on our faces. There is a collective shout. The silence is over. We are looking into each other's souls. I know we're going to win.

39 HOURS AFTER THE CHAMPIONSHIP BOUT

I am pacing the halls outside the surgical waiting room. It has been a day and a half of crazy anxiety. First, Evan Gordon's collapse at the arena, then waiting in the hospital while they stabilized him, then getting through all the pre-operative steps, and now waiting for it to be done. Nina and I had our worst fight ever last night, about me not wanting to go home and get her the clothes she wanted, but really about her going through with this. "I don't want to leave you, I heard myself saying to her. I'll get your clothes later." But what I meant was, "I don't want you doing this. Please don't do this. I don't want to leave you, but if you do this, I will." But with her father lying there, dying for lack of what she was going to give him, I couldn't bring myself to say it.

Now I'm sitting with a gaggle of worried people, and their hand-wringing and hushed conversations and other expressions of anxiety are freaking me out. Not to mention having to share the space with Nina's mother, who is stoic one minute and in muttering meltdown mode the next, fuming in anger at her ex-husband one minute, then weeping hysterically that he might die the next. I have no idea if she has spared a thought for Nina at all. When she talks to me, she is either talking about herself or talking about Evan. Funny that I feel I am on a first name basis with him now. I've only just met him. And Nina never calls him Evan; he's always "my father." Nina's mother hardly calls him by his name either. "Nina's father," she says most often. Given the fact that I know Nina's mother really doesn't like me, I know she's only talking to me because I'm here, stuck paying attention to her. In the time she has been sitting here, she has alienated the intake nurse, the rent-a-cop guard at the door, and every doctor and orderly who has come through, whether he or she has any knowledge of what's going on in operating theaters five and seven or not. She is aggressive with her questions and angry and judgmental about the job she assumes every employee of this hospital is doing poorly. To me, she recites statistics and medical trivia. She is a wealth of miscellaneous information. She blurts facts at me as if we were in a rational ongoing conversation.

"Do you know how lucky he is that Nina has agreed to be his donor? At any given time in this country there are over a hundred and twenty thousand people waiting for kidneys, and the median wait time for a kidney donation is over three years. He'd be long dead without her. There are over three thousand new patients added to the waiting list every month."

I think she thinks this is supposed to make me feel good about what Nina is doing, proud of her maybe. But it's like she's tightening a vice around my head. Evan is a bad candidate for a transplant. If he was on the general donor list, he would never get one. It's only this system of jumping the line if a family member can be dragooned into donating that allows bad risks like Evan to get one.

Now that I've gotten to know him some, I think he's a decent guy. Thinking he's a bad candidate has nothing to do with him as a human being or a father or a dentist or a husband. It's about him as a patient. I feel like I'm the only one who sees how unlikely he is to treasure this gift. He's not going to change his habits. He as much as said that to Nina trying to dissuade her from getting tested. He's not going to take care of himself. But I can't say that to either Nina or her mother. I have no rights here, and no lever to sanction her. Nina is doing the most selfless thing she knows how to do. I know that's her perspective. This is pure goodness. It is goodness inconsiderate of herself or of me or of anything but her father's continued life. And I suppose from one perspective it's admirable. But all the wishful thinking and pep talking in the world won't make him a different person. I know people have epiphanies. Or at least people in books and movies do. Maybe this guy will have one, and change his life, and have a lot more years, and do something good with them, including somehow making real amends with his daughter. Maybe he will forgive her for being a lesbian and embrace her life and her choices. Maybe that happens. But if I were a betting woman, I would bet against it. Call it a hunch, call it a feeling, call it a sad premonition. This is not going to end well for any of them. Despite all the magical thinking, no one is going to get what they want out this. That's my bet.

Nina, obviously, has a different view. This is one of the mysteries of Nina. She has complicated relationships with her parents. Her mother's impact on her is obvious. Whatever her mother wants, Nina wants the opposite. Until Nina folds. I suspect that they have been this way all their lives. Nina's mother has no inhibitions about telling her daughter (and everyone else) what she thinks, what she wants, what she wants them to do, and how it is going to help her. She is the most selfish person I have ever met. She seems to have no shame about her self-interest. If it serves her needs, she feels entitled to ask for it. And so, resisting her was the natural response, first for a teenage girl who had a mind of her own, and then for an adult woman for whom that kind of mothering was obnoxious and overwhelming. But in the end, something always seems to sway Nina to do what her mother wants. But this decision to give her father a kidney was not motivated simply by her mother's pressure. Nina's reasons are more complex than that. She is not simply saying yes to her mom's selfish need to arrange the world around her particular idea of how everything should work. And that is where I get hung up. I know there are other factors. I'm just not one of them. Or not enough of one to make a difference.

Nina's relationship with her father was invisible to me for a long time. She called him occasionally, visited almost never, talked about him with a kind of regretful nostalgia for the idyllic childhood she felt he betrayed when he refused to acknowledge she was gay. Or refused to engage with, is maybe a better way to say it. Because he was smart enough to understand it, to know what it meant for her to say it and come out to him. But he just didn't want to hear it, didn't want to imagine her life, didn't want to see her that way. I don't think this is so unusual for parents of queer folks of Nina's or my generation. Our parents grew up being told that being gay was bad, that deviance was evil, was godless, was harmful to our futures, and was illegal. To have to admit to yourself that you raised a deviant was shameful. Easier to ignore the fact. And for a long time, it was easy. If we had all just stayed in the closet, we wouldn't have made our parents so uncomfortable or angry. For Nina's father, a relationship at arm's length was cleaner; he didn't have to acknowledge what he didn't allow himself to see. For Nina, the desire to have her old indulgent, loving dad back was an underground but driving force. If only he could love her, if only he could get over that one thing, everything they once had, all the fun and literary joking and snobby highbrow disdain for plebeians like me would return and the world would be right again, and everything would be fun and fine. It occurs to me now that that's how some women think about lost lovers. If only, if only. And saving his life, if this works, is what? Proof she's okay? That she's still his good girl? That daddy was wrong about her deviance? Because only a good girl steps up like this, right? Only a good girl gives away her organs to save a man who in the harshest light one might accuse of being a withholding bastard, a dismissive asshole, not to mention a self-destructive guy with bad instincts and poor self-care skills? Okay, that's me judging. But really, even if I tone all that down to the facts and not the judgments, here's a man who told his only child she wasn't worthy of his time or attention or his love, all because she is in love with a woman. Isn't that enough to make one question whether giving a piece of yourself away to save the guy is the right thing to do? Especially when there are other options? If all of this happened under pressure, maybe I would say, okay, I get it. But she made the decision weeks ago that if it came to a crisis she would jump into the breach. And in all that time, did we have a real or serious or open conversation about it? No. Not once. The minute it became an option, it was the only option, the one she would exercise no matter what.

So here I am. In the waiting room, heart in my mouth, awaiting word that she's all right, that she has come through the operation without any problems – because there can be problems – and at the same time furious at her for choosing to do this. And every time her mother opens her mouth, I want to strangle her. I want to punch her in the mouth. I want to yell into her face, 'shut up, you stupid cow.' I want to tell her she is one of the worst parents I have ever met, worse than my own, because there is a difference between behaving badly because you are ignorant like my folks and manipulating someone else to do what you want so that you never have to look like you are the bad one or ever take responsibility for the damage you have caused.

This is the Nina conundrum I cannot untangle. In a derby bout, in her work, in her life, she is all aggression. Full steam ahead, take no prisoners. It's what I love about her. But with her mother, she acquiesces. She ignores me and rolls over. That is not how you live with a partner.

FORTY-FIVE

NINA'S RECOVERY JOURNAL

I am not able to say if the things I remember experiencing immediately after the operation were actual or hallucinations, dreams or reality. Things were jumbled. Things I was sure I heard people say turned out not to have been said, and visions I thought must be imaginary turned out to be real. I assume all of this was caused by the drugs I was taking. There was the general anesthesia during the operation, and then morphine for pain for a few days afterward. That stuff twists your thought process up.

I didn't do much except sleep for a couple of days afterward. I began to recognize that I was having strange dreams. The oddest thing about them was how many I remembered. I never remember my dreams. Sometimes I wake up knowing I've been dreaming something, but I can never recall them. Or I couldn't until I was recovering in the hospital. There was one that was amazing. It was a surreal replay of the operation, and I remembered it in detail when I woke up, so well that it has stayed with me.

The dream starts with me being wheeled into an arena. It's funny to use that word since I mean a surgical arena, though in my dream state I knew somehow that I was at a derby match and the arena was more ambiguous, medical and athletic at the same time.

As it usually happens, the teams are warming up. My team is wearing green scrubs. The other team is my father's. They're wearing blue. Both teams are wearing surgical gloves. I can't tell you how I know the other team is my father's, but I do. Dream logic. I am strapped to a gurney and my father is strapped to another gurney and the other members of our teams are racing around somewhat out of my view, but I know they're on skates and pushing us along. Occasionally my father and I are alongside each other and we exchange glances. He shakes his head at me. I shrug. I realize that in this bout, my father and I are the opposing jammers. Our blockers form around us. An announcer introduces the players by their Derby names. When called, each team member rises from a skating crouch and waves both arms over their head. I try to follow suit when I hear my name, but I can't because I'm strapped down.

Somehow, I know that the announcer is Butchy Trucks, the same guy Rachel told me about from her dream. "Ladies and Gentlemen," Butchy says, "boys and girls, cowboys and Indians, it's time to begin the jam. Let's start by meeting our visiting team. From the far reaches of Cherry Hill New Jersey, and appearing for the first time in operating room five, with a won-lost record of none and two, including wife and daughter who fled from his self-indulgence and confusing permissive love, in need of a kidney transplant and coming in this morning at 98 percent negative function, the team jammer and kidney recipient, the **nearly dead diabetic guy,** Evan Gordon. **Evan skates under the name Renal Failure.** Butchy elongates the name Renal Failure the same way the TV announcer I heard as a kid said Moose Kaboosky. On his gurney, my father lifts his arm which has an I.V. line running into it.

"Next up on team Evan, wearing the pivot stripe and number 40 – for the number of whacks Lizzie Borden gave her parents – it's Nurse Hatchet. Give it up for this nasty nursemaid!" There are cheers between each of Butchy's introductions.

"Bringing twilight sleep to the about-to-be-in-deep, in the hubba-hubba scrubs, the gas passer master, anesthesiologist P. P. Le Pétomane." This is a joke that comes out of a story my college roommate told me one night when we were smoking weed in our dorm room. There was this guy during La Belle Époque **in** Paris who did musical farting shows downstairs at the Moulin Rouge, a musical gas passer. He was the sensation of Europe. He would go behind a curtain where he was backlit so his shadow was visible to the audience, and he would drop his pants. Then his assistant, always a woman, would pump his ass full of air with a bellows. Then she would step out from behind the curtain to the edge of the stage, and he would fart the **La Marseillaise** and other French musical hall favorites. In college, I thought that was a scream. His stage name was Le Pétomane. I must have conflated farting and peeing, and added the initials P.P. How the brain works when drugged.

"Next," Butchy continued, "we have Nephrology Resident and Surgical Assistant, wearing number one for "having one's as good as having two as long as you don't do anything too coo-coo," our beta blocker, Cool Hand Luka. Heat up your hands for Cool Hand.

"Now, give it up for our next skater, wearing the same number as his broker's key on his speed dial, our saw bones himself, the cutest cutter who ever cracked a body cavity, Dr. "Flesh" Frenzy, Board Certified Surgeon and kidney kanoodler. Let's hear it for Dr. Frenzy." That was my father's team. I'm not sure I ever met the surgeon who cut my dad. I met the guy who opened me up, but he was on the other team, my team, which Butchy introduced next.

"And now, Ladies and Gentlemen, let's welcome our starting jammer, the offspring of the nearly dead diabetic guy, the donor daughter, the Yid who put the Kid back in Kidney, Nina Gordon, skating under the name Renal Reviver, and tonight for the first and only time, wearing the star of David as her surgical chapeau. Let's hear it!" There's a lot of cheering and I know I'm supposed to acknowledge it, but I can't lift my arms. I try to get someone's attention, afraid there's something wrong, but everyone skates by patting my arms or offering hands for high fives. No one notices I'm agitated.

"Next, passing gas and pushing oxygen, our alt-rocker alta-cocker, smack your palms together for the one and only antithesis of awkwardness, our anesthesiologist, Needa Killdaddy!"

I was already panicking about my paralysis when I hear him say that. I try again to sit up. I want to shout, "Kill Daddy? No, wait. I don't want anyone on my team named Killdaddy. Please."

To my surprise, Butchy seems to hear me. "You just lie back and relax, Nina. Everything is going to go wrong. Just kidding. Everything will turn out terribly. Ha. No. I'm such a card. You'll be fine. Now turn up that gas, Needa."

I'm in full panic mode now. "What about him? Is he going to be fine?" I was trying to shout, but no one is responding and Butchy goes right on.

"Next, from a no-status training school somewhere out in the Midwest, we have our blockers, I mean un-blockers. First, direct from Urine town, give it up for Nephrology legends, Di and Alice Cis, operating room superstars. They've done more operations on less sleep than anyone in the nation. On their right wing, sporting the number 100 liters, wearing watersports yellow, is Piss in Boots, our Surgical nurse. Her left-wing ally, sporting the moniker 99 Bottles of Beer on the Wall and dishing out pleasure to deflect pain, nurse anesthetist Bailey Buzzkill. Give it up, people."

There is more applause. Then there is a reverent silence. I know my team's surgeon will get the biggest intro; that's the way stars are always presented. The lights dim. Butchy starts in a low voice and builds. "Ladies and gents, we have come at last to the man of the hour, wearing the pivot stripe, please twist and shout, do the hokey-pokey and turn yourself about for my favorite, your favorite, everyone's favorite surgical god, Dr. Bradley Ballinger," At which point the arenas, surgical and athletic, go wild.

I could see Rachel in the stands, but she seemed to be completely unenthusiastic about my team. This didn't make any sense to me. You need to root for the side you favor, right? You need to have a favorite. That's the way it works. I thought maybe she was confused, and I try to wave to her to show her I'm here, but then I see her sit down next to Butchy in the broadcast booth.

The next thing I know, Dr. Ballinger is talking to the crowd in the stands as if they are a class of medical students.

"You are here today to observe a kidney transplant. All of you first-year surgical residents have seen this procedure before, but it is worthwhile reviewing what we will be doing. Team Nina, the donor team, my team, will remove a kidney from Miss Gordon there."

I hear Butchy's voice say over the loudspeaker, "Let's have a great big roar for Team Nina!" Then the doc goes on.

"Can someone from Team Nina give us a little background on Miss Gordon?"

Di and Alice Cis give my history in unison. "Nina Gordon, a thirty-one-year-old white female, in good physical condition, has O negative blood, works as a physical therapist, plays a lunatic skating game, and fucks women. She has issues with her mother and her girlfriend, the latter being conflicted about this decision and thinks the gift of a kidney to a sick and possibly dying man is an empty gesture based on guilt and appeasement. And though her girlfriend does not want to say it aloud, she is angry that this woman she loves does not love her back well enough to honor her feelings. She feels abused by this decision, as if her girlfriend, Nina, I mean Renal Reviver, is giving away a piece of herself that rightly should belong to her, Rachel."

I try to protest. "Rachel, wait. That's not fair. That's not accurate. It's more complicated than that." But they move me away and I can no longer see anyone but the doctor.

"Thank you," Dr. Ballinger says. "The process of kidney removal from the donor is called nephrectomy. Today we will use a laparoscopic video camera to see inside the donor's body. First, we make a small cut, inflate the abdomen with carbon dioxide so we can get around better in there, then insert the camera and some instruments. Blood vessels and the ureter are clamped and cut and, once it is detached, the kidney is removed. We try to keep the hole small. This promotes faster healing and causes less pain."

After that, things got weirder. My kidney starts talking. It's up on a video screen over my head, being broadcast to the whole arena, as if it's a celebrity being interviewed at a sports event. It looks exactly like the one on the chart in Dr. Wolfe's office, with tiny hands and feet growing out of its kidney body. I feel completely exposed, opened, if you will. I feel like I'm watching a parody on a cable comedy show. This guy, the kidney, is like a cross between a self-impressed teenage dude and Rodney Dangerfield.

"Hey. Hey. Can you see me?" my kidney begins. "This is so fucking cool. Hey, Pancreas boy. Check this out. I'm on reality *fucking TV. While you're being all hormonal there on the Islet of Langerhans, I am about to get voted off this island. Only on this show, exile from your host body is a good thing. Getting chosen for this, it's like getting a call from god. 'Hello? We need you for the resurrection. Sure, you have to leave your cozy cavity in this beautiful and healthy girl's abdomen. And yes, you'll be stuffed into this other guy's belly and they won't even take out the ones you're replacing so it'll be like moving from a sleek condo to a crowded inner-city tenement where there's shit decaying around you, but hey. You want the sickly old guy to have a few more mediocre years, right? For all his failings, and believe me there's been plenty, he's an okay guy with good intentions. You want to honor the wishes of your biological host of origin. For the greater good and all that, right? We know this guy was a careless asshole with his life, has a fatal disease he ignored, drank like a fish, smoked like a chimney, and still carries an extra fifty pounds. But you're a smart, liberal, independent organ. You make sacrifices when they're required. That's what you do. You're honorable. Hey, here's a kidney joke. A kidney walks into a bar. He says to the bartender, 'Give me a Urine Collins.' The bartender says, 'You want that up or on the rocks?' The kidney says, 'You have a lot of stones asking me that question.' The bartender says, 'Very funny. Have you tried our special Daiquiri? Piss and Vinegar?' The kidney says, 'No. What are the proportions?' The bartender says, 'Are you asking about the drink or my wife?' The kidney says, 'Speaking of your wife, what did the wife say to her husband when he asked for her kidney? She said, 'After fucking around with my sister the entire time we were married, you'll get a kidney over my dead body.' The husband says, 'A man can dream.'"*

Then there's a shadow across the kidney on the screen and a giant forceps comes into view and grabs hold of him. I hear Dr. Ballinger's voice. "The transplantation is just the opposite of the donor operation. The kidney is implanted above the pelvic bone but below the existing kidney. We leave the old one in there unless there is likely to be a problem with infection. We suture the non-functioning kidney to the recipient's iliac artery and vein. We attach a right-side donor kidney upside down to the recipient's left side because flipping it allows for easier at-tachment of blood vessels and the ureter. Everyone ready? Time to make the donuts." That's all I remember.

48 HOURS AFTER THE TRANSPLANT OPERATION

I have been sleeping in this chair for about ten hours now, getting up only to change positions or use the toilet or get a cup of vending-machine coffee, which does nothing to keep me awake. Perhaps I don't want to be awake, to be thinking forward about what will happen now. I am up about twelve seconds, looking at her, gray and puffy from the effects of the anesthetic when her mother breezes in. Her mother is keeping vigil in the other recovery room, the room where Evan sleeps with his new young kidney taking root in his smelly old body. Okay, that's unkind. Right now, tired as I am, I'm not above it.

"You awake?" she asks me as she enters Nina's room, to wake me if I'm not. It is this kind of behavior that makes me understand why Nina is so wary of her, this selfishness that assumes she has every right to barge in, wake you if you're sleeping, and impose herself on you even if her imposition is the last thing in the world you want. I start to answer, but she cuts me off. "Talk softly. She's still sleeping." Like I don't know this.

"We were both sleeping."

"You can take a break now if you want. I can be here if you need to relieve yourself or get something to eat."

"What time is it?"

"About seven. P.M."

I stretch and rearrange myself in the chair. There's a mirror over the small built-in dresser facing the bed. I can see myself from where I am sitting, and I look nearly as bad as Nina, puffy-eyes and matted hair. The only visible difference is I'm wearing street clothes and the remnants of make-up. She's in one of those stupid hospital gowns that opens in the back. Her covers have slipped off; her left leg is exposed. Her mother is fussing with the bedclothes, which I am sure is less an effort to fix them than an attempt to wake her.

"Leave her alone. You'll wake her up," I say in my snarkiest voice.

Her mother glares at me, gives the covers a last defiant tug and backs off. There is only one chair in the room, so unless I give her the chair I have been sleeping in, she will have to stand.

Her mother stands with her hands on her hips, waits for me to move. When I don't, she asks, "Any signs of life from her?" It seems like a rude question to ask about a woman who has just been operated on and anesthetized, but Nina's mother is oblivious to the niceties of conversation.

"Snoring. Seems like a life sign. She's still blissfully asleep. Which is more than I can say for myself."

"Hospitals are not interested in the comfort of visitors. Who cares if you're comfortable? You think they should spend money making you feel good at the expense of patient care or patient comfort?"

"No reason not to do both."

"Of course, there is." Because she's the expert on this too, as she is on so many things.

We are in our usual positions now, dug into our dislike of each other, not interested in playing nice. Even though I could use a stretch, I stay seated. "How's Mr. Gordon?"

"He's out. They tell me he could be out all night. I told them where I'll be. I want to be available when they wake up."

"So, you can horn in." It was out of my mouth before I could stop myself.

"I beg your pardon?"

"Sorry. I shouldn't have said that."

"No. You shouldn't. I'm her mother. I have a right to be here. More right than you, I want to point out."

"I'm sure you want to point that out. But I was talking about your ex-husband, whose life is no longer yours to control." She ignores me.

"She's my baby. I need to be sure she's all right."

"She's not a baby."

"I said 'my baby.'"

"The one useful thing my mother taught me was not to borrow other people's troubles. But that's all you do."

She raises her voice. "Your kids aren't borrowed trouble." I'm not sure she hasn't increased her volume just to wake Nina. If that's her intention, it works.

"Is it over?" Nina asks, not opening her eyes.

With as much surprised irony in my voice as I can muster, I say, "You're awake."

Nina's mother says, "Yes, it's over, Baby. It's over. How are you doing? What can I get you?"

"I feel – my head. My arms. I can't..." her voice trails off.

"It's the drugs. The doctors told me you might feel woozy when you came to. You don't have to talk."

"Sore. Throat. Dry. Need water."

"I'm not sure if you are allowed water yet," I tell her.

"Why don't you go find the nurse and ask her," Nina's mother says. I know she just wants me out of the room. She'll give Nina water before I come back with the answer.

I am about to get up when Nina says, "Rach, I had the weirdest dreams."

Her mother tries to redirect her attention, as if Nina was not aware that her mother had been talking to her already. "Hi, Honey. I'm here, too," she says.

"I know, Mom."

"Okay. Just wanted to be sure."

Then Nina asks, "How is he?" I watch the dark cloud pass across her mother's face.

"Still out, last they said. Don't worry about him right now. You have your own recovery to think about. You want anything? Are you cold? Do you need more blankets? This room is freezing."

"I'll go ask the nurse about getting you water," I say, giving up my chair. Nina's mother slides into it before I reach the door. As I'm heading out into the hall, I hear Nina tell her mother she wants to see her father as soon as she can. I'm sorry I can't see her mother's face, but I'm sure she's not happy Nina wants to focus her attention elsewhere.

I head to the nurse's station and tell the duty nurse Nina is awake and ask her about giving Nina a drink. She says, "Hold off on water for the moment until we get a temp and her current vitals," but as predicted, Nina's mother is holding a straw to her lips by the time I get back to the room with that instruction.

56 HOURS AFTER THE TRANSPLANT OPERATION

Nina sleeps fitfully, waking suddenly and then drifting back off for hours. But in each short period of wakefulness, she shakes off the delirium faster. Doctors come and go, take her vitals, check her surgical scars, two tiny holes and one larger one, the drains and bandages that cover them. Nina complains about discomfort but doesn't have the strength to be her usual agitated self. She's weak, docile. Waking up at one point, Nina sees me standing in the doorway. Her mother has gone down the hall to see how Evan is doing. She smiles at me. "Hi," she says.

"How are you doing?"

"What did I miss? Anything important happen while I was out?"

I laugh. This is Nina at her best. No acknowledgment of her discomfort. The tough girl.

"Are you comfortable? Can I get you anything?"

"I'm hungry. Am I allowed to eat?"

"I'll ask. Don't ask your mother. I'll get the answer. She'll give you the wrong one."

"Where is she? I'm surprised she's not breathing down my neck."

"She was here. I think she's with Evan now. When she was here, she was writing down everything you said in your sleep. I thought you were babbling, but she thought you were spouting pearls of wisdom. 'She might be saying something important.' she told me. I told her I have heard you talk in your sleep for months. You never say anything important."

"Thanks a lot."

"It's true."

"Crazy."

"Yeah. Do you have any memory of these monumental

speeches you were making?"

"I remember that I had a dream that the operation was a derby bout. My dad and I were opposing jammers. My kidney was talking. He did a little stand-up routine. You were cheering from the sidelines, I just couldn't tell what for."

"Vivid."

"Before they put me out, they told me I might have more intense dreams, but I wouldn't remember them. But that one I remember. One other is crystal clear. My kidney was screaming at me that I better wake up or you would think I was dead, and you wouldn't take care of me. You'd be gone."

"I don't think what you experience in dreams has anything to do with waking life. You didn't die. I'm here." I'm trying to keep my tone even. I don't want to be reassuring about our future exactly, but I don't want to give her anything to worry about when she is just recovering from surgery and anesthesia. We have things to talk about, but I don't want to include Nina's mother in the conversation. I know in my bones she'll show up the minute we start to talk. That's her mother's M.O.

"I'm going to take care of you. You don't have to worry."

"Are you angry at me, Rachel? I mean so angry you won't get over it? Tell the truth. Can you get over it?"

"You rest now. We can talk about it later."

"Shit. That sounds like a no."

And as I predicted, at that moment her mother waltzes in. "What sounds like a no?"

I say, "It's an I don't know." And I walk out.

SESSION NOTES RACHEL WILLIAMS

CONCLUSORY NOTES SESSION SIX: We continued discussing Nina and Rachel's circumstances, and explored the coping mechanisms Nina employs to deal with Nina's family in light of her experiences with her own. She has not come to any resolution about what she is going to do moving forward.

PATIENT NAME: WILLIAMS, RACHEL SESSION # 7
DSM CODE: 300.02 Record # 447/26
DESCRIPTION: Generalized Anxiety Disorder
PRESENTING ISSUE(S): Trouble sleeping with bruxism; anxiety about the future; fear of loss of primary relationship; self-doubt
REFERRING ENTITY: Self
INSURANCE: Fonterra Healthcare HMO (Submitted, could be denied. Patient will pay if unreimbursed)
SESSION: $175
CO-PAY: $40

5 DAYS AFTER THE CHAMPIONSHIP BOUT

"I saw you."

"You saw me?"

"At your girlfriend's championship   what do you call it? Match? Contest?"

"Bout."

"Yes. Bout. I guess I heard the announcer say that. I was way up at the top of the stands. I dragged my husband, and you know, even though I didn't know exactly what to tell him to expect, we had a really good time."

"Wow. Never would have predicted this."

"I know. I didn't want to tell you I was thinking about it in advance in case I didn't get there, but you piqued my interest. We live close to the arena and we just walked over. It was packed."

"Yeah. The championship games bring out the crowds. All the hard-core fans were there, plus a lot of other people who always wanted to come but never did. People came down from New York, too. You saw some really good jams. The first half anyway."

"Those women were amazing. So fit and self-assured. I loved watching them. It did my heart good. That's some big secret you're keeping from women my age. I think a lot of us could become big fans. There's something amazing going on there.

"I told you so. But no one's keeping it a secret. They'd love it to become more popular."

"It's not just the athletics either. There's that. But something else you feel right away when you walk into the arena. Even though it's a physical sport, brutal at times, there's something very different about watching an all-women sports

team than watching men. Something about the spirit of cama-
raderie. It's supportive, not just competitive. At least, not the
way men's sports always feel. I like baseball and football. I
grew up with them, and in my house, we lived and died by the
Phillies and Eagles and the Flyers. But there's a different spirit
to this. You can feel it. Less about winning than about playing.
I'm not articulating it very well. And I should stop taking up
your session time talking about it."

"No. It's fine. You got to see Nina at her best, and so now
you have an idea why I felt the way I did about her."

"She's pretty dazzling. She has real joie-de-vivre about
skating and playing. You can see it in the way she charges
into it. But I didn't understand why she wasn't skating most
of the second half. They needed her. They were killing New
York in the first half, and then she was gone and the team sort
of fell apart. Was she injured?"

I was stopped. I'd been talking like she knew what happened, but how could she?

"Nina's father? I've told you about him. He needed a kidney
transplant. He was at the bout. He hadn't told her for sure he
was coming so she didn't know he was there. At the half, he
started to come down toward the home team bench to say
hello to her, and he had some sort of episode. He collapsed
somewhere in the corridor behind the stands. Nina's mother
was in the arena, but not with him. She had come down to see
Nina at the half too, and she saw someone being put onto an
ambulance gurney. She had a premonition it was her ex-husband. She says things like "I had a premonition" and who
knows if she did or if she just made that up afterward to put
herself into the picture. But whatever happened, whether she
had a premonition, or she recognized him, true to form, she
took charge at that moment, and she got someone to tell Nina.
She could have let that wait until after the bout was over, but
she wasn't thinking. Or she was only thinking of herself. Or
she was thinking, and it was sabotage. Take your pick. When
Nina heard, she freaked out. The message her mother sent
was that she should stay, that Mrs. Gordon would get her old
man to the hospital and that Nina should join them there after

the bout. But Nina wanted to go. The coach told her the team needed her, that this was their moment, and that an extra hour wouldn't make a difference. Nina wasn't persuaded by this argument. Words were exchanged. That made it worse.

If I had been included in that conversation, I would have told him that she would be a wreck on the track, that she would be dangerous to herself and other skaters, angry and reckless. She was worried that her father was going to die, and she wouldn't be there. The coach, I don't know, he wasn't thinking clearly either. He should have just let her go. He should have known she was going to be useless. But she stayed and started the second half.

It was a disaster. On the first jam, she fell. In the next one, she crashed into one of her own blockers. She misjudged where opponent skaters were and collided with them, or she didn't and tried to push them down. She drew penalties and sat for time outs, and when she was in, she made the New York team angry with her violent play, so they came at her. Then things just fell apart. Her head wasn't in the game. Without their lead jammer at the top of her form in the second half, it was awful. By the time the coach pulled her, less than twelve minutes into the second half, the damage was done. New York was so keyed up, they crushed the Freedoms. Through all that, no one thought to tell me. I was sitting in the stands with some friends, trying to figure out what was wrong with her. When she got pulled, I saw her skate into the tunnel and head for the locker room. I went down to see if she was okay, but by the time I got there, she was gone. She didn't even change out of her uniform. She tossed her skates and left. I had no idea what was happening. I went out to the arena floor and stood behind the bench until I got the attention of one of the other skaters and she told me Nina had gone to the hospital. At first, I thought her mother had gotten sick because I had no idea her father was there."

"What happened?" Dr. Gray asks. "Was he all right?"

"No. He was in total renal failure. They scheduled him for surgery. Nina gave him a kidney. It's a done deal. They're both still recovering."

FIFTY

NINA'S RECOVERY JOURNAL

Skating in the championship bout against New York was heaven. And it was hell.

The first half was pure rapture. If I have ever played as hard, or skated as well, or been as fired up, or been as deadly focused, or ever been just plain as good as I was in that period, I do not remember it. I remember thinking afterward, when I had time to think about it, that there had not been one moment when I felt any doubt about our winning, or felt over-matched by the New York team's stars, or felt anything but pure, confident, transcendent joy. Say it was my adrenalin cranking, call it exuberant teamwork, say it was simply good juju, I was so deeply and powerfully in my groove that I felt like there was no one and there was nothing that would ever bump me out of it.

When the arena filled and all the pre-bout shenanigans were done, like introducing the junior squads and letting them skate around for a moment of glory in the spotlight as a recruiting advertisement for anyone who might want join the team in the future – and giving the sponsors their shout-outs, and observing the patriotic ridiculousness of getting the crowd to stand for the national anthem – which I have never understood as having any relation to sporting events but apparently we're obligated to do contractually, believe it or not, by our agreement with the arena – the championship teams skated out for their intros. New York went first. They were styling their crimson and gold lightning-streaked uniforms, the colors and design of which reminded me of my high school's marching band outfits. The tradition for intros is that each team skates slowly around the track in a pack, everyone clustered together, each skater bent low in a semi-crouch until one by one each player is announced by her derby name and number. At the call of her name, that player stands up and waves to the crowd, acknowledging the cheers (or boos) of fans. There were cheers for the New Yorkers, since they had a lot of hard-core partisans in the stands, bussed down from their home arena or part of a caravan that came down following the team bus, but the derisive hoots and Bronx cheers were nearly as loud. A group of women near the top of the bleachers turned their backs and their tee-shirts spelled out Philadelphia FreeDoms in large letters, letting the world know our inside joke. When it was our turn, their fans returned the favor with hoots and boos of their own. When our opponents were back at their bench, we started our intro skate. We were a pack, just like Coach wanted, keyed up and ready. We had new duds too, or newish, I should say. We had been skating in them for the last couple of practices, to get used to the feel. A local designer had done the work, black pants and jerseys with orange accents, the colors of a jaguar's coat and eyes. No one looking at us would immediately think of giant predatory cats, but we were feeling the connection. We were hunters, angling to kill the antelope prey who were our opponents.

As we skated our intro lap, people in the stands were on their feet, cheering, blowing air horns, making a racket. No one will ever convince me that given a team to root for, women fans aren't just as rabid as those face-painted football fanboys or chest bumping hockey fanatics. The New York disciples did their best to be heard in counterbalance, but they were vastly outnumbered. I remember thinking as we skated that intro lap that, on tickets alone, we had won the day. The arena holds about four thousand fans and by the time the bout started, it was sold out. Four thousand times twenty-five dollars a head was a hundred thousand bucks, not to mention the money we were making on concessions and merch. There were costs to be sure; there was the negotiated split with the New York team, and the arena rental and the costs of personnel – rent-a-cops for security, and refs that had to come from elsewhere than the competing teams' home cities, trainers and bench personnel, and the stand-by ambulance and EMT's, in case someone got injured in the bout, and there were the pre-game costs of uniforms and laundry and all that. But when all was said and done, we stood to clear over forty grand, enough to ensure

Coach's per-diem for next season, pay for our practice facility rental, and the other incidentals of running the team. We'd be in the black with money to spare after tonight, and if we won, we'd be invited to skate in out-of-town exhibition bouts, which would make us more money. It made me happy that we had built this, we women, we bunch of outsiders and misfits, we sexual outlaws, punks, and rebels, all of us so ill-fitted to bourgeois goals, a capitalist's nightmare. We had made this, and we were about to give our fans the show of their lives.

After our warm-ups and the intro skate, despite the serious nature of our challenge, we were loose and jokey. We talked trash about everything from their uniforms to their hairstyles. We had a scouting report from a fan who had seen New York in their last bout before the championship, who told us that their second jammer was new and less sure of herself than their star, who was a kid of twenty-two but had blazing speed and astounding talent. Their lead jammer had the rep of being slippery as soap in a stadium shower, outrunning every other jammer in the league and slipping past blockers like she was a greased pig at a southern barbeque. (Rachel would tell me "enough with the metaphors.") If there are marquee players in derby, so far, they have all been on the New York team, and they were crushing the star thing – getting endorsement contracts and posing for fanzine features. When they skated their intro, we watched those women gesturing to their fans in the crowd, taunting the Philly fans, strutting their stuff and showing off. Samantha Silvera, who skates as Silver Star, their lead jammer, was the Queen Shit. Even the Philly fans knew her, and I suspect some were hot to see her – the way sports fans always are about stars, even stars on opposing teams. Stars are stars, and I give her all her props. She deserves her reputation. If I wasn't on this team and skating against her, I would be fawning over her myself. I watched to see her footwork. There are some skaters who are so confident, whose stride is so swift and whose cross action when they skate so clean, they seem to be moving without effort. She was like that. She was tall and lanky, and I could see what made her special, even when she was warming up. She was muscular. She was tight.

I'd skated against her once before, a year ago, when she had just become New York's lead jammer and was not yet quite the bullet she was now, but a lot had changed in that year, and I knew, if she was anything like me, she was going to be a laser beam tonight.

The Freedoms were being derisive in a good-natured way, but everyone on our bench was watching their position's opposite as she made the rounds. The Hot Broadway were formidable, and we knew the play would be tough against this team that had a title to defend and pride to lose.

Then it was time to begin. There was a captains' meeting in the center of the ring for a handshake and a recitation of the rules of fair play, which is a pro forma thing that happens before every game skate. I've heard the rules so many times I could recite them in my sleep, but there is something comforting about the ritual. I skated out with my helmet hooked around my arm, the jammer panty already in place. I wanted the fans to see me, doing a little of the star turn thing myself I admit, my moment of glory. The recitation of the rules tonight was really for the crowd, and so the refs could see the jammers up close for a minute since they did not know us. As the lead ref read and his voice boomed out on the stadium speakers, the crowd quieted down, the last time they would be quiet for the next couple of hours. Standing there listening splashed a little cold water on my energy high. We want people to be interested in the game and everything is marketing, but I was twitchy. I just wanted to get started. I made momentary eye contact with Sam Silvera, who looked away fast. Then I caught Coach's eye. He was standing behind our bench, saying something to himself over and over, reciting some sort of self-calming mantra, I think. I could see his lips moving. But whatever he was saying, it was not working. He was twitchy, too. Like me, he just wanted the bout to start.

After the mid-court meetup, we captains skated back to our benches. Even though we knew who the starting five were, Coach pointed to us and sent us out one by one, as if he was making the choice on the spot. This was supposed to convince the other side we were so deep with good players that there was an endless number of combinations that might be tapped for each bout. I'm sure they were playing the same game on their bench. Funny how many silly mind games the coaches play. In a few seconds, we would be lined up, then the whistle would blow, and we'd be racing off the line, the women around me blocking and slamming into each other, and we'd be off. There'd be no psychology at work in what happened then. It would all be physical. Then we were lined up and ready, just waiting for the whistle to start the match. The rink was as loud as I had ever heard it, a wall of sound, ready to roil up into cheers. I bent into my starting crouch. I was pumped.

SESSION NOTES RACHEL WILLIAMS

CONCLUSORY NOTE SESSION SEVEN: Rachel's girl-friend's father has had a kidney transplant, and Nina is the donor. Rachel is now Nina's caretaker. This has put a further strain on their already precarious relationship. She will return for one more session next week. I am not confident she will make any more progress. We have had cursory conversations about medication for her anxiety. She has rejected that idea.

PATIENT NAME: WILLIAMS, RACHEL SESSION # 8
DSM CODE: 300.02 Record # 447/26
DESCRIPTION: Generalized Anxiety Disorder
PRESENTING ISSUE(S): Trouble sleeping with bruxism; anxiety about the future; fear of loss of primary relationship; self-doubt
REFERRING ENTITY: Self
INSURANCE: Fonterra Healthcare HMO (Patient will pay if unreimbursed)
SESSION: $175
CO-PAY: $40

I WEEK AND 5 DAYS AFTER THE TRANSPLANT OPERATION

When I get home from my session with Dr. Gray, I ask Nina if she feels well enough to stay awake and participate in a conversation. She says she does. I tell her right away that I've decided to make a break from her. It's just under two weeks since the operation. If it was up to her, we'd forgo this. When it comes to relationships, she'd rather read the headlines, get the spoiler, skip to the end of the story, hear the punchline. I'm pretty sure when she reads novels, she skims the descriptive parts. Okay, that's not fair. She doesn't do that. But she doesn't suffer deep analysis very happily. She always thinks she understands everything before anyone else. She aims for the heart of the matter and hacks her way through the thicket of nuance as fast as she can. But I need her to understand why I'm leaving, how I've come to this. Having her semi-immobile gives me an advantage. She can't run away.

I start by telling her what I have talked about in my sessions with Dr. Gray. "Talking to a therapist is something I am still not sure I completely trust. There's a certain amount of voodoo to it. For the first five sessions, I felt like I was just telling my life story to someone who was only partially interested, but not particularly invested. She didn't seem bored exactly, but it was business-like, a professional encounter. It was always slightly unsatisfying. In the beginning, I wanted her to say more than she did, though that did not end up being my desire. She sometimes interjected a personal reaction, something that made me laugh or she said something that felt offbeat or out of left field. That made her feel more human and less like an insurance-assigned professional, and it made me like her more but didn't exactly make me believe she was responding specifically to me. I wasn't feeling any better week to week. You know what I mean?"

"Sure. You wanted a friend. An ally, though that makes it sound like war. Allies and enemies. Am I the enemy, or is she? Did talking to her make you feel like you were at war?"

"It did sometimes. At war with myself over you. I told her a lot of history and a lot about you, but I kept asking myself how it was supposed to help me. It wasn't like last time when the counselor practically saved my life by guiding me through coming out. Dr. Gray wasn't going to tell me anything. After a few sessions, I got the message I was supposed to figure things out for myself. She pointed out patterns and recurring ideas, things she thought were traps in my thinking, but I couldn't see how knowing those things would help. I wanted to know what to do. I wanted to feel the relief that comes with understanding. I wanted to choose a path, and I wanted her to certify I had chosen the right one. How would I know if I was doing the right thing when she said so little? Because isn't the point to get new insights and make adjustments in relation to that? Sometimes I felt like she was working to keep herself interested. I know she has heard every fucked-up relationship story a thousand times."

"Is our story fucked up? It seems pretty common to me, people with different agendas."

"I'm just one of dozens of patients she sees and listens to every week, and so logically that would mean her method is probably similar for everyone. But I wanted to feel she was my confidant, my enlightened friend, my wise aunt, my sage older sister, someone who cared deeply about me, always told me the hard truth and was always on my side."

"That's a lot to expect. Therapists are just people with some training and, one hopes, good instincts about people and about how to use what they know to move their clients along."

"I get that, or at least I get it intellectually. But you're right that I wanted something more. I know a good therapist should be neutral, should be a sounding board, on your side but skeptical, supportive enough to encourage you to get on with thinking about yourself in helpful ways, responsive to the specifics of your story, but also not judgmental. She should ask good questions."

"Did she ask good questions?"

"Yes, she asked good questions."

"Okay. Sorry, can you get me some water?"

I do, though I'm a little annoyed at the interruption. I put out of my head that asking me this is a tactic to throw me off my game. When I sit back down, I say, "During the session today Dr. Gray told me straight out what she was thinking. This was not how it had gone in the previous seven sessions. She told me that when she asked me about myself, I always answered about you as if I didn't exist as a separate entity, as if my life was only in motion when I was around you, as if everything that mattered in my life was in response to you. She pointed this out a few times before, but this time, I heard it differently. It stopped me. Maybe I had just reached a turning point, or maybe I saw through the fog of my perspective, or maybe up against the finish line I let my guard down enough to give her a way in."

"The finish line?"

"In terms of how many sessions I could pay for. I would hate to think the reason I heard her is that shallow but who knows? That could have been why."

"Okay." I can hear a certain wariness creep into Nina's voice, as if she is finally getting it that this is going to come to a hard stop. I know she'd be okay if we went on the way we've always been. But I'm not negotiating. I'm quitting her. I begin to see that fully register.

"The question that broke through my defenses was would I ever be happy if I was constantly living my life in relation to yours? If I was constantly gauging my happiness as a function of your happiness? She told me that's what she heard me saying. Then she asked me 'Is this the relationship you want?' She wanted to know if I thought there was any hope that you'd change and not assume I'd comply with your wishes about how the two of us should be together. I didn't say anything right away, so she kept pushing. Did I want to organize my life around yours? Could I think of a way I would be happy if the best I ever had was the relationship exactly the way it was at that moment? I didn't have any answers. Then she said something like, 'As genial as you are, Rachel, I know you're in pain.' I remember her using the word genial. It seems like such a wimpy way to be. Like I was a doormat. Then she asked me again if I thought I would be satisfied with the status quo. If you never changed? If I never felt like I was the first blip on your radar? If I always felt like I was the second car in your caravan. Would I be happy?"

"She really used all those phrases?"

"I don't know. I think so. That was the gist. It's what she got from what I said. The disregard, the neglect. These were the words I used to describe my feelings."

"Wow. Is that what you think? That I disregard you? Okay, about the kidney donation, I did. But not only you. My father. The transplant psych. I couldn't make any of you understand what was important about that to me. You just rejected that out of hand. He's my father."

"I told Dr. Gray I really didn't like what she was saying. I protested. I told her your disregard wasn't the whole story. It wasn't all I said. But she said, 'But that's what brought you here, the feeling that Nina wasn't paying attention to what you wanted. That's your recurring theme. More than the unresolved issues with your parents, that's the reason you're here, the thing you needed to unpack. Your dissatisfaction with your relationship.' She was asking the right questions, alright, and I knew it. Was this the relationship I wanted?"

"Is the 'second car in the caravan' metaphor one of those weird out-of-the-blue things she sometimes said that surprised you?"

She's trying to make me laugh, but I'm deep in it now. "She asked me if I had known you were like this, would I have started living with you?"

"Would you?"

"I didn't have an answer. Lots of things would change if we all had twenty-twenty hindsight. But the thing is, I did know almost right away. Then she wanted to know if there were any compromises, I could make in myself that would make staying with you okay. And if there weren't, why was I sticking around? What was preventing me from moving on and looking for someone who could give me more of what I wanted."

"She was suggesting that?"

"She was asking me questions. I don't think she was making suggestions. She wanted me to examine my indecision."

"Why are you telling me all this?"

"I want you to understand. I just don't think you're likely to change, Nina. I wish I did. I love you. I just don't like you all the time. I don't think you'll ever take me seriously about wanting kids. I don't think you'll ever get better at compromising about anything."

"Like giving my dad a kidney."

"Like making life-altering decisions without regard for what anyone else thinks. Like giving up skating and being in the jam."

"How's that important? It's a game."

"That's bullshit and you know it. It's what you love. And how you play it is what I love about you. You play with your heart out."

We're silent for a while. I think the conversation is over. I think Nina has hit her limit on hashing things out, especially since she can see the endpoint, which is where we are.

Then Nina says, "I can't take it back. I can't undo anything. I know everything's fucked up now. My parents' relationship is weirder than ever, my dad's health might be better or might not, the championship bout is lost, we're done, all of it is fucked up. I wish I could get back all the practice time that was for nothing."

"That's the thing you regret?" Nina doesn't answer. "That wasn't for nothing."

"I can't make it up to you."

"You wouldn't do it any differently. That's the point."

Even though I've made up my mind, I'm a little hurt she is not pushing back harder. She's arguing, but it's weak. She's not hitting me with her best stuff. This is not like her. Where is the Nina I love? Or does this civility and passivity prove that the damage is already done? She's not who she was. I hate feeling this.

"You know what else Dr. Gray told me? She said that love was the easy part. She knows I love you. But figuring out how to like each other well enough to stay together for the long run, that's the hard part. When I feel ignored or like you don't take me seriously, I'm resentful. It's like acid eating away at metal. I don't know how to stop it. Pretty soon there's nothing left."

"How much of this is about not having kids?"

"I told Dr. Gray we couldn't get through that conversation. When I told her about the night we had before your father's collapse she actually came over and sat next to me on the couch, as if the twin subjects of sex and kids were too intimate for her to hear from across the room. It was frightening having her that close. She told me that some of her clients like constantly rejiggering their relationships. Some like things on an even keel. But it sounded to her like we were too dug in to agree. We want what we want, and we want the other one to bend. I want kids. You don't. She said that when couples who are at war over kids come to see her, she wants to hide in her own foxhole. Those were her words. She told me kids are the hardest problem. She sees it on both ends, couples arguing over whether to have them and on the other end who wants them and who gets them after a divorce."

"Some people must make sacrifices for their spouses. Give up what they want."

"I told her, I know some people accept the 'til-death-do-us-part' thing. I'm sure my mother was unhappy nearly all of her marriage, but she would never have thought of leaving. I'm just not wired like that. Probably because of watching her. Maybe if I felt trapped by economics or I was afraid of being alone like my mother was, I'd feel different. But I don't."

I want Nina to understand why I've come to this decision. Suddenly I feel overloaded, flooded, burdened. Nina says my name, but I don't respond. I hear her ask if I'm all right. Finally, I say, "I'm sorry if it's hard to hear me say these things.

But this is the point I've come to. I think I owe it to you to hear me say why."

We say nothing for a while. Then she says, "I'm sorry." I have no response. I help her get ready for bed and then sit by myself on the couch in the dark. I feel depleted. I feel bereft. I think about going in and making love to her. I think about walking out of her apartment, boarding a bus and going somewhere, anywhere, away from here. I think about quitting my job and starting over in a new city. I think about changing my name, dying my hair, making up a new life story.

What I don't tell Nina is that in that session with Dr. Gray, after she asked me all those questions, I completely lost it. I was furious at her. I told her I thought she was meddling. I told her I thought she overstepped. She said, "I am just trying to get to the heart of the matter."

I felt like I'd taken a slap in the face. This wasn't what I wanted. It didn't feel supportive. I was seething at her for holding this mirror up, forcing me to look at an image I did not want to see. I knew it was reflecting me accurately. I resented it. I resented her.

"I need to think about this," I told her. The session was over even though there was more time. I was desperate to get out of her office. I reached for my sweater. "I'll call you if I decide I want to come back and talk to you again."

Dr. Gray said, "I know money is an issue for you, so let me take that off the table. If you decide you want to come back, I won't charge you for the session. Or you can pay me what you want. I don't want to promise more than one, but I don't want you to feel that you need closure and you're not getting it because you can't afford it."

I don't know how I got out of her office. I was propelled by my anger. I heard myself say goodbye. I saw myself open the office door, walk down the hall, take the elevator from her floor to the street level, and walk to the corner as if I was watching someone else in a movie. Then I was sitting in the back of a Starbucks with a cup of coffee. I don't remember ordering or paying for it, though I must have done both things. For a long time, I stared at the wall. When I finally took out my phone, I saw that Nina had texted me. She wanted me to bring her some ice cream when I came home. I started to text "fuck you" and then deleted it. Who was my anger for? Then I wrote it again and deleted it again. By the time I got home, I was calmer. I knew what I had to do.

FIFTY-THREE

NINA'S RECOVERY JOURNAL

Last night, sleepless for the second night in a row, not sure if it is the pain in my side or the pain in my head, I start to imagine what my parents would say to each other if they could talk about anything important. I wonder if my mother would take credit for convincing me to become his organ donor, or if my father would thank her for convincing me to save his life. I wonder how they would talk about me, how they would talk about their relationship, how they would reconcile themselves to the way their only child had grown up. I wonder if either of them would ever take any responsibility for themselves about anything, but particularly for their individual contributions to the destruction of their relationship. As it is, they blame each other for the inflexibility and anger, blame they have recited as catechism since I was nine years old.

There is a way in which pathology gets visited on each next generation down the line. My great-great-grandparents on my mother's side came from Germany in the eighteen-eighties. My great-grandmother was born here, in New York City, on the lower east side, in the Jewish ghetto. But they did not stay there for long. My autocratic great-great-grandfather, Saul, brought his skills with him. He was a furniture maker, an upholsterer. He set to work making chairs, started selling them to Macy's, and soon was hired by Isidor and Nathan Straus, who by then owned *Macy's, to supervise a factory producing his furniture designs. He was never rich, but he made, as my grandmother once told me, "a comfortable living" and his family lived well. They had six children, only two of whom survived to adulthood. Two were taken in the 1918 Spanish Flu epidemic. One was killed as a seventeen-year-old soldier in the trenches during World War I. And one was killed in an accident when she was seven, kicked in the head and trampled by a horse startled by a car backfire. My great grandfather became morose after her death, so family lore goes, and with his gloom, also more rigid with his surviving children. He was a spare-the-rod-spoil-the-child parent. It was likely only because she was a girl, and therefore less likely to engage in the kinds of behavior that elicited his wrath, that my grandma was spared his harshest discipline. But she grew up believing that children needed limits as well as encouragement, and though enlightened enough to want her own daughters to get an education and "be something" she expected them to have high standards, as she called them, in everything. Her husband followed her father into the furniture business, opening his own store after he returned from service in the Second World War. My mother was their only child.*

All of this is in my head now as I think about the conversation I had with Rachel right before my father got sick, the one about having kids. Why is our desire to recreate ourselves so strong, even among us non-traditional types? What is so special about us that we think we can escape the traps that forged our own parents? I am pretty sure that I don't want to visit onto any child the things I know are the worst of my personality. But is there something I'm missing?

2 WEEKS AND 5 DAYS AFTER THE TRANSPLANT OPERATION

From the couch in my living room, I am watching the changing of the guard at my front door. Mother in, Rachel out. I am still in significant pain, not so much from the incisions themselves, which are healing well but in my shoulders and back. This pain is from expanding my abdomen and chest with gas so the doctors could see inside the cavity with their tiny cameras, a procedure routinely employed in surgery, except that no one told me how much time it would take to recover from it. When I ask the doctors if lingering pain is normal, they're evasive. They don't even want to admit having caused it. "You'll be over that in a few days," an intern told me during a post-op check-up. That was two weeks ago. "We're more worried about your incision and how that's healing than a little muscle ache. When I look at your vitals, and how well you're doing overall, this is nothing. It will pass." Easy for him to say; I still can barely straighten up to walk to the bathroom. I didn't say anything. What would have been the point? Wouldn't have made the pain go away. That much I know from being body slammed in derby. Bitch all you want, you spend the same amount of time hurting. Though I admit, depending on your audience, there is a certain pleasure to be derived from bitching. I've tried not to be awful to Rachel. She's been here since my discharge from the hospital. I admit, once a day or so I look for ways to get under her skin, hoping for a different reaction from her than the cold professional efficiency she's turned on while fulfilling her promise to take care of me. She hasn't taken the bait.

Which brings me to my mother. She arrives with two suitcases, having come from two weeks living at my father's place, taking care of him. Even though her apartment is less than a half hour drive from mine, she moves in. I don't need such hovering care. She could stay at home and just come over during the day to check on me. I'm recovered enough to be on my own now, but she's in Florence Nightingale mode and there's no stopping her. We fall right into our old patterns. She orders me around, I only comply when I want to. It's an easy groove to find. Familiar. Despite the friction, she waits on me with little complaint. I'm only slightly ashamed to admit that given license to be self-indulgent, I too often take it.

I didn't see much of her the two weeks she stayed with my father, though she called every day to remind Rachel what she needed to do, even though Rachel had the exact same post-operative care instructions my mother had. My father's insurance paid for his nurses. He hired an aid from a home care agency to do his laundry and housekeeping, and the hospital signed him up for visits from a wound care specialist. None of this mattered to my mother. She took it upon herself to supervise the paid specialists. She's left him to come here because, she insists, "You still need care and his helpers can take over now that I'm convinced they won't screw up and kill him."

My mother's arrival at my place causes her to cross paths with Rachel who is moving out. Rachel has already piled the bulk of her stuff in the hall outside our apartment door. She'll take an Uber to her new place, an apartment she's sharing with a woman she met on Craig's List. I'm surprised how little she has to move, how easy it is for her to extract herself from this place she's called home for nearly a year, from me. Her clothes, in two suitcases and a garment bag, a pasta maker, some cookbooks, her toiletries, her laptop and the cords and plugs for her phone. Roughly the same volume of stuff any college student moves into her freshman dorm. It makes me sad that there isn't something more dramatic, something she has to struggle with, a large painting or a piano or some furniture. But there's no bed; she shares mine. There's no dresser; plenty of room for her in my drawers and closet. There's no comfy chair; she commandeers one end of the couch if we're sitting opposite each other. In less than half a day, she packs and cleans and removes all evidence of her months here. Well, all the physical evidence.

Is it too petty to suspect that my mother times her arrival so she has a moment to gloat over what I am sure she considers a victory? I'm sure she feels she has won her battle with me over Rachel. She watches Rachel carry out the last of her things. Rachel and my mother do not speak to each other, or rather, do not speak in actual communicative words.

"Aha," my mother says when Rachel opens the door for her.

"Of course," Rachel says, shaking her head, meaning, of course, my mother shows up while she's still there. Rachel is furious at me for going through with the transplant. For that and other things. I wonder if she is taking some pleasure in how hard my recovery has been. She needs something from me, a demonstration of commitment that I'm not giving her. Something about what we have feels wrong to her, broken or misshapen or ill-fitted, not what she wants to hitch her wagon to.

At the door, my two caregivers dance around each other like battlefield enemies enduring a Christmas truce. Rachel moving the last of her stuff out and my mother bringing her suitcases in. They glower at each other's backs as they cross paths but avoid each other's eyes. If this were in a movie, there would be a shot of each of them staring daggers at the other, then a shot of me rolling my eyes, like that scene in *Moonstruck* when Olympia Dukakis lets both of Cher's lovers into her kitchen and rolls her eyes between each arrival.

I've given in to my mother's need to "be here for you" because I do not have the strength to resist her. She'll cook and clean and make things easier, in exchange for which she'll give me advice about everything from the arrangement of my furniture to keeping safe in the neighborhood where I live, from my clothing choices to my occupation. She'll have things to say about my "lifestyle choices" I am sure, meaning my sexual orientation. We'll argue. I'll fume. I have a limit to how much hectoring I can absorb before I explode like an over-inflated balloon. I've told her I reserve the right to throw her out. She absorbs that assertion with a snort.

When we left the hospital, I thought I might be done with my mother's quarrelsomeness for a while. We were a funny parade, all of us, leaving the recovery floor. We were wheeled out to the parking lot in tandem wheelchairs, my mother pushing my father, Rachel pushing me, our bags of clothing and flowers and cards in our laps. We were headed to different places, but I'm sure my father and I were each feeling the same wariness about the people who were taking us to those places. Someone sent my father a helium balloon, but five days after its arrival the balloon was wilted and floated low alongside his chair. For me, the balloon was a perfect metaphor. Half inflated was exactly how I felt. Closer to the floor than the sky. And tied by a string to people I was uncertain would ever be able to buoy me up. Five days of recovery in the hospital had not softened either Rachel's or my mother's view of the other. When I was feeling well enough to spend a few minutes with my dad, and I convinced Rachel to help me walk the fifty miles down the corridor that twenty steps felt like, and she and my mother found themselves together with us, there was the kind of stony silence that must accompany the reading of a will to a contentious and fractured family.

My father felt much better after the operation. He needed more bedrest than I did – his procedure had been longer and harder than mine, but he was bouncing back faster than predicted. They took the dialysis drain out of him two days after the operation. Not that he wasn't in pain or didn't feel all of the aches the assault of major surgery and anesthesia visit on a body, but because his blood was being cleaned to a degree it had not been for quite some time, he felt more awake and alert. "It feels like being high," he told me on one of my visits to his room. Because he felt well, it was hard for him to maintain his annoyance at me for deciding to give him my kidney and thus "cripple myself" as he kept saying. Feeling good also frightened him. Once he recognized how much better he felt, every small postoperative complaint became magnified. My mother claimed the nurses told her he rang his buzzer more than any patient they had ever had, a confirmation for my mother of what she considered his babyish behavior. When they told him on his second day of recovery that the dialysis drain was coming out, he protested, worried that the doctors had not given his new kidney "enough time to prove itself."

"What if I reject it?" he asked them. "What if her kidney doesn't like me? What if it doesn't want to be in the body of an old fart like me? My daughter has lots of reasons not to want to hang out with me," he told his surgeon. "What if her kidney just shuts down to spite me?" This made the doctor laugh. I was not there. This was reported by my mother. The doctor told him he was sure that even the worst parent-child issues did not travel with transplanted organs from one body to another. "There is no such thing as literal bad blood."

"I was pissed at her for doing this," my father told him, not letting up. "She could want to torture me to get back at me." My mother told me that the doctor laughed off all my father's postoperative paranoia, though the doctor repeated my father's concerns word for word to the surgical residents and interns during grand rounds. I told my mother to tell him that once given, the organ was his and I took no further responsibility for it. I did not tell her about the dream I had that my kidney had its own television show and mouthed off like Rodney Dangerfield. I was sure she wouldn't find it funny, and I could only imagine how distorted her recitation of the dream to him might be.

That is how our communication continues. Whisper down the lane from me to my mom, from him back through her to me. For the five nights we were recovering in the hospital, my mother slept on a chair in my father's room. After the operation, she readied my father's apartment in Cherry Hill for his return, taking her own clothes there, ready for two weeks of overnights. Now that she has invaded my place, I know how weird her invasion of his apartment must have been, his long-time ex-wife staking out her territory in his domain. I'm sure she went through his stuff; I know she'll be poking around in mine. Before he consented to her camping out there – which he did under the influence of pain killers on the eve of surgery – she had never been there. Other than a few stop-overs, she's never spent more than an hour at a time in my place. She reported after her first visit there that his place was "a depressing mess." I told her I had been there and didn't find it so. "It's filled with things he loves, books and magazines and art. He's not the neatest housekeeper, but the place is clean and hardly depressing." My mother dismissed me with a wave of her hand. When I tell her now not to start moving my things around, she gives me the same gesture.

"You always forgave your father his worst habits, Nina," my mother says. "I can't. And it is obvious some of them have rubbed off on you." I'm sure by the time she's gone nothing will be in its usual place. She'll take it upon herself to "straighten" the place up to her standard of order. She will rearrange or remove whatever strikes her as out of place, unnecessary, or offensive. She will do this without giving a thought to the invasive nature of it. She will categorize my books, alphabetize my DVDs, Windex the TV screen, put my spice bottles in order by size, hang my shirts and pants in the closet by color, and rewash everything that doesn't drape four-square on its hanger. I am sure she has already done this at his place. Rachel called my parents' relationship the most fucked up divorce she ever encountered. When I warned my mother not to alter his living space or move his stuff around, she laughed at me. "He needs someone to make order there. He lives in complete chaos. After I'm gone, he can do what he wants. But if I'm going to take care of him, he needs to indulge me in this. Besides," she asked me as if there was an actual answer to the question, "what else do I have to do?" Now she is bringing her whirlwind to my place. I hear her on the phone engaging a cleaning service, the "same one," she tells me, "that did a good job at your father's." The day after he got home, he told me on the phone, "The air in this apartment smells so perfumed I thought I'd sneeze my stitches out."

Being camped out at the hospital allowed my mother to keep an eye on both of us, which she told me she found comforting. She was the only one. When Rachel took me home, we had a reprieve from the tension my mother propagates everywhere. And while I knew that Rachel was pissed at me, for the two weeks she was here she undertook her Florence Nightingale duties with grace, if not good humor, though I must admit that other than the fact that she'd made a commitment, I do not know why. She's long-suffering. She made a promise and she kept it. Thinking about it now, I realize the fact she has moved out suggests that her tolerance for suffering may be changing.

We had a few nice moments during the two weeks she was here. She cooked for me, her usual interesting and fussy meals, homemade pasta dishes with ethnic seasonings, elaborate salads made with root vegetables and herbed dressings, frittatas and quiches filled with julienned vegetables, pot pies, pepper cornbread muffins and olive rolls, banana breads, and apple turnovers. She had some dietary guidance from the hospital about what might cause me distress; everything she cooked was appealing and digestible.

While she was here, she went to work late or took time off, an hour here, an afternoon there, scheduling her clients around my needs and naps. She ferried me to doctor appointments. Even though we shared the bed, we didn't do anything except sleep. We didn't have sex. In the abstract, I wanted it; I thought it would distract me from feeling crappy. Practically, I was sore enough I couldn't imagine how I would accomplish it. I still am. If she had been inclined to bring me off with her fingers, I would have liked it. That's what I've been doing for myself when she's out at work. But she wasn't. We were done with that, sad as that makes me.

After dinner every night, I stretched out on the couch to watch TV. Sometimes Rachel turned one of the counter stools around and watched over my shoulder. Sometimes she went into the bedroom and read. I missed her sitting next to me or stretching across the couch with her feet in my lap. When we talked, it was about the practicalities, what she should get from the store or my medicine routine. She walked me to the bathroom, changed the sterile bandages on my shrinking incisions. She had made up her mind about leaving me, and there was nothing to talk about. Neither of us saw the value in trying to deconstruct her decision. If she was not satisfied with me after months of living together, what could I say that would make her feel otherwise?

We use the same words to describe what we want, Rachel and me. We want to be taken for who we are, to give to the other unstintingly, to not have to ask for what we need. But it turns out, when we bear down on the specifics, we mean different things. Words fail us. Good intentions are less than the whole story. The best outcome in one way is the worst in another. My father told me if I loved him, I should not consider giving him my kidney. My mother told me if I loved him, I had an obligation to do it. I put Rachel's love in the balance and now I've lost it. I'm feeling the true gravity of this today as I watch Rachel cross paths with my mother and then walk out of my door.

FIFTY-FIVE

NINA'S RECOVERY JOURNAL

It has been a little while since I felt like I wanted to write in here, but I'm awake in the middle of the night and thinking about why I have not thought about my teammates or the championship game since that day. When I was still in the hospital recovering, a few of my teammates stopped by and Coach sent me flowers with a card that everyone on the squad signed. The visits were awkward. We didn't talk much about the game. I couldn't. I apologized to all the women who came to see me for deserting them at the half, and they all said they understood, but I felt ashamed that I didn't do my job or help lead them to victory. Everyone was reassuring, very understanding, and yet and yet and yet. I knew I wouldn't have been. I would have thought "why couldn't you put your personal stuff out of your mind for another hour and finish what you trained and practiced for? Why let yourself be so rattled that you couldn't perform the thing you were primed for and best at?" I know that's not charitable. I would not have been charitable.

There are certain sports, I am convinced, that are better participant sports than spectator sports. Maybe everything in life can be divided up like that. In the old days, for my parents' generation, sex was a participant sport. Private. And then the Internet turned it into a spectator sport for everyone to see. Amateur couples post their videos, and now anyone who hasn't had a threesome or foursome or more-some is a total square. Tourists walk the High Line in New York specifically hoping to see other people having sex in the window of the Standard Hotel, or in midtown looking up at the floor-to-ceiling windows in the Yotel, and people go to that hotel to have sex in the windows. But somehow, I can't shake the feeling, all of this has diminished sex. I never got golf or bowling as spectator sports. Or fishing. I spent a lot of time watching TV while I recovered from my operation. There are fishing tournaments on ESPN. I heard a commentator say bass fishing had a bigger audience than NASCAR. How big is NASCAR? I never got auto racing, though, with that, I understand the spectator appeal. Crashes and fires and speed and the chance of death. But fishing? I watched these people lining up on the shores of the St. Lawrence for the Bassmaster Championship. I could hardly make out the boats let alone the fish. Baffling. But Roller Derby is the ultimate spectator sport. Easy-to-understand, fast action, high scoring, high potential for danger. What's not to love? But it's not on TV. There's a channel with some bouts on the Internet. I've been trying to watch it. I've been thinking about how much I once loved watching it. Long before I was good at doing it. When I discovered Moose Kaboosky. Now, it's all muddled up. My love for it and my shame about it. On my computer screen, it looks dinky. I think derby could be the ultimate big screen sport. I want it to be huge. Why has it become so small?

7 WEEKS AFTER THE TRANSPLANT OPERATION

My father and I have a new routine. Every Tuesday night, after work, I arrive at his place with take-out food from DiBruno's. I shop carefully. They have breads and rolls, interesting salamis and cheeses, prepared salads, pickles, and vegetables dressed or prepared in exotic ways. Tonight, I am bringing white asparagus sautéed in saffron olive oil, cold boneless chicken thighs with a rosemary-sesame drizzle, and tabbouleh. I pay attention to the portions as well as the flavors, honoring the gourmet tastes my father taught me to love as a kid, while also trying to respect his not-too-terribly restricted diet. I'm not sure he cares about food the way he used to, though he always acts delighted to unwrap the dinner I present him with and effuses over my choices.

In his kitchen, unpacking the grocery bag he has taken from me as I enter, he reads the printed labels on the containers and says, "These look delicious. Wonderful combinations. As usual." Though I do not know what he means by "usual." This weekly get-together is a recent occurrence in our social history, after we each recovered from our operations enough to socialize without pain getting in the way or causing one of us to run out of steam midway through the evening.

"It wouldn't kill me to have some potatoes, you know," he tells me, "or pasta" he adds when he has everything laid out on the counter. He knows I steer away from starches, as much as I love them, because keeping his weight down is part of stabilizing his recovery and keeping his sugar numbers down. Also, if I eat them, I put on weight, and somewhere in the back of my mind, there is this itch that someday I'll get back to athletics again. Though right now, I'm still stiff enough that anything but light exercise is completely off the table.

Overall, my father is a lot healthier than he was before his operation, but he's not altogether better. He has ups and downs. I do not know if that's because his eating habits are bad when I'm not supplying food, though his refrigerator seems free of any evidence of self-indulgence when I come over on Tuesdays. My father is crafty enough to be sure I don't catch him cheating, but that doesn't mean he isn't. Although there doesn't seem to be any evidence of alcohol consumption, he might schlep the bottles out to the trash before I arrive. I know he gets his neighbor to take him to market on Wednesdays, so when I see him on Tuesday night he is at the end of his week and his larder looks a little bare. My father is nothing if not a serious tactician of deception.

His neighbor, though he never names her, is the same woman who heard him hit the floor when he collapsed before his operation. I do not pry. Like most children, I do not want to imagine my parents having sex; I don't want to imagine them having sex with people other than each other, which my long-uncoupled parents have not had in some time. In all the years I have known her, I have never asked my mother about her love life after she split with my father. It's not that I don't believe she had one. It's that I don't want to know. For years, I assumed that if someone became important enough that she wanted me to meet them, she would have made that happen. Someone would be introduced at a dinner, or their name would creep into conversations and eventually the person would appear as if I had been party to his appearance all along. After some amount of time, I would realize, oh, wait, that's a boyfriend. I assume boyfriend because of my mother's long-standing disdain for my relationships with women, but then again, who knows? It's not like she isn't capable of being contradictory.

With my father, I think the resistance to including me in this aspect of his life after my mother or even providing information about it, was that his objects of affection were always temporary. My father discovered that he liked the bachelor life, liked serial monogamy, liked dating women one after another in succession. He's charming, my dad. He liked to turn on the charm, and he had old-fashioned ideas about dating and courtship. He liked the chase as he called it. I am sure he treated the women he dated well, similarly, I suspect, to the way he treated me, which, I'm loathe to admit my mother correctly characterized at one point as a seduction. With me, it was not a sexual seduction, but part of a zero-sum game he played with her, battling for my affection. He took me to the best restaurants, to the theater, to special exhibits at museums. He made our time together feel important and fun. He knew the city in a way that made him a denizen of its most interesting corners, as only someone with a deep understanding of its secrets would be. He knew the best places to shop for everything, the best places to get croissants and truffles and squid ink pasta, the best places to buy ties, the best places to buy hand-made suits, the best bars to encounter famous writers and celebrities, rubberneck at rock stars, see reclusive artists. When he put on his cosmopolitan clothes and set out for an evening of fun or frivolity or serious food, he delivered. Hard not to be swept along. I know. I was. And so, I imagine, were the series of women he saw over the years. I always knew that when he took me on his arm and we hit the street, heading from his apartment to some opening or play or concert, that I was in for something special. New Yorkers, even people who considered themselves jaded and in the know, would have had to go some distance to be more wired into the pleasures of their city than my father. Though I can imagine that this may have been obnoxious, a kind of showing off that might have been maddening, might have reduced the impulse to assert one's own taste or desire to a minimum, I am sure that for most people, for a while at least, it was dazzling. How often did I ride somewhere in a taxi badgering him to tell me where we were going as he sat smiling next to me, assured that the experience he was about to usher me into would delight me? As a teenager and young adult, this was a persuasive trick. I was learning the world on his arm, and he was winning the war of affection that raged between him and my mother.

But what would it have been like to have been his date, to have been hoping for a long-term relationship with him? At a certain point, did it become clear he was not interested in the version of socializing that his dates might have in mind? When meeting the kids from their first marriages would have been the next step, or vacationing together in Montauk or on the Cape would have been a logical summer plan? Did he duck out just when the routine aspects of a relationship came into view, moving in together, sharing nightly dinners in an apartment kitchen together, opening a joint bank account, shopping for a bed or a car or furniture? When effort got wearing, when there was something more serious looming, when commitment would have had to have been declared? At most, I would estimate, his relationships with the women he dated after my mother lasted a few months or half a year. Even with me, as I got older, the time between our visits stretched out with longer and longer breaks between. He made excuses to skip his weekend parenting and my mother, ever possessive, agreed to let him shrug me off, so I would stay at home with her. Nor did he ever whine or object when my own social life began to get in the way of our father-daughter weekends. If he never expressed relief at not having to entertain me, I cannot be sure he didn't feel it. Perhaps even with me, the seductive trick just got harder to turn.

And it occurs to me now to ask if this is not a lesson I learned from him, as much as I want to reject it, that tying myself too tightly to someone is a gateway to pain? This was certainly the lesson he took from his relationship with my mother, even though, in some bizarre way, they were a perfect match. It's easy to think that once out that door, he swore to himself "never again."

Once I left New York and moved to Philadelphia, when I visited him, he never mentioned anyone serious. I heard names of women he dated, most often just first names. Occasionally I met a woman he was involved with, but no one was presented as a serious partner or potential partner. The fact that I don't remember the names of any of these women is proof they were not ever supposed to seem important. Not anyone to get attached to. I came to assume, as I met them, that they would be replaced by others.

My father was a sensualist. He liked good food, good wine, the good life he lived in his man-cave of a Manhattan apartment and cultivated it in the restaurants and theaters and galleries of New York. His place, with its deep leather couches and tall bookshelves and fine art prints, was part of his allure. It was calculated to impress, to enfold, to promise immediate comfort if not long-term company. He liked smart and classy women, of whom my mother was the foremost example, albeit the certifiably crazy version. In his prime, he was elegant, he knew how to "clean up good" as he would have called it. He always owned a well-tailored tux and a fleet of silk Italian-cut suits. He would have been any woman's perfect date until his diabetes kicked up and his kidneys started to fail. Now, in his generic apartment in an uninspiring New Jersey suburb, I am amazed to discover that he still has enough juice to attract the downstairs neighbor for what I assume is a little hanky-panky. Or maybe they just sit, hold hands, and talk. What do I know? She is nowhere in evidence on Tuesday evenings when I come calling.

For all our newfound engagement, and the regularity of our contact after all these years, my father is not forthcoming about very much. We talk as we always did, about music and books. He doesn't go to the theater anymore, not to New York, and though I love the scrappy and fringy theater scene in Philadelphia, he is disdainful of it. He wants to see virtuosos. I tell him that ninety percent of New York theater, except Broadway, is new plays by edgy companies, the same as in Philadelphia, and that in some ways, because it has so much less to lose, the scene in Philly is riskier, edgier, the kind of work he once went out of his way to take me to – not to mention his dates. But he is no longer interested in the new and edgy. He wants the familiar, the safe, the comforting. When he tells me what he is watching on TV, police procedural shows he can figure out long before the final commercial, and old movies he has seen before and for which he already knows the plots, I am shocked by the complacent nature of his desires. Is this what it means to age? He tells me he longs for an older standard of quality, one that perhaps was never as posh as he romanticizes it to have been. He will no longer sit in a base-ment theater to see a work of genius by a twenty-five-year-old. He will no longer sit on a hard church pew to hear concerti by young Juilliard students, who in ten years will be defining the canon. He wants Shakespeare by actors trained by British royal academies, Beethoven played by the New York Philhar-monic, Mozart by the Vienna String Ensemble.

Sitting across from him now, eating the dinner I have brought him, he sighs and reaches for my hand. "I cannot tell you how grateful I am to spend this time with you," he tells me. There is a resigned quality to his speech now, that fills me with sadness. "Sometimes I do not know what I'm doing here."

"Here, in New Jersey? Because I've been asking you the same question ever since you left New York."

"Here on earth," he says, and squeezes my hand.

FIFTY-SEVEN

NINA'S RECOVERY JOURNAL

This morning, for the first time in months, I notice when I get out of bed, I'm no longer hesitating at all. I'm no longer wary that I'll feel the ping of pain that for months has reminded me of what my body has been through. I just get up, like I once did, and do my morning routine. It occurs to me that the self-protective way I have been getting out of bed for months, turning my body to the side, using my arms to push myself up to a sitting position, then polling my limbs and abdomen for negative feedback before I stand, I'm no longer doing. I'm back to the un-self-conscious way I blasted through things before the operation, not thinking about every little movement as if pain might punish me or incapacitate me for a foolish overreach. I'm carrying a little extra weight around my middle, a result of being responsible for my own meals the last few months rather than relying on Rachel's careful and healthy cooking, and also from doing less exercise, but I'm not overweight, not carrying pounds anyone would look at and think gross. I'm just softer. Softer in all its several meanings. Softer in the belly. Softer in my being. Is this what Rachel feared for me, this loss of my tone?

So, without noticeable pain, I step out of the shower and wrap myself in a pair of towels; one is a turban, the other a gown. I stand in front of the mirror and perform the familiar work I have always done to keep my body fresh and robust. I brush my teeth. I roll on deodorant. I put moisturizer on my face, and, removing the top towel, rub a small amount of gel into my hair. By then the towel around the middle of my body has absorbed enough of the shower's moisture that I drop it and inspect myself.

This is the new part of my ritual, a new routine. I run my fingers over the scar where my kidney exited for its new home, the only tangible marker left on me after I made this contribution to my father's life and health. The other tiny scars on my side have faded to the dimensions of pencil erasers, and their discoloration only hints at their once angry pink tenderness. But this line, this stitched scar mark that looks like railroad tracks, this has become my combination touchstone, talisman, fetish, and badge of honor. It is the stronger sister to my piercings and tats. Compared to this, they were placeholders on my body awaiting this marking, signifying its deeper purpose. They were mere fashion statements, decorations. This scar line is defining, uplifting, magical. It gives me power and character. It humbles me and it makes me proud. If it is still visible when I go to the ocean this summer, I will wear a suit that displays it. I will slather Coppertone on it before sunbathing, put aloe vera lotion on it as a healing balm after. But here, in my bathroom in the morning I perform my new ritual, rubbing my index finger and thumb up and down the raised line, pinching the picket-fence scar between my fingers, and I smile. For all of the pain I suffered and, I immediately add, caused, and all the worry I continue to carry about my father's recovery and health, in a separate and personal way, this ropey ridge of swollen flesh reminds me of what I have done, and it fills me with pleasure. I will never have babies, my evasion in conversation with Rachel about this idea persuaded me of that, but I have given my father this precarious rebirth, and in its honor, I rub my forefinger and thumb up and down the now reclosed avenue of its delivery. In another moment in my life, I might have wondered if some future lover would be repulsed, would find a scar this prominent a reminder of the decline toward mortality that life and hardship bring to all of us. Now I relish the chance to test some lover's reaction. Love me, love my scars, I want to say, and then wait for her to bend and kiss it, make love to it, and affirm with her lips and eyes that she will love me regardless of the choices I have made. This scar is the cross, the crescent, the star of my new religion, the altar on which I pray. Looking at it in the mirror – at myself showing it – may be the first time in my life I feel truly beautiful.

11 MONTHS AFTER THE TRANSPLANT OPERATION

At home, on a Friday afternoon after a grueling work week filled with fights with insurance companies and the Medicare office, I am self-medicating with a glass of pinot when the phone rings. "If you are trying to reach Rachel, she has a new number." I hear my recorded voice say the number for the caller, and then go on. "If you're looking for a call-back from Nina, go ahead and leave a message on this machine. Here comes the beep. You know what to do."

The machine is in the kitchen. I strain to hear who's calling. Through the tinny speaker, I hear my mother's voice. "Nina, it's your mother. Call me. It's urgent."

I don't need to hear anything else but the catch in her voice to know my father is dead. He never quite regained what anyone would call a normal standard of life. He was coasting. It wasn't just his kidneys. It was everything. He just fell apart inside. Heart, liver, lungs. They think he may have had a TIA on the table. They should probably never have let him go through with – no. I'm not going there. We had almost a year. Now, I am left with – what? I don't know. Anger sometimes. Helpless rage. Emptiness. I touch my side. I want to feel what I have lost, a space, a negative. But things have filled in. Some adjustment has occurred. "Organs migrate," one doctor told me when I asked her why I seem as solid to the touch as I did before the operation. I may be the only transplant donor ever who wants to feel like there is some space inside where the kidney used to be, like a footprint in the sand. Healed, I am some version of whole. I look in the mirror; there's little left to see. A thin raised line and two bumps so tiny they look like healed mosquito bites, scars so inconsequential no one would ever guess their relation to actual and emotional pain.

In some odd way, the person who has lost the most in all of this is my mother. My mother has been defeated by the aftermath of my father's surgery, and by my father's death. By persuading me, or guilt-tripping me, or whatever part she played in getting me to do this, she thought she would have won. It's a perverse equation. If she persuaded me to do what he did not want me to do, and it saved him, she won. She had the last laugh, the last word. But it didn't work, and now I'm without him and she's without him and she feels responsible for all of it, but particularly for what I went through, 'my sacrifice' she keeps calling it. She means my kidney, of course. She is not talking about the loss of the sport I loved or losing Rachel. I doubt that my loss of Rachel is something she feels bad about, but who knows? My mother feels things she refuses to admit, says absurd things to hide what she feels. Maybe among her other misgivings, there's some small regret for the part she played in the demise of my relationship with Rachel. Or maybe she has some regrets about the fact I have been alone for most of the past year. I have never seen evidence of that, though I know she feels she is responsible for something. I'm just too numb to feel or care much.

My mother gave the eulogy at my father's funeral. She wept through her whole reading. True to her fashion, she gave out printed copies. She announced, as the ushers handed them around, that she printed them out so she would be sure to remember to say everything she wanted to say because her sadness had her muddled. You think she was muddled? Who prints copies enough for everyone in attendance at a funeral unless they want the muddle to continue for everyone who walks out of the funeral home holding a copy? My mom.

She wrote, "Nina will tell you I wasn't Evan's biggest fan. I thought he had a hard time taking the important things in life seriously. He was glib, about people, about his health, about the value of life itself. I never thought he lacked gravitas and verve, just good sense and consistency. But he loved his daughter. He accepted her better than I could. He never wanted her to be anything other than who she was. And for that, it is my duty to honor him."

Oy, right? He accepted me? That's what she believes? Or does she mean he didn't argue with me the way she does? I ask myself these questions, and then I ask myself if I want the answers. So, there's that. It's amazing the stories we use to comfort ourselves when everything is far more complex than we admit. And way more fucked up. Funny thing is, right now, fucked up complexity seems okay to me.

This is how most of us die, I now think. Not with a bang. You give away your heart. It gets broken. You give your organs away, they go the way of all flesh. My kidney is buried now, in the Jewish cemetery where my mother believes I won't be able to get buried because of my tats. My mother arranged for my father to be buried there, in a family plot they bought together years ago. I'm not sure how he would feel about that if he had an opportunity to express his opinion about it. He might think it was a perfectly ironic end to a ridiculous relationship. Or he might be outraged. One way or the other, I'd bet he'd have some choice words about it. Not least about my mother's belief that in eternity we will be a happy family again. Most Jews do not believe in a corporeal afterlife, well, the ultra-orthodox do, but not the rest of us. But my mother needs to believe that anyone stumbling on that grave any time in the future will assume that there was a marriage and that neither life nor death put it asunder. There is no way I will be buried there, I can tell you that. I have modified my will to forbid it. But in a snarky way, I guess I can count my father's burial there with my kidney in his chest as a partial victory. Despite the tats, at least part of me has snuck in.

I wonder if this partial death will make my actual death easier. If I believed in heaven would I believe I would meet my kidney there? Does the fact that one part of me is dead make me partly dead? Insert zombie joke here. This is what your parents do. Kill you by bearing you. Where does all this sadness lead? My father is gone. Rachel is gone. She saw me through my recovery but in the end, she saw that I was less. I had given up something I would not hold on to for her. I chose it, and I was different afterward. She was right. Doing this changed me. Not skating changed me. I am not the wild kite she attached her dreams to. How do you love someone who chooses something – anything – over you?

Researchers know the weight of the kidney in relation to the weight of everything else in your body. I Googled it. On average, the human kidney weighs four to six ounces. The kidneys are organs whose function is essential to maintain life. Filtration of blood. Passing the waste from the body as urine. Returning water to the body. Regulating blood pressure. Stimulating the production of red blood cells by releasing the hormones. The kidneys are shaped like kidney beans which are named for them. I have never liked kidney beans.

I went to the practice facility today. Yes, where the team works out. There's a weight room there, and I want to get back into shape. It's the first time I've gone over there since the operation. It has taken me a while to get motivated to do it. It was hard to go back to work, and for months the energy to accomplish anything meant that by the end of the day I was completely drained. That depletion discouraged me for a while. But I have begun to reclaim my life. I snuck into the practice facility after Coach called the warm-ups. I didn't want to see anyone. I'm sure they all hate me for fucking up the championship bout. But I wanted to be there. I watched the track fill up with skaters. I imagined myself stripping out of my street clothes, pulling my skanky workout duds from my duffle bag and re-dressing into the workout uniform. From the shadows of the women's room door, I watched the skate around, the whips and races, the squats and falls. I watched, and for the first time, I let the tears for all I have lost flow free.

FIFTY-NINE

NINA'S RECOVERY JOURNAL

It's been a full year since the start of the season I missed, a year and a half since the night of the championship bout and my father's collapse. Team publicity called last season "a re-building year." Since the start of this season, I've been coming to jams and hiding out high in the bleachers under a cap and hoodie, watching my former teammates play and the newbies' train. It's been mostly local bouts so far, but the regional season starts soon. Marianne has been killing it as lead jammer, and the rest of the team looks sharp.

Today is the last day of open tryouts. I'm not here to watch. I've decided. I'm out of shape and I'll spend a while being fresh meat again. That's okay with me. I need to do it. Sacrifice and penance. I'm going back into the skirmish, back to into the fray. I miss it more than I can say. I know. Self-destructive. Self-in-dulgent. Call me completely selfish. The minute my father's back is turned I'm building a ramp again. Like an addict jonesing for a fix, here I am. A woman on a mission. Like a pil-grim seeking god. The transplant psych warned me about the consequences. And that's what Rachel would say. Will say, when I call and tell her, beg her, to please give me another chance. If she does, I know we'll have a lot to work out. It'll be starting over.

I tie on my skates and step out on the rink. Coach blows his whistle. There is a collective gasp that I have the temerity to show up, or at least I think that's what I hear. And then Coach smiles at me, turns to the rest of them and says, "All right. All right. Time to get this party started. Line up for a two-minute race. After that, skills drills in this order. Interval sprints. Snakes. Lap the line. Then partner up for pushes and pulls. What's our mantra? Drills build skills. Drills build skills. Every-one say it." When we all have, he says, "Ready to skate?" I wobble at first, a fawn, shaky on her spindles. But I will find my balance. I will find my ease. I will find my stride.

He blows his whistle, and I'm off.

ACKNOWLEDGMENTS

This novel would not exist without the involvement and generosity of a number of amazing women: Ninni Saajola, roller derby competitor and a true tough girl, who introduced me to the sport and brought me to her team's bouts; Ronna Serota, who is the partial inspiration for this story and helped me to understand the practicalities and challenges of being an intra-family kidney donor; Bonnie Gordon, who has read and reread all of my drafts, and whose honesty and insight in editing them has made this book broader and deeper; Cheryl Berg, who read for the authenticity of the therapists' voices; Jess Conda, Lee Ann Etzold, and the cast of the BRAT Productions staged reading of the play WHAM BAM, precursor to this novel, who strapped on skates and gave me the first look at what this story could be; Leslie Rudy Rothman who read and commented on several early drafts; sensitivity reader Minou Pourshariati; Jennifer Cappella who encouraged me to submit to Sunbury; Chris Fenwick, the editor at Sunbury who has guided this book to publication; and Diane Loebell, first reader, unwavering supporter, and all around kick-ass human being.

ABOUT THE AUTHOR

LARRY LOEBELL is a writer and teacher, best known for his plays *La Tempestad* and *House Divided* and for having been one of the EMMY-winning writers on the first season of the animated series Rugrats. He has published two previous books of fiction, *The Abundance League,* a collection of short stories, and *Seven Steps Ahead,* a collection of novellas. His plays and monologues have been published by Playscripts, Indie Theatre Now, NY Theater Experience, Smith and Krauss, and Applause Books. He is the author of several other full-length plays including *Memorial Day, Pride of the Lion, The Ballad of John Wesley Reed,* and *Girl Science.* His playwriting career highlights include a "Best New Play" Barrymore Award nomination, four Pennsylvania Council on the Arts Fellowships, a Pennsylvania Playwriting Award from the Theater Association of Pennsylvania, a grant from the EST/Sloan Science Foundation, and a grant from the National Council for Jewish Culture. He has taught film history and screen writing and led undergraduate creative writing workshops at the University of the Arts, and taught playwriting, dramaturgy, and theater history at Arcadia University. His fiction has been published in local and national periodicals and presented in Philadelphia's *Writing Aloud,* and was a recent finalist in the Marguerite McGlinn National Short Story Competition. Larry has written and directed two low-budget feature films, *Dostoyevsky Man,* loosely based on *Notes from Underground,* which was a "Fringe First" in the Philadelphia Fringe Festival, and *Portrait Master*, a political thriller. Since 2005, he has been under commission to write and annually revise *Living News, a* "living newspaper" style theatrical experience, which performs during the school year at the National Constitution Center in Philadelphia. Larry has an MA in English from Colorado State University and an MFA in Film and Television from Temple University.

https://www.larryloebell-writer.com/

www.ingramcontent.com/pod-product-compliance
Lightning Source LLC
Chambersburg PA
CBHW020633260626
47157CB00008B/2722